NO ONE LEFT

PINTER P.I. SERIES

BOOK 2

LISA BOYLE

No One Left

ISBN: 978-1-7366077-8-7 (Ebook)

ISBN: 978-1-7366077-9-4 (Paperback)

Copy Editor/Proofreader: Constance Renfrow

Cover Designer: Rafael Andres

This book is for Lloyd.

2012–2024

I almost didn't finish this without you. I had to include a little fictional friend you would have liked. A silly mutt like you. I miss you every day, and I can't wait to see you again at the Rainbow Bridge.

[1]
ADRIEL

WHEN ADRIEL first opened his eyes, it was pitch black. He blinked a few times, trying to spot the difference between awake and asleep. The truck had slowed only a little, and Adriel shifted in the passenger's seat so that his cheek was against the cool window.

He could hear soft music coming from the speakers. He thought it would be church music. That was what his dad normally listened to. But it wasn't. It was slow and sad, and Adriel sort of liked it.

He could hear his dad humming, too, off and on. His real dad. Not that scary man his mom had taken him to visit before she was killed. It didn't matter whose blood Adriel had. George was his father. And even though he'd been frightened at first when George told him, very seriously, that they were leaving, that Aunt Kay wasn't coming with them, he knew George would protect him.

Adriel closed his eyes again and let the gentle rocking of the truck lull him back to sleep.

JUDGE WINTERS

As Bartholomew Winters stared down the barrel of the .357 Magnum, he realized two things. He would not be able to save himself, and he would not be able to save his wife, either. He thought of Cathy with a painful yearning. He hoped that heaven was real. He hoped he would see her there.

Judge Winters did not feel regret or even fear in those final moments. He felt sorrow. He was the only one left. The only one standing in their way. Now, he knew, these assholes would do whatever they wanted.

He picked up his glass of whiskey, swirled it with his wrist, and listened to the clinking ice cubes. He didn't look back at the gun's barrel until he'd finished off his drink. It was then that he noticed how steady the gun was. There was no tremor in the killer's hand. There were no second thoughts. That hand was steady.

"Rot in hell," Judge Winters said.

As he lay on the floor of his office, bleeding to death, he smiled. Of course heaven was real. Cathy was an angel. She was perfect. In her own way, she was even stronger than he was. That was why they would kill her next. If they hadn't killed her already. Because she wouldn't give up. He closed his eyes. He would see her soon. He almost already could. He could feel her. She was so close.

JAMES

THE TRAILER HAD BEEN dusty when James and Molly moved in but otherwise in good shape. No major repairs. No mold as far as James could see. He knew issues could come from seemingly nowhere, though. In the middle of a shower or a load of laundry. He remembered the apartment he had rented with Dorothy before Molly was born. One day, the bathroom door just fell off, sending Dorothy running out of its way. That time, it had just been a rusty screw, but there'd been worse things in that apartment, too.

James sighed and put his hands on his hips. Molly was at school, and he'd just hauled in two desks for the far corner of the living room. Their temporary office. Had it not been for Kay, he probably would have looked for an apartment in Gallup. An office there, too. But their relationship had taken off quick. The night of their first official date, James had intended to go back to Wayne's—where he and Molly were staying—after only a long kiss goodnight. Instead, he'd ended up sweaty, in Kay's bed, with his clothes strewn on the floor in a trail from the front door to the foot of the bed, where he'd somehow pulled off his socks at the last second.

James liked Kay more than he could remember ever liking a woman. Even more than Dorothy in the beginning. He supposed it was useless to compare them, though. He'd practically still been a child back then. Still made decisions like one, at least. He wasn't rash anymore. And he wasn't attracted to flaky or confusing women anymore, either. Kay was definitely not flaky. She was solid.

Driving an hour each way to see Kay would've been inconvenient to say the least, but he would've done it. Luckily, though, Wayne had thought of a way for James and Molly to stay on the reservation.

Wayne and his wife, Barbara, put in for some money from the Bureau of Indian Affairs for an expert consultant on staff to assist with big investigations, like the Linda Morris murder. Barbara even added some language about the "war on drugs." James had had enough experience with that in Vietnam to last him a lifetime, though he knew he couldn't be picky about what kind of cases he took on. Not this early on in the life of his P.I. business. He was satisfied with bail jumper warrants and larceny cases, but being on the reservation he suspected it would only be a matter of time before something more serious came along or a body was found.

Then Adriel and George disappeared. And then George was accused of murder. It was quick like that. One day and then the next.

He and Kay had both been suspicious of George after some questionable behavior during James's last investigation, and James was keeping an eye on him. Still, he couldn't very well camp outside the man's front door, and so when George took off with Adriel in the middle of the night, James didn't know until the following evening, when Kay arrived at an empty house with a large pepperoni pizza from the Pizza Hut all the way in Farmington. She searched the trailer—which took all of two minutes—and then called Thelma Long to see if they were at her place. Then she called James, because George's family was all the way in Arizona, and she couldn't think of one other place they might be. Not on pizza and movie night.

James called Wayne and then went to the Church of the Open Door, where Fred—the maintenance man, janitor, and assistant pastor all in one—told James that he hadn't seen George since Sunday.

Then he and Wayne made calls. To George's sister in Shonto. His mother in Kayenta. His great-aunt in Tuba City. His brother in Tsegi. His grandmother in Flagstaff. George had a big family, and while some didn't answer the phone, those who did hadn't seen or heard from him or Adriel. James thought they would wait, then. What else could they do? George was Adriel's father. He was allowed to take him somewhere. And he was allowed to do so without telling anyone.

But then, a day later, clear as day on the news, the police dispatch, the radios, there was George's name again. George Morris, suspected of killing a judge and his wife in Albuquerque. Then, everyone was on it. Other chapters of the Navajo Nation police department; the state police of New Mexico, Arizona, Utah, and Colorado; all the big city police departments. Albuquerque, Santa Fe, Flagstaff, Phoenix.

And the small ones, too. Gallup. Farmington. They all had Adriel and George's physical descriptions, George's truck's plates.

James knew that Kay was practicing great patience. She hardly went home. She left school at the end of each day and went straight to the station. Wayne had given her the cot in the back. Finally, on the fourth day, she jumped into her baby-blue Toyota Hilux and disappeared herself. She called James that night from a hotel, crying so hard that he just sat on the line and waited for her to get it all out. Finally, she clearly said, "I failed him. I failed Adriel."

James assured her that she had done everything she could. Yes, George had been acting a little strange in the wake of Linda's murder, and yes, he'd probably been hiding something. But no one could have predicted the man would up and leave with his child and then be accused of killing two people.

James had told Kay she needed to come back home. She couldn't chase after them. They could be anywhere. She had come back the next day but still didn't know what to do with herself. Even her students were worried. One boy showed up at the station to tell "that white guy that hangs out with Miss Kay that she's not doing so good." He said she'd been showing the class movies all week. And not even educational ones. Something wasn't right with her.

"We're watchin' out for her," James had assured the boy.

Now, James sat at the desk with the metal folding chair. The upholstered one with wheels would be Molly's. He scooched his chair in and got ready to call the next number on George and Linda's phone bill for the month of May—the real one, the one that hadn't been tampered with—when the phone rang.

"Pinter P.I., this is James Pinter," he said.

"Pinter, it's Sanchez." The line cracked, and Sanchez's voice sounded distant.

"Sanchez. You in a cave or somethin'?" James asked.

"A payphone. Listen. I need you to pay a visit to a guy in Albuquerque."

"Why's that?"

"It's the son of this murdered judge and his wife. I told him you'd be contacting him."

"Hold on, now," James said. "Why would you do that?"

Sanchez took a deep breath. James could hear horns in the background. The whoosh of traffic.

"He's convinced they've got the wrong guy. I think he suspects someone, but he won't tell me who. He insisted I look into it, but I told him I couldn't. Not officially. But that I know someone who might be able to help him."

"Let's meet and talk about it," James said.

Sanchez said, "I'll come to you."

"Fine. When?"

"Tonight. When I'm off shift. I'll meet you at the Shiprock station."

"See you then." James hung up and stared at the phone bill again, thinking about what Sanchez had said. How the hell Sanchez was involved in this, James couldn't figure. He guessed he'd find out soon enough.

James picked up the phone again and dialed the last number on the bill. The phone rang once. Twice. Three times. On and on before the machine picked up again, just like it had the first time he'd called. "Hello. You've reached

Janice Stone. I'm unable to get to the phone right now. Please leave a message after the beep."

James did not leave a message. He stood, stretched, and scribbled a note for Molly before grabbing his hat and heading for the station.

[4]
MOLLY

It was the last period of the day on a Friday, and Molly just couldn't focus any longer. She stared out the window. Twirled her hair around her finger. Thought of Adriel. Of where he was. If he was afraid. She thought of the weeks they'd had together before George ripped him away again. George. With his fake smiles. He'd seemed so gentle and attentive to Adriel. It made Molly a little sick to think about now.

Something soft hit the back of her head, and she looked down at a crumpled piece of paper on the floor beside her sneaker. She glanced behind her and saw Paula mouth, "Sorry."

Molly smiled and bent down, pretending to tie her shoe. She sat back up and unraveled the note slowly, keeping her eyes on the chalkboard. She glanced at the note.

Compound? it read. Then, *Mr. Pinter* <3 <3

Molly bit her lip to keep from laughing. A few days ago, her dad had brought Kay coffee at school and caused a bit of a sensation among some of the sophomore girls. It was excruciating to listen to them, but she was glad only Paula knew that Mr. Pinter was, in fact, Molly's dad. She assumed it would come out eventually, but for now, she let Paula tease her about their little secret.

While Paula was a member of the Navajo Nation, she had been raised in Albuquerque. After they were evicted last year, she and her mom moved to the reservation to live with her grandmother. Paula was Molly's bridge to the rest of the Navajo kids—an outsider, but not really. Paula and Molly also both knew what it was like to be looked down upon for not having a father at home. It was something that the two bonded over at first. That in Albuquerque and Dallas they had had a life other kids couldn't understand.

But on the reservation, it didn't seem to matter. Plenty of the kids at Molly's school only had one parent. Or lived with a grandparent or other family members. Molly had asked Paula's grandmother about it one day. She had told Molly, "Paula has already learned to shoot a gun, shear a sheep, and weave on a loom since she moved back. I can tell you *I* didn't teach her all of that. A child needs many adults in their life. So we share them. We share the children." She glanced at Paula and sighed. "Even when they become moody teenagers."

Molly doubted she'd find another friend as good as Paula. They were already inseparable. Paula had started calling James and Molly's trailer the "compound," since it was technically their office, too. She also helped with the P.I. business. She and Molly had gone door to door, asking the neighbors about George and Adriel, and she'd tried to help Thelma remember any details from the few days she'd had with Adriel after he returned from Shonto. Paula was good with people, as if she'd known them for ages. She had a big, warm smile and a familiar manner. She said she'd learned it from her grandmother.

The bell rang, and Molly stuffed her notebook into her backpack, stood, and swung the bag over one shoulder. She walked to Paula's desk.

"Yes, compound," Molly said. Paula grinned.

"Good. Because if I even have to smell my mother right now, I'm gonna lose it."

"Gross," Molly said. Paula and her mom had a complicated relationship. Much more complicated than Molly and her dad—and they hadn't even had a relationship until a few months ago. Paula vented occasionally, and so Molly knew bits and pieces of their story. But Molly never talked about it unless Paula brought it up. She knew how painful a broken relationship with a parent could be.

"Do you think George's family is telling the truth? They really don't know where he is?" Paula asked, as they rushed to the high school's front doors with the rest of the kids.

"I don't know," Molly said. "I keep thinking my dad's gonna have to go check."

"Road trip!" Paula squealed, and Molly laughed.

"Road trips with my dad are not that fun. He listens to these Sherlock Holmes tapes. He's such a nerd." Molly rolled her eyes.

"Of course he does," Paula said. "He's a detective. Sherlock Holmes is probably, like, his hero or something."

Paula popped a stick of gum in her mouth and chewed fiendishly as they exited the building and made their way down the outside stairs. She was quitting smoking, she'd told Molly. For real this time.

Molly's bike was an old one Kay had found propped up in the back of her barn while cleaning it out right after George and Adriel disappeared. Kay had been looking for something. Molly didn't know what and didn't ask.

James had fixed the bike up. "Good as new," he'd said. But the handlebars kept turning away from Molly, and she had to keep tightening them with a screwdriver.

The two girls hopped on their bikes and slowly rode through the huddled groups of high schoolers scattered around the parking lot, leaning against cars, giving piggyback rides, stumbling over one another in fits of giggles. Some gave Molly the side-eye, but most ignored them both.

Up ahead, one girl was sitting on a boy's shoulders. Julie. She was one of the popular girls. Straight, shiny hair. White teeth that looked like they had never once encountered a cup of coffee or a cigarette.

"What if I just gently knocked over Pocahontas up there?" Paula mumbled.

Molly turned pink. "You can't say that," she whispered.

"*You* can't say that. I can," Paula said as they breezed past Julie.

"Why do you hate her?" Molly asked, a little louder now they were out of earshot.

"I don't *hate* her," Paula said. "It's just . . . what is she hiding? Nobody's *that* perfect."

Julie's father was a lawyer. The head of DNA legal services on the reservation. Her mother owned a deli. They did seem like the perfect family. Still, Molly had nothing to say. She had learned over the last few months that plenty of people had plenty to hide.

WAYNE

WAYNE SUPPOSED he ought to be used to children being taken from the reservation. Hell, it was happening for generations before he was even born. But did a person ever get used to a thing like that? Did they ever see it as part of the job? A way of life for an Indian? It was the boarding schools before, but more recently, since Wayne had become an officer of the law, it was slightly more subtle than a bus hauling children away from their families, away from their traditions, away from everything they knew and loved.

Now, it was only one person or two people from child protective services. Coming to do wellness checks. Not understanding the way Diné raised their children. The way they taught. The way they loved. Now, it was families in tears, asking Wayne what they had done wrong. Asking Wayne because they didn't know how else to get their babies back. It was Wayne going to the tribal courts, Wayne explaining. Sure, the boy's mom is a drunk, Wayne would say. But she's trying to quit. Sure, the girl's father has fallen on hard times. Lost his job. But the child has a perfectly able and willing grandmother, adult brother, neighbor, the list goes on. They all want to look after him. Or her. Please. Get the child back.

Sometimes the kids came back, and Wayne would know because the family would tell him. Thank him. But sometimes the kids didn't come back. And Wayne would know because he would drive by their house whenever he made the excuse to do so. He would hope to see a basketball left outside. A bike leaning against the side of the house. A sweatshirt hanging from the railing. But he wouldn't. He would never see those things again there.

And though this situation was different because Adriel was with his own father, Wayne couldn't help but notice the lack of Adriel. He missed his smiling, curious face. His little hands waving to Wayne when he pulled down Kay or George's driveway. He wouldn't allow Adriel's absence to become the new normal. He would only think of finding Adriel. Of what he needed to do to find the boy.

That morning, he had gotten off the phone with George's sister, Sandra, in Shonto. The call had confirmed something for him, and he was glad of it. Glad to finally make the decision. He paced his office now, deciding what to pack.

The station's bell dinged, and James's footsteps—with his familiar slight limp—resounded down the hall. James's wounds from the summer were mostly healed, but the limp wasn't quite gone.

"What's the news, LT?" he asked, hanging his hat on the coatrack just inside the door.

Wayne shook his head. "Sandra's not telling me something."

James took Wayne's chair and propped an ankle on his knee. "Now what makes you say that?"

"She calls me every day. If you were a worried sister, convinced—as she says—that her brother is innocent, being framed, and out there somewhere with your nephew in tow, what's the first thing you would say to me?"

"Heard anything? Are they back? Have you found them yet?"

"Exactly," Wayne said. "Want to know what Sandra says? She says, 'I still haven't heard anything from him.' Then she goes on and on about why he wouldn't have come to her anyway but that she also knows he didn't do what they're saying he did. She *knows* it."

James nodded. "You goin' there?"

"I think I need to," Wayne said.

"Agreed."

For a moment, there was silence. A still silence. An unspoken understanding between the two law enforcement officers about the odds of a kid missing for a week coming home alive. A kid in the hands of a suspected murderer.

Finally, James asked, "When you plan on leavin'?"

"Tomorrow?" Wayne guessed.

"I have a meeting with Sanchez tonight. He's coming here. He seems to think there's more to this judge's case than what the police are sayin'. He told the dead couple's son that I'd be able to help."

"Help the state police?" Wayne asked.

"Work on it privately, I believe. I guess I'll find out tonight."

"What time?"

NO ONE LEFT / 17

"After his shift," James said. "Around eight or so. You joinin' us?"

Wayne looked at his watch. "Yeah. Count me in."

"You got it, boss."

Wayne grabbed papers from his desk drawer and stuffed them in an envelope. "I'm stopping by Kay's," he said. "See if she's got any last requests before I leave."

"There's just one thing Kay wants."

"I know," Wayne said. "Adriel."

[6]
KAY

EVERY TIME KAY SAT DOWN, she felt itchy. But not somewhere she could scratch. She felt itchy on the inside. It was as if her soul was telling her that without Adriel, she couldn't be still. For about the thousandth time in her life, she was angry that she couldn't be patient. If there was something productive she could be doing on the reservation, she couldn't think straight enough to figure out what it was. She tried the obvious things. She burned cedar. She sang the songs her father had taught her. Prayed for so long and so hard that the only thing left in her at the end was a hollow sadness. And even then, she couldn't be still.

That afternoon, Kay scoured every inch of her home for things that belonged to Adriel. A blue and orange windbreaker. A stormtrooper action figure. A Scooby Doo sock. Just one.

She was under the guest bed—the one where Adriel slept —looking for the other sock, when Wayne let himself in.

"Kay?" he shouted into the house. She backed up in a sort of Army crawl.

"I'm back here!" she shouted.

She heard nothing for a moment and then Wayne's soft footsteps. He had left his boots at the door. Always polite, Wayne. Always thinking of others. Kay sat with her back against the bed, studying the popcorn ceiling and waiting for him to appear. She felt his presence more than she heard it. He crossed the room and sat in a rocking chair in the corner.

"I've been thinking," he said. Kay watched a spider crawl across a web that stretched from ceiling to fan. "I ought to pay Sandra Morris a visit. It's about time that I do in-person checks on George's family members. At first, I thought he couldn't get very far without one of our people spotting his truck. Now, I think it's clear he had help. Somewhere to stash the truck. Another vehicle to use. And Sandra has been calling every day. Being strange all around."

Kay looked from the spider into Wayne's eyes. She thought she knew the answer but asked anyway, "Can I come?"

"No," Wayne said. "Wherever George is, we have to assume he's dangerous. This is official police business."

"It's dangerous for Adriel!" Kay wasn't surprised that Wayne didn't want her to come—but he was wrong.

"I know," Wayne said. "I don't like twiddling my thumbs any more than you do. Which is why I'm going to Shonto. Still, we have to run this through official channels."

"I know Adriel better than anyone. And maybe George, too, nowadays. I'll see things other people won't." She was on her feet now. Her mind raced. She would not let Wayne leave without her. "I promise, I won't be stupid. I won't be in the way."

Wayne sighed. "Kay . . ."

"Come on, Wayne. Please. I'm useless here. My poor kids at school are learning nothing. I'm barely a babysitter. And what if you do find them? Adriel will need me."

Wayne set his jaw, but Kay could tell he was considering it. She held her breath. She didn't know how the school would take it if she up and left for an unknown duration. She had only ever taken off a handful of days. Days she was too sick to get out of bed. She didn't take vacations. Her students needed her. But Adriel needed her more. She would figure it out. The school would figure it out.

"Tomorrow," she said, letting out her breath. "We'll leave before the sun is up."

Wayne raised his eyebrows. "This is serious, Kay. Your interference could throw out the entire case."

"That won't happen. I'll listen to everything you tell me," she said. Wayne breathed heavily for a moment.

"Fine. But officially, you're only visiting family. This is a personal visit for you."

Kay tried to smile. "Thank you, Wayne."

He looked at the pile of Adriel's things on the floor and motioned to it with pursed lips.

"Pack all that, too," he said. "Just in case."

Kay's heart sped up. Just in case. Wayne probably didn't want to get her hopes up, but Kay woke up every day expecting to see Adriel again. She hoped so hard, as if her hopes were strong enough to pull him back home. Adriel couldn't speak, and he might never be able to. But Kay knew he could listen. He was good at that. And so, she sent her hopes, her prayers, her love out every day. She asked the Holy People to carry it for her. To attach it to the wind. To whisper into his ear, *Your aunt Kay is waiting for you. Your aunt Kay loves you so much.*

She would prepare tonight. Wash the sheets. The towels. Go to George's and find a stuffed animal. The stuffed lizard— Sunny, Adriel's favorite—was gone, she knew. Disappeared along with Adriel. It was an orange-and-black lizard Kay had gotten for him years ago. It looked like a Gila monster. A protector in the Diné stories. Her heart had broken when she realized it was missing, even though she knew, logically, it was probably a good thing. George might have been rushing him, but Adriel still remembered to take Sunny. Or maybe George had grabbed it for him. Sunny belonged with Adriel, but his absence only made Adriel's all the more painful.

Still, Kay would find something to bring to Adriel. She would be ready.

"I'll see you in the morning, Wayne," she said, hurrying him out of the trailer. He turned as soon as she shut the screen door.

"I'll talk to the school," he said. "I'll tell them where you're going and that you might not be back for a little while."

"Really?" Kay asked. She looked at the creases starting to appear at the corners of Wayne's mouth. The few strands of gray newly streaked through his two braids.

"I'll handle it."

7

SANCHEZ

IT WAS dark by the time Gabriel Sanchez reached the reservation. He had watched the sunset—a beautiful one—on the drive, thinking about what he was about to do. Sanchez had always been a cop's cop. His father had been a cop, too. Offered the job in order to stay in the country. Although, Gabriel supposed, "offered" was putting it generously.

His father had come to this country as a part of a temporary program during World War II to be a bracero—a farm worker. With so many American men off fighting, food still needed to be grown. Cattle raised and slaughtered. Hands were needed, and since Mexico hadn't sent any hands to pick up guns and pilot airplanes, they were honored to do the work the soldiers had left behind.

Emmanuel Sanchez enjoyed the work. And he enjoyed talking to the farmer's daughter. Their young love blossomed, and though both knew, on some level, that Emmanuel was not supposed to stay in New Mexico, neither thought of the future. So, when Renee got pregnant, Emmanuel refused to leave her and the baby. They had no plan, and their beautiful love story could have become a tragedy had it not been for Renee's uncle.

A police officer and Renee's closest confidant, her uncle offered Emmanuel a job with the state police. They needed more bilingual officers. The uncle would handle Emmanuel's paperwork, and in turn, Emmanuel would marry the young woman.

Though some people might have seen the job as a last resort, Emmanuel saw it as an opportunity. A blessing.

Gabe Sanchez thought his father had been loyal to the department to a fault. He'd ignored the low pay—much lower for a Mexican—and the shitty assignments, and the way he was often treated as a simple interpreter. But still. Gabriel respected the department, not only for what it had done for his own family but for his community, too. Policing was an important job. A noble one, even. Especially with the rise of crime the drug trade of the 1960s and '70s had brought.

The lights were on inside the Shiprock police station, and Sanchez could hear Pinter and Tully's laughter seeping into the hall. He found them in the conference room, empty Styrofoam coffee cups lining the modest table. He should've guessed Tully would be there, too. *Partners in the true sense of the word.* He gave them a tight-lipped smile. They both stood and shook his hand and said their hellos.

"Sit," James said. "I'll get the coffee."

"How are things down in Albuquerque?" Wayne asked after James left. They both sat.

"Other than this case? Fine, I guess. Busy."

"Crime never sleeps. And your family?" Wayne asked.

Sanchez sighed and let his shoulders sink just a bit. "Good. Parents are waiting very impatiently to become grandparents. Always wondering why I haven't found a nice girl to settle down with yet."

"They won't let up until you do."

"Don't I know it?"

James came back with a cup of coffee in each hand and one tucked in the crook of his elbow.

"Black for the LT. Cream for the trooper." He set them down on the table, in a little circle away from the documents. "You brought some goodies."

Sanchez thumbed through the folder. "A copy of the reports." He handed them to James before glancing apologetically at Wayne. "Sorry, I only brought one copy."

James started reading the first aloud as he slowly took a seat next to Wayne.

"Fifty-eight-year-old male. Judge Bartholomew Winters found dead at 20:21 on the floor of his office. Single gunshot wound to the chest. Coroner report estimated the time of death at 18:10. Cause of death by arterial hemorrhage. Bloodied documents were found on his desk referencing the legal parentage of one Navajo Indian boy named Adriel Morris, father George Morris." James looked up at Sanchez. "That all they got on George? Some papers?"

"Check out the next report," Sanchez said.

James flipped to the next page and scanned it for a minute. "Cathy Winters, fifty-six-year-old female also found dead. Three gunshot wounds to her back. She was at home in the kitchen, found by Isaiah Winters, her adult son, who came to the house for a scheduled dinner date. Isaiah Winters, twenty-six-year-old male called the police at 19:37. Coroner report estimated time of death at 18:20."

James looked up at Sanchez. "No one noticed the judge dead in his office for two hours?"

"After hours, I guess. Isaiah finds his mother first. Police call the judge. No answer. Go to his office, which is maybe a five-minute drive from the house. Find the judge dead."

James nodded and set the report down. He looked at Sanchez. "Still don't see anything other than some papers connecting George to all this."

"I know," Sanchez said. "Here's the connection." He handed James the evidence custody documents for all recovered evidence at the scene.

James ran his hand through his hair. "That's Adriel's all right." He passed it to Wayne.

"I'd assume so. Checked it out myself. Says *Adriel* right on its tag. Labeled, and not recently." Sanchez took a deep breath. "Here's the thing: The lizard wasn't at the crime scene."

James's forehead wrinkled. "You're sure?"

"I'm sure. I was there. And look at the photos," Sanchez said, laying the photos of the crime scene out on the table. "You won't find it there anywhere."

"But it's in the evidence locker now?" Wayne confirmed.

"That's right."

"Is the department looking into the discrepancy?" Wayne asked.

Sanchez shook his head. "I don't know."

"Sanchez, I gotta ask. How'd you get involved in all this?" James asked. As far as he knew, Sanchez was still a patrol officer, recently transferred to Albuquerque. But there was more to the story, of course.

Sanchez sighed. "The reason I'm in Albuquerque is because I'm an agent now with the narcotics division."

James grinned. "Congratulations, man." He stuck his hand out, and Sanchez shook it.

"Thanks. I'm working toward homicide, but this is a step, I guess."

"Well, looks to me like you're already knee dip in the shit."

Sanchez nodded. "I was the first on scene, believe it or not. A fluke, I guess. The son? Isaiah? He happens to be one of my informants. He called me right away, and I showed up. Requested additional units. Then I went to the judge's crime scene, too, because, hell, I was already part of the investigation at that point."

James nodded. "Do you know the detective assigned to the case?"

"I do now. His name's Duncan."

"Who is this judge?" Wayne asked.

"He's with the New Mexico Second Judicial Court. But not the regular court. Children's court."

"Children's court?" James asked. "So his enemies were . . ."

"Maybe some of the most dangerous enemies out there," Sanchez said. "Parents."

"You think this is personal?" James asked.

"Possibly."

"But why his wife?" Wayne asked.

"Haven't got a clue. Yet," Sanchez said. A rock formed in his stomach at the thought of helping James, of continuing to investigate the case in secret.

"You know of anyone within the department who has personal business tied up in children's court?" James asked.

"No," Sanchez said.

"Not exactly the kind of dirty laundry one is eager to air, but I had to ask," James said. "Okay, so this son. Isaiah. What can you tell me about him?"

"He's an informant of mine." Sanchez paused. He thought of what he ought to tell Wayne but wouldn't. "He's convinced it isn't George. He's got an idea of who did it, I can tell. But I can't get it out of him. The man is scared, that much is clear. I told him there wasn't much I could do for him unless he thinks it's tied up in the work we do with narcotics. All I got was a headshake, so I told him that I knew a guy who could help."

"I suppose I'm off to Albuquerque in the morning, then," James said. "I'll put Molly on Judge Winters's court cases. See if she can't find something fishy."

Wayne stood to shake Sanchez's hand again. "I'm off, too. Pleasure as always."

Sanchez could never tell if Wayne Tully was being sarcastic. He shook his hand anyway.

James stood, too. "I'll be back in a minute to make copies of those photographs," he said.

"One last thing," Wayne added at the threshold. "What's a judge's son know about narcotics?"

"I can't exactly tell you that. It's close hold in NARC division. I'm already stepping out of bounds a bit. But Isaiah can brief Pinter if he'd like."

Wayne nodded. Waved as he left the room.

"See you, Wayne."

When Sanchez was alone again, he scrubbed his face

with his hand and breathed deeply. At first, he hadn't taken Isaiah's pleas for help all that seriously. Sure, he trusted his informant, but grief could do strange things to a person. But when he went to make copies of the evidence and the photos as "part of his own report," he saw that lizard. It was orange, bright, obvious. Sanchez might not be the lead homicide detective, but the scene didn't make sense. He was certain that plush toy had not been at Cathy Winters's home. Something was wrong with this case. Isaiah Winters was right.

8

GEORGE

It didn't feel far enough, but George doubted anywhere would. At least there was protection here. That's what he'd been told anyway. George had made so many mistakes. He couldn't believe what he'd almost done. He hadn't planned any of this. When he left Sanostee that morning, he'd thought the afternoon would find him in Shonto, visiting Sandra. She was expecting him. But then everything changed, and when he left that office, he knew he and Adriel would have to move quickly and that they would need another vehicle. And that was before George found out he was wanted for double homicide.

So far, George had managed to stay focused enough to avoid getting caught. Which had to mean something, considering every police department in the surrounding four states was looking for him. At first, Adriel had been upset. Of course he was upset. He'd lost Sunny. And he would've felt even worse if he understood what was happening. But George managed to calm him down by acting like they were on a big adventure. Adriel seemed to buy it. Maybe. He seemed to want to, at least.

George was tired. So tired. Tired in his bones, his hair, his fingernails. Now that they were here, he felt like he could sleep for a week. But he knew he couldn't. And wouldn't be able to if he tried. George had to be vigilant until . . . when? He didn't know.

He felt like the world's biggest fool. Now that they'd stopped moving, he could think about what he had done. What he had been doing. He thought about Linda's anger the day she found out. George had been so stupid to think he had an answer for everything. That he could explain it all away. Justify it. He would never forget how hardened her eyes had become when he tried. It was the first time something had shifted inside of him. Doubt. Just a glimmer, and it had made him uncomfortable.

And then to do what he'd done after Linda died? It was inexcusable. When he let himself think of it, he felt such panic that his throat seemed to close off. His thoughts tumbled. And so, he tried to focus on Adriel. To look at his face. To remember why he had made the decision he had. For love.

[9]

MOLLY

EVEN THOUGH PAULA was eager for a road trip, she did not want to go to Albuquerque.

"Place is a shithole," she'd told Molly.

"Isn't that where you lived, like, your whole life?" Molly asked.

"Yup," she said. "Have fun!"

Now, Molly packed the last of her things into the trunk of the gray Ford Thunderbird her dad had bought just a few weeks ago. Camera. Sketchbook. Colored pencils. Notebook. Clothes and shoes and bathroom things. And in her purse, her revolver.

She was excited, and she could tell that James was, too. Not only because of this new case and the meetings they had set up in Albuquerque, but also because of Wayne and Kay's trip. Though she would miss them, they had all been so anxious to do something—anything—for Adriel. Their trip felt like a relief.

Molly and James had woken before the sun to see them off. Kay gave Molly a big hug.

"I hope you find him," Molly whispered. Kay said nothing, only nodded, but when Molly pulled away, Kay's eyes were wet. Then, she blinked it away.

Molly was tired from waking up so early, and just outside of Gallup, she asked to stop for a coffee.

She and James leaned up against the bumper, sipping coffee—Molly carefully, James taking large gulps. He handed her a folder with a few papers slipped inside.

"Two lists for you in there," he said. Molly pulled them out.

"Names?" she asked.

"I was thinking when we get to Albuquerque, you could visit the courthouse and check out Judge Winters's cases."

Molly sipped. Felt the hot liquid warm her chest. Noticed the sweet aftertaste of the creamer.

"All of his cases?" she asked.

"That's where these lists come in. One is from Barb. A list of important politicians in New Mexico. The other is from Sanchez. Law enforcement officers in New Mexico. Not all of 'em, of course. But as many as he could think of and dig up. If you find a case involving any of these names, make a copy."

"Are you coming?"

James shook his head. "I'm gonna pay a visit to this Janice Stone. She's probably just a friend of George's. Or maybe a friend of Linda's. But now that we're down here, I need to check up on her. She hasn't returned any of my calls. Tomorrow, we'll both go see Isaiah Winters."

Molly sipped again. "Why can't I come to see Janice?"

"Just a time thing, honey. We've got to get you back to school on Monday."

"All right." Molly hated being left out, but if she had to decide between the two meetings, she'd pick the murdered judge's son. "Anything else at the courthouse?"

"While you're scannin' the cases for names, keep an eye out for cases where something feels off. If you read something that doesn't smell quite right, trust your gut."

Molly liked that her dad was trusting her with this. That he was allowing her discretion and not just giving orders. It was Molly's job to find the judge's enemies. The thought made her heart hammer in her chest. Or maybe that was the coffee.

James took one last gulp and then tossed his cup at the trashcan across the sidewalk. It tumbled in.

"Nice throw," Molly said. She tucked the papers back into the folder and the folder under her arm, all while balancing her still piping-hot coffee.

James glanced at his watch. "Not quite two hours until we get to the city," he said. "Chimichangas for lunch?"

"Always."

JAMES

WELL-KEPT but humble houses lined Janice Stone's street. Family homes. No more than four bedrooms inside, James guessed. Small courtyards. Slightly rusted gates. Bikes propped against stucco walls.

Janice's house was different. For one, it was pink. Not gray or tan, like most of the desert homes in the Albuquerque suburbs. It was, for another, at least twice the size of the others in the neighborhood.

He whistled to himself as he pulled up. The crown jewel of the neighborhood sitting at the very end of a cul-de-sac. He shut his car door carefully and walked up the winding concrete path. There was a small Welcome sign under the house number. He knocked. No answer. Not entirely surprising, since there was no car in view. He walked around the property and saw a large courtyard with a pool and multiple tables and chairs. No sign of life there, either.

He went back to his car and waited. Maybe Janice Stone had gone away for the weekend. Maybe this was a waste of time. That was all right. James had time to waste. He thought of Molly at the courthouse. Plenty of time.

He grabbed the folder with the copies of the documents Sanchez had given him. Pulled out the report for Judge Winters and the one for his wife, Cathy. He made a few mental notes as he reread them and compared them to the photos.

A whiskey tumbler on the desk. Less than an inch of water inside. Melted ice cubes, James guessed. One set of fingerprints on the tumbler: the judge's. Documents next to it regarding George Morris being Adriel Morris's legal father. Blood spattered on each. Beside them, typical office items. Engraved pens. Framed photos of the family. Then, the body. Unaccompanied. One entry wound to the chest and an exit wound causing spatter on the chair to the final rest on the floor. Victim was seated. There were no signs of a struggle. No physical altercation occurred before he was shot. This could have been intimate, personal. The unknown subject was close in proximity. There might have been a final discussion. He or she might have even let the judge finish his drink. This was an intentional, precise execution. There was no additional trace evidence or signs of forced entry. The victim might have known him or her. The scene was not sloppy but organized. Nothing about it struck James as a crime of passion, of a killer acting in the heat of the moment.

Then James looked at the wife's crime scene. Cathy had been in the kitchen. In the photos, she was face down, arms above her head, also in a pool of her own blood. She had been shot from behind. A knife and a partially sliced watermelon were on the counter behind her. The island held her car keys and a water bill still in the envelope. She had left her presumed melon-chopping to do something. Answer the phone? James flipped through the images, looking for a phone. He couldn't find one in any of the photos and definitely no plush orange lizard.

Just then, a car passed by and went up the driveway to Janice Stone's house. James waited for someone to emerge.

Janice was older than he had expected. Maybe late fifties, early sixties. Brown hair graying at the roots. A casual denim dress. Thin but muscular arms for a woman her age. She was circling the car—on her way to the trunk, James supposed— when he got out of his car to greet her. She looked up, startled.

"Good evening, ma'am," he said.

She squinted at him and used one hand to pull the glasses hanging from her neck onto her face.

"Can I help you?" she asked.

"Are you Janice? Janice Stone?"

"Yes." Her tone was not welcoming.

"My name is James Pinter. I was hoping we could chat for a minute."

Something about Janice's stare reminded James of a strict teacher he'd had as a child. She didn't reply at first.

"I have some questions about George and Linda Morris. I believe you called and spoke with one of them on the phone back in May."

Janice's eyebrows furrowed. Still, she was quiet.

"Maybe you'd like to sit down?" He gestured to the bench beside her front door.

"I haven't a clue who you are," Janice said, not moving.

"I'm a private investigator, ma'am," James said. "Linda

Morris was murdered a few months ago." He didn't elaborate, didn't tell her that the killer had already been found. Instead, he watched her face turn pale. Her eyes widen.

"Goodness." She touched her chest. "How terrible. I haven't got anything to do with that."

"No, ma'am," James said. "But I was still hoping you could tell me a little about your relationship with Linda. Or with George."

James could see she was taking deep breaths, her hand still resting on her chest. She looked all around them for a moment, as if the whole neighborhood were watching.

"I didn't know Linda Morris at all," Janice finally said, quietly enough that he had to lean forward to hear.

"And George?" James asked. "George Morris? You must have known him, then. He's a member of the Navajo Nation. Devout Christian?"

Janice's chin lifted just a bit. Her hand came down and found the other. She clasped them together in front of her.

"I'm sure George can explain the nature of our relationship," she said, her voice gaining strength.

"I'm sure he could. But I can't locate him right now. And wherever he went, he took his son with him. So any information I can gather will help us bring them both home."

James saw something curious pass over Janice's face, then. Anger? Fear? She seemed to be at a loss for words again.

"How do you know George Morris, Miss Stone?" James asked. "Friend? Distant family member? Y'all meet through the church?"

"No," Janice said. She cleared her throat and brushed down the front of her dress. "No, I hardly knew him at all.

Now please, Mr. Pinter. I would appreciate it if you would kindly remove yourself from my property before I call the police."

11

KAY

KAY WAITED on the doorstep of Sandra Morris's yellow house. It had an attached garage and three clothing lines strung up across the front lawn. She tugged at her blouse again and tried to ignore Wayne's composure. She wished it didn't bother her. Not everyone had to be as high-strung as she was. And yet, his apparent lack of urgency annoyed her.

She couldn't remember the last time she had dressed up like this. She didn't know why she had packed this bright-green top with oversized flowers and boxy shoulders. It wasn't like Adriel would care what she wore. Not that Adriel would be here, behind the door, his eager, sweet face staring back at her, his scrawny little-kid arms ready to hug her. She knew it wouldn't be that easy, and yet with every step, every movement, Kay felt like she needed to be prepared for that very thing to happen.

Maybe the top was for Sandra. To make some kind of impression. And what was that impression? Responsibility? A good caretaker for Adriel? Or maybe Kay just wanted to appear as if she was better than Sandra. Better than George. Maybe she wanted to intimidate the woman.

Kay didn't feel like she was that petty or mean, but here she was anyway, in slacks and a blouse. Itching, still, for what had been taken from her.

Sandra answered the door with a baby on her hip and another young one hiding in her skirts. She smiled warily. "Can I help you?"

Wayne stuck out his hand. "Lieutenant Wayne Tully from over in Shiprock. We've been speaking on the phone about the disappearance of your brother and nephew."

Nephew, Kay thought. He was this woman's nephew, too. Kay knew that, of course. But the word seemed to belong to Kay alone. Adriel belonged to Kay.

Sandra's smile widened. "Lieutenant Tully! Please, come in."

Sandra led them from the foyer to the living room. Kay could smell something cooking. Something with garlic in it. Her stomach rumbled. She'd been too anxious to eat much the last few days. But this? Whatever she smelled? She could eat it.

"Please, sit," Sandra said, reaching a hand toward the sofa. Two more young children were playing together in this room. None of them had shoes on, and Kay noticed how faded and discolored their clothes were. Both looked up for a moment and smiled at her and Wayne.

"I'm sorry," Sandra said, looking at Kay now. "I don't think I got your name."

"Kay," she said. "Kay Benally. Adriel's aunt."

Sandra nodded once. "I am so sorry for your loss. I only

met your sister a few times, but she really was a lovely woman."

Kay felt her throat closing up. She wondered when speaking about Linda would become any easier. "Thank you," she said, quietly.

"So, you came all the way from Sanostee?"

It was the first time she had detected any hint of apprehension in Sandra. *Good*, thought Kay. So Wayne was right. This trip wouldn't be a waste.

"We couldn't sit around and wait for Adriel any longer," she said, staring at the woman. She knew she ought to soften her tone. She could feel Wayne's eyes on her.

"And George." Sandra returned Kay's stare. There was a challenge now in those soft eyes. "Surely you're worried about George, too. Being falsely accused of murdering two people."

Kay opened her mouth to tell Sandra that, actually, she wasn't sure that George *hadn't* murdered those two people and she wouldn't care if she never saw his face again, when Wayne cut in.

"Of course," he said. "We want to get to the bottom of this and bring them both home safely."

"Well." Sandra tore her gaze away from Kay and focused on Wayne. "I'm not sure how else I can help. I've told you everything I could over the phone."

Kay looked at Wayne, too, who nodded.

"And Rich came to check up, too. Officer Frazier, I mean," Sandra went on.

"Of course," Wayne said. "I wanted to put faces to names for the both of us. Ask around the area in case others may have seen or heard anything. Officer Frazier, I'm sure, is doing a fine job. We're just here to assist for a bit."

He put his hands together between his knees. "It's likely that George tried to go home. Go somewhere familiar." Kay wasn't sure if that was true or not. She suspected Wayne and James often bullshitted people.

Kay studied Sandra's face for any clues that she knew exactly where George was and what he was doing. Stealing Adriel, of course. But why? He could've murdered two people all on his own without involving his son. What was he doing with Adriel? Kay wanted this woman—this woman who might know George better than Kay did, better, maybe, than anyone alive did—to give them answers. She wanted something more than that stupid, plastered-on grin. She tried to be patient, though. Tried to let Wayne do his job.

"It's still crazy to me that anyone could think George would do what they're accusing him of," Sandra said, chuckling nervously. "He's not a killer. He's not even a fighter. He's been as straight as an arrow ever since finding the church."

"So where did he go? Why did he leave if not to go commit this horrific act?" Kay asked.

"Slow down, there, Kay," Wayne said. "We don't know what George has or has not done. And we're not accusing him either."

Kay was studying Sandra, but she didn't look at either of them. She looked at the baby she was holding. Switched him to her other hip.

"Maybe he was intending to leave anyway. Before all of this happened—before he was framed. Maybe there just wasn't anything left for him in Sanostee now that Linda's gone."

"If that's the case, he could've told us. He could've said something. Who rips a child away from everything they know? From his family?"

"Who's his family?" Sandra asked, glaring at Kay. "You?"

Kay breathed deeply. She was surprised Wayne wasn't jumping in to stop her from saying something terrible. But she stopped herself. Maybe Adriel loved this woman, too. This wasn't about Kay's anger. It was about Adriel.

"Adriel has me, yes. But also Thelma Long, his teacher. He has friends. You should know how far family extends in the community. Or maybe you don't, because you've been lucky enough to have plenty of brothers and sisters and children. But those of us who don't have that, we know that our neighbors, our friends, *are* family. Adriel has plenty of people who care a great deal about him in Sanostee. They are his family as much as we are."

Sandra's face reddened. Kay wasn't sure if she had embarrassed her or angered her, but she didn't wait for a response.

"Besides," Kay went on. "George loves his church there. That's his spiritual family. And he had a good, steady job. It doesn't make sense for him to leave without warning."

Sandra was quiet. Even the children on the floor had stopped playing to watch the two women. Outside the back window, two older children screeched in delight. Kay turned to watch them play with the hose.

"We need to know where they are," she said, staring out the window.

"I don't know." Sandra's voice was low. Quiet. "George is my brother. I always answer the phone when he calls. But that doesn't mean I know any more about his life these days than you two do. I don't know where he and Adriel are. But I know my brother is not a killer."

Kay stood from the couch, and Wayne followed her lead.

"We'll be in town a few days," he said, handing Sandra the phone number for their hotel in Kayenta. "If you think of anything. Any detail about the last time you spoke or something that George did or said at one point that you think might help us, please call."

Sandra nodded, her smile gone. "It was nice to meet you."

[12]

WAYNE

THE INFURIATING thing about Kay was that she was usually right. Her delivery wasn't great and her timing was terrible, but she was smart. She knew it, too, which annoyed Wayne a little. He sympathized with her, he did. After all she had been through, she was still here. Still fighting for Adriel. If he could only soften her up a little. Make her more approachable, more understanding. Not so brash. But he had brought her along with him knowing all that about her.

He took a deep breath and opened the passenger door for her.

"I know, I know," she said, as she ducked in. He walked around to the driver's side and got in. Then, he sat there for a moment, staring at the house. This was, he was pretty sure, the house George had grown up in.

"I actually held back a little, if you can believe it," Kay said.

"I do," he said.

"Maybe next time you go alone," she offered.

Wayne chuckled. "Hopefully there is a next time."

"Awww, come on." Kay nudged him with her elbow. "I wasn't *that* bad."

Wayne smiled but shook his head. Put the car in reverse.

"Where to now?" Kay asked.

"Let's go by George's old church before we leave Shonto. There's bound to be a few old friends still there. Maybe some staff. A pastor or someone."

"Is Sandra all that's left of his family in this area? Of his gazillion siblings?"

"Not quite. He's got a brother in Tsegi, and his mother lives in Kayenta now."

"His mother's still around? Why didn't we visit her first?"

"According to a good friend of George's at the Church of the Open Door, George and his mom are very estranged. Sandra's his favorite of the family. Maybe the only one he's in regular contact with. You know, the kids get along well with Adriel."

Wayne glanced over at Kay as he stopped for a red light. Her eyes grew wide.

"The kids!" she cried. "We should talk to the kids! If they've seen Adriel, won't they tell us?"

Wayne smiled. Smart indeed. "That was my thought, too. Talk to them when their mom's not around. Maybe pay them a visit at their school this week."

Kay nodded vigorously. "Okay, so the rest of the family. Where are they?"

"Scattered," Wayne said. "Mostly to the big cities."

"His father?"

"Passed a few years ago."

"So, we'll visit the brother next? Or the mother? After the church?"

"Mother's next. We can take our time here in Shonto, though, if we need to. Miss Tammy Morris's apartment is close to our hotel. We can always visit her tomorrow," Wayne said.

"Okay. . . ." Kay dragged out the word. "You're the expert."

Wayne pulled into the church's parking lot. *Patience*, he reminded himself. *Be patient with Kay*. Wayne was an observer. He worked best when he was able to watch. To notice things. People, places. He could draw plenty of conclusions. It helped him know what to ask next. But Kay was a doer.

He opened his door and stepped out to get a good look at the church. One level. Flat roof. Only a few windows visible from the front. Nothing to announce its purpose other than a small sign next to the door: Nazarene Living Word Church.

Kay plowed ahead, though, so Wayne followed her to the front door and stepped aside to open it for her. They walked in. The lights were dim, and it smelled musty. The foyer was covered in a light-yellow wallpaper with small flowers. It peeled a bit where it met the ceiling and floor. Double doors stood to their left. To the right, a short hallway led to what looked like the bathrooms, a janitor's closet, and possibly a few offices.

Wayne tried to take it in. This was where George had been saved as a teenager. It wasn't much. Nothing about this building was impressive. What had even brought him here?

"It's Saturday," Kay said. Her voice seemed to echo down the empty hallway. "Do you think anyone is even here?"

Wayne nodded toward the hallway. "Let's see."

Kay led the way again, and Wayne looked up at the

ceiling as they went. At least half the lightbulbs were out. Past the men and women's restrooms were three doors. Two on the left, one on the right. The signs next to the doors read Pastor Hogue, Nursery, and Staff. Both the staff door and Pastor Hogue's were slightly ajar. Soft music trickled into the hallway.

Kay let Wayne do the knocking. He heard scuffling. Papers being moved, a chair sliding out.

Pastor Hogue was a wide, sturdy man with a head shaped like a block. His hair was tied into a bun at the nape of his neck, and he took up most of the doorway. Wayne shook his hand.

"Pastor Hogue. It's nice to meet you. My name's Wayne Tully, and this is Kay Benally." Pastor Hogue gave them both a closed-lip smile. "I'm the police lieutenant over in Shiprock."

Pastor Hogue took his hand off the doorknob and crossed his arms. He nodded.

"Nice to meet you both," he said, stepping aside. "Please come in."

As he followed Kay into the small office, Wayne noted the rows and rows of shelved binders behind the desk. A painting of a resurrected Jesus in the clouds, arms extended, hanging on the opposite wall. A framed photo collage with smiling men and women with their arms around one another. One at a potluck. Another at what looked like a concert. Many more inside the church's nave.

"What brings you to Shonto?" Pastor Hogue asked, standing beside his desk. Without being invited, Wayne took a seat. He wanted the man to know he intended to take up a little of his time.

"Working on a missing persons case," he replied. He prayed that Kay would keep quiet this time, and hoped with them in His house, the good Lord would abide. "I'm not sure if you've heard about the man they're looking for in Albuquerque. He's been accused of killing two people and is on the run. He's got his young son with him."

Pastor Hogue's eyebrows went up. He crossed his arms but didn't reply.

"The man in question is from around this way. I'm not sure how long you've been preaching here, but I was hoping you might remember him. George Morris was a member of this congregation, oh, about ten years ago now. Maybe a little more. He likely would've come alone. His family were not believers."

Pastor Hogue rubbed his chin. "Would Officer Frazier have already come around asking about him?"

"I hope so," Wayne said. "It's been about a week now since George and his little boy, Adriel, went missing and two days less than that since authorities in Albuquerque asked the reservation to be on the lookout for him."

Pastor Hogue nodded. Kay had not yet spoken up, and it was about this time that Pastor Hogue seemed to remember she was there, too.

"And Mrs. Benally," Pastor Hogue said. "Are you George's wife? Or a relative?"

Kay snorted. "Sister-in-law," she said. "He was married to my sister."

"Was?"

"She died about five months ago now, Pastor."

"I am very sorry to hear it."

"Murdered, actually," she added. "Not by George."

Finally, the good pastor looked concerned. He took a few steps toward Kay, put his hands on her shoulders, and said, "That is truly a terrible thing. Please accept my condolences. Was she a believer?"

"She was," Kay said. Wayne watched her shift her weight under the pastor's touch. She was clearly uncomfortable, and Wayne didn't blame her.

"Then she is with Jesus now. Take comfort in that."

For a moment, Wayne saw amusement dancing behind Kay's eyes. *Don't offend the man*, he silently pleaded. *Play along.*

He could almost see her bite the inside of her cheek. Adjust her face. "Thank you," she said.

Wayne let out a long breath as Pastor Hogue finally made his way to the swivel chair behind his desk. He sat back and placed his arms on the armrests. He did not offer Kay a seat and she did not take one.

"I do remember George," he said. "Young. He came to the services alone, as you say. I remember him being serious but kind. Quiet."

"Do you know anything about his family? The Morrises? There were quite a few of them."

Pastor Hogue nodded. "George did bring his sister to a few services, but she wasn't particularly interested. Sure, I knew of the Morrises. From what I understand . . ." He paused. Sighed. "I can't say George's family life was the happiest."

"In what way?"

"His father was gone a lot. They never really knew when or if he would return. The mother . . ." He stopped again. Leaned forward. Folded his hands together on his desk. "She isn't a happy woman. She wasn't good to those kids. They tried their best to raise each other. At least, that's the impression I got from a distance."

"Did George ever open up to you about these things?"

Pastor Hogue shook his head. "Like I said, he was quiet. Shy. But I could put you in touch with our youth pastor at the time." He pulled a pen from a mug that read *God's #1 Fan* and scribbled something on a pad of paper. He ripped out the page and handed it to Wayne.

Jeff Natonabah, it said. With an address.

"Jeff is retired now. But he worked with our youth for years. He'll be happy to talk. I can't say whether George Morris was more open with him or not, but if there's anything to learn about young George, Jeff is your man."

"Appreciate it," Wayne said. "And what exactly did Jeff do with the youth? What does the youth program entail?"

"Oh, you know. After-school basketball. Summer trips to the lake. Stories and songs by the fire. Just giving the kids something to do, somewhere to go."

"Your teenagers are into that kind of stuff?"

"Not many," Pastor Hogue admitted. "It's a struggle to get the teenagers to come. And to keep coming. Most of them are getting into trouble instead."

"But not George."

"The ones we do get tend to be a little different from their peers."

"So, George didn't have many friends?" Wayne asked.

Kay cleared her throat, and Wayne wondered what she was thinking about all this.

"Like I said, I didn't know him very well. But the fact that he came here alone, that he wanted to be involved with the youth activities at his age? It's a safe assumption."

Kay very pointedly and unnecessarily looked at her wristwatch. Wayne understood. They had exhausted all information here. He stood and shook the pastor's hand.

"Thank you for your time."

"Please, anything else I can assist with."

Wayne nodded once and steered Kay out of the room.

As soon as they got outside, she said, "That man is weird."

"A little strange, sure," Wayne said. "He doesn't seem to understand people."

"This whole place is weird," she said. "And George was weird. Still is. Makes sense he would go to this weird church."

Wayne chuckled. "Things aren't always as they seem."

Kay raised her eyebrows. "Can we find a place to get a burger? I'm starving."

"We can try," Wayne said. They got in the car and shut their doors.

"I didn't realize George's parents were so awful," Kay went on. "Linda never said anything about that."

"Maybe George never talked about it."

"To his own wife?"

"They must have had secrets."

"Do you and Barbara have secrets?"

Wayne thought for a moment before shifting the car into gear. "I don't know," he finally said. "I don't keep secrets from her. But I can tell you from twenty years on the job, I'm the exception. Most people keep secrets. Even from their spouse."

13

MOLLY

MOLLY HAD THOUGHT that looking through court cases would be exciting. Like watching a courtroom drama on paper. But she didn't understand half of what she was reading, and as the minutes wore on, she felt a deep worry that she would disappoint James and he would never again assign her something so important. She read the first three cases multiple times, trying to make sense of them. Finally, she started to skim and made peace with the fact that if James wanted to come read them himself, he could. It wasn't like Molly had a law degree. She would look for the names and that was it. She could manage that. It wouldn't be a complete failure.

Two cases showed up for two names on the list. Both seemed, to Molly, simple. They weren't pages and pages long, like others she had flipped through. Both were divorces. Custody cases. One involved a police officer from Sanchez's list, and the other involved a state representative from Barbara's list. Molly copied them both. She had noticed something else, too. A lot of the judge's cases had the same lawyer. She supposed that could be completely normal. Lawyers probably had specialties, and though this man's cases seemed on the complex side—or at least long—she supposed there was a reason for that, too. Still, she copied a few of them just in case it wasn't normal. *Trust your gut*, James had said. And Molly's gut told her it wasn't a coincidence.

The sky was changing colors, the sun starting to set, when James entered the office where Molly was sitting alone, going back through the cases she had simply skimmed the first time around. He sat across from her at the small table.

"Find anything good?" he whispered.

Molly shrugged. "Maybe."

He pointed to the papers in her hand. "You've got more there?"

"These are ones I've already looked through. I'm just looking again in case something shows up that I didn't notice before."

James nodded his approval. "Want some help?"

Molly breathed a sigh of relief. "Sure. I swear some of this isn't even in English."

James chuckled and looked at his watch. "We've probably got about forty-five more minutes until they kick us out. Hand me that stack next to you."

Molly gladly slid it across the table. "Oh," she remembered. "Look for a Bobby Tate. He's a lawyer."

James didn't raise his eyebrows or even cock his head. He just said, "Copy that."

Molly saw a light flick off down the hallway just as James returned from copying a few more cases. He looked at his watch. "Yup. It's about time. Let's get packed up here."

She stood, and they both gathered their papers into folders. Stacked them in the crooks of their arms. The woman at the desk gave them a tight smile as they exited.

"Good night," James said.

They piled the folders in the back seat. Molly thought she ought to sit next to them to keep them from spilling all over the floor, under the seats. But she was too tired to care enough. James drove to a pizza place with an illuminated sign outside and a picture of the Colosseum. Empire Pizza Pie. Windows wrapped around the building, and Molly could see teenagers huddled around two tables, sitting backwards on chairs, laughing, rolling their eyes. In a corner booth, a mom with two young children looked exasperated. By the teenagers or her own children, Molly couldn't tell.

Molly carried the stack of cases inside, careful not to drop anything. She thought about dripping pizza sauce on them and held them tighter.

James ordered while Molly found a booth. She eyed the teenagers. She knew that vibe. They were plotting some juvenile nonsense. Not that any of them were about to come steal the case files. Molly sighed. She was tired.

A few minutes later, James slid in across from her with four giant slices of pepperoni pizza and two bottles of Dr. Pepper.

Molly pushed her plate away from the papers. "No grease, no sauce on the cases."

James grinned. "I've got a strict boss. Okay, you got it. Eat first. Yes, ma'am."

He took a big bite and pulled the slice away, the cheese stretching between his mouth and the pizza before breaking and falling onto his chin.

"You're a creature," Molly said, shaking her head.

James shoved the rest of the cheese into his mouth. "It's a miracle that such a lovely lady like yourself came from me," he said, once he'd finished chewing.

Molly took a bite of her pizza. They ate in silence for a minute before James spoke again.

"So. Bobby Tate. Notice something about his cases?"

Molly thought, took a sip before answering.

"Not really. Lots of pages. Maybe more complex cases? Or maybe they took longer to decide? Needed additional . . . things? Evidence?" Her face turned red as she grasped for legal terms and realized she didn't actually know what any of them meant. But James looked thoughtful. He nodded.

"Good, good. There's something else I noticed about Mr. Tate's cases. A decent number concerned Navajos. Have you noticed that some last names are popular on the reservation?"

"Sure," Molly said. "At school, there are lots of Begays and Nezes and Yazzies and Benallys—like Kay."

"Exactly," James said. "Navajo names from the Navajo language. Saw lots of 'em pop up in Mr. Tate's cases."

"Clients?" Molly asked.

James shook his head. "Not one of 'em."

"So he's arguing cases for the state?"

James shook his head again. "We'll have to take a closer look, but I don't think he's doin' that, either."

"Hmmmm." Molly took another bite of her pizza. "What if we need more help understanding what the cases mean?"

"We'll ask Barb for some insight," James said.

"I thought she was in politics."

"She is. But she also went to law school."

"She did?" She was already impressed with Barbara. But law school, too? She chewed her last bite, wiped her hands thoroughly with a napkin, and took a deep breath.

14

ISAIAH

Isaiah slammed another cabinet closed. There was nothing for breakfast. He hadn't gone grocery shopping. Hadn't cleaned the kitchen—or anything else in the house. Hadn't been able to do much of anything but show up to work, get lost in the monotony of the job. Pouring drink after drink, opening the cash register, bringing change, barely speaking to clients on busy nights—and on not-so-busy nights making a show of cleaning to avoid conversation. He would come home in the middle of the night and stare at his ceiling as he lay in bed, trying to fall asleep. Sometimes, eventually, in the early hours of the morning just before the sun started to light the sky, he would drift off to a restless sleep. But never for long.

If anyone else was aware of what Isaiah knew, he might be dead by now, too. Most likely would be. It was both comforting and nauseating. So, if they didn't know now, how long would it be until they did?

He hadn't even hesitated when his mother, Cathy, asked for his help. He'd taken the chance to be a part of her world, if only for a brief time. It was a kind of acting. Just like bartending. Isaiah was good at pretending to be something he wasn't. He had a lot of practice.

He had just started to brew some coffee when the doorbell rang. He tensed. Let it ring again. He took a deep breath. Maybe it was the cops. Maybe they had decided to do their job properly. He didn't know if that would be good or bad for him. Or maybe it was Agent Sanchez. Asking Isaiah to do his *other* job again. The one that required him to lay a secret on top of his other secret. Isaiah felt buried in secrets.

He peeked out the living room window at the front door. There was a man there. And a girl. A teenager. Isaiah let out a breath. They probably had the wrong house. Still, he opened the door to tell them so, plastering on a tight smile.

"Can I help you?"

"Hi there." The man smiled easily back at him. "My name's James Pinter, and I'm here to speak with Isaiah Winters. Is that you?"

"Yes, that's me."

The man stuck out his hand, and Isaiah shook it.

"I'm a private investigator up on the Navajo reservation, and this is my daughter, Molly."

Isaiah smiled at her and nodded. "Hello." The girl stuck out her hand, too.

"Nice to meet you," she said.

"I'm sorry to hear about your parents," James Pinter said.

"Yes, thank you," Isaiah managed to get out. He swallowed. "They were wonderful people. Both of them."

"Do you have a minute to talk?" James asked. "I took a look at the case. I think the state police might be missing a few things."

Isaiah studied the private investigator. So this was the man Agent Sanchez thought could help him.

"All right," he said, letting them in. He thought about a father and daughter working together. They must be close. Like Isaiah and his mother. Maybe this man would understand. The sound of the coffee dripping out of the machine welcomed them into the kitchen.

"Would you like some coffee?" he asked.

"Sure," James said.

Isaiah looked at the daughter next. "Yes, please," she said.

He served them coffee while James talked.

"I'm sure you know Agent Sanchez with the state police."

"Yes," was all Isaiah offered.

"He mentioned you might need some help. He told me you don't believe that George Morris killed your parents. I have some experience with cases like this one. Cases tied up in political knots, involving heavy hitters."

Isaiah placed a jug of milk in front of the guests for their coffee.

"Political crimes?" Isaiah asked.

"I was in the Army. Investigating higher-ups can be difficult. You need to tread lightly."

Isaiah nodded. This man was quick.

"How much did you know about your father's career?" James asked.

"As much as anyone else, I guess."

"Did he ever talk specifics with you? A particular case that may have troubled him? Maybe he complained about something simple, like a sleazy defense attorney or a spaced-out stenographer?"

"Both of my parents were quite public about the things they cared about," Isaiah answered.

"And what did they care about?" James asked.

Isaiah watched the girl. She was taking notes. Maybe even transcribing. She seemed to write very quickly.

"My father did everything he could to keep children with their families. He made sure the parents had support, even after a child was taken. Rehab, temporary housing, whatever they needed. Sometimes he even called the electric company and paid a bill. Edited résumés. If the parents wanted to be good parents, he helped them become good parents. If they didn't, my father was adamant about finding a relative. An aunt, an uncle, a grandparent. He just . . ."

He paused. "He didn't like the foster care system we have here in New Mexico. He tried to keep children away from it. He thought it was deeply flawed."

"Huh," James said.

The girl—what was her name? Isaiah had forgotten. He wasn't good with names. James's daughter bit her lip. Furrowed her eyebrows.

"What can you tell me about their marriage?" James asked. "Did they fight a lot?"

"My parents loved each other. They had fights, of course. Every couple does. But they always made up."

James nodded. His daughter was scribbling away again.

"Now . . ." James leaned over the kitchen island, interlaced his fingers. "I understand you found your mother. That must have been difficult. I don't like to ask you to recall those memories, but it would certainly help with the investigation if you could tell me your version of that night's events."

Isaiah's chest tightened. He took a deep breath. Looked

up at the ceiling. He hadn't let himself think about the details of that night yet.

"I . . . um . . ." His voice shook. He cleared his throat. "I have a standing dinner date at their house every Wednesday. It's one of my nights off work. I come a little early sometimes to help my mom cook."

He sipped his coffee. "That day, I called to ask if she needed me to pick up anything at the store. She said to grab some dessert. She said she was making haddock. My father's favorite. But that she'd had a long day and wouldn't have time for dessert."

Isaiah bit the inside of his cheek before continuing. "I could smell the fish as soon as I walked in. I yelled, 'It's me, Mom!' But she didn't answer. I hung up my jacket and went around the corner. I could smell something else, then. Something metallic. Blood. Lots of blood. I saw her lying face down and sort of froze at first. It was like it wasn't real. Like I was waiting to wake up. But the smell brought me back. The fish and the blood. It made me gag. I had to turn away."

The words caught in his throat, and he stopped talking.

"Do you remember calling the police?" James asked after a moment.

He nodded. "I called Agent Sanchez. I don't know why I didn't call 911. I guess I thought he would respond quicker or something. After I hung up, I sat next to my mom. On the floor. In her blood. I still hadn't touched her. I yelled in her ear at first. It was obvious she was dead. I was thinking, she was all alone when she was killed. She must have been afraid. I didn't want to touch her. But I didn't want to leave her, either."

"What happened when Sanchez came?"

"He called more police. He led me away from her and sat with me, and I guess he talked to me. I don't remember what he said. Then more cops came. They asked me questions, like you're doing now. They asked me to come to the station. That's when I realized I hadn't called my father. I told them I needed to call him."

"And did you?"

Isaiah nodded. "He didn't pick up. Of course."

"Did he always work that late?"

"Always."

"Do you happen to remember seeing a stuffed animal at your parents' house?"

Isaiah's forehead wrinkle. His mouth turned down. "A stuffed animal?"

"A lizard, actually," James said. "An orange lizard."

Isaiah shook his head. "No. I didn't see anything like that."

"If there had been a stuffed animal there—say, somewhere you didn't notice—do you have any idea why it would have been at your parents' house? Are there any children that your parents often have around? Neighborhood kids? Family friends?"

Isaiah had no idea what this was about, but he tried to rack his brain. "I don't think so." He glanced at his watch. He didn't have anywhere to be yet, but he was exhausted from this conversation. He wanted to wrap it up.

"You said your mother had had a busy day," James said. "What did she do for work?"

"Nothing," Isaiah said. "She never had a job. She raised me, and then she got really involved in the community. She volunteered tons of places. Sometimes she helped campaign for local politicians, though she always had to be careful with my dad's position."

"And you? Can you tell me about your work? What you do for Agent Sanchez?"

"I work at a bar. I'm a bartender. It's also where I gather information for Agent Sanchez."

James nodded but waited a beat. Maybe he was waiting for Isaiah to give more information, but he wouldn't.

"I'd like to help investigate this further," James finally said. "Would you be open to that?"

"What's your rate?" Isaiah asked.

"I don't ask for payment until I bring you new information," James said, which surprised him. The man must have been confident. Or arrogant. "Hourly rate is twelve dollars. Plus gas and expenses. I provide receipts."

Isaiah nodded. It seemed reasonable.

"So, your mom didn't have an office, then. Do you have keys to your parents' house? Your father's office?"

"I've got keys to their house," Isaiah said, walking to the table that held his key chain. "They've asked me to come clean out his office. I haven't yet."

"Can we set up a day and time to do that together?" James asked.

Isaiah nodded again as he slid his parents' house key off his key ring. He handed it to James.

"Do you know who did this?" James asked outright.

Isaiah froze. His heart pattered faster and faster inside his chest. *Did* he know who had murdered his parents? No. He wasn't certain.

He shook his head. But James's eyes said that he was too smart for Isaiah's wavering.

"So what makes you think it wasn't George Morris?" James asked.

"My mother had secrets," Isaiah said, quietly. "I think you ought to find out what they were. The police didn't even look." He turned away. He didn't want to see James's reaction to that. He didn't want to answer any more questions. He led James and his daughter to the door.

"I hope you can find who did this," he finally decided to say. "My parents deserve that much."

James shook his hand. "I intend to."

[15]

JAMES

JAMES KNEW he ought to walk into the Albuquerque division of the New Mexico State Police with some humility. After all, as far as they were concerned, he only had crumbs.

"The police normally don't have a hard time workin' with P.I.s. As long as they feel like we're workin' together," he told Molly.

"But we're not," she said.

"Correct. But we're gonna make it seem like we are for as long as we can."

Molly cracked a small smile. "All right, then. Scooby Doo," she said.

James chuckled and opened his car door. "Turn on that sniffer."

They locked the bundle of evidence Sanchez had provided in the trunk. The same documents they were about to request access to. As they walked past the checkered cement walls to the front doors of the station, James watched the sun blotch Molly's cheeks in quick patterns like a movie effect. Her profile was serious.

Shoot, James thought, holding the door open for her. *She truly is incredible. She's handling this like a pro.*

He shook his head to clear his thoughts. Then, looked up at the heavyset woman at the front desk. She wore a mean scowl and a black collared shirt, and her jet-black hair was pulled into a bun. Despite her frown lines, James would guess her younger than him. "Hi there, ma'am," he said.

"Yes?"

"I'm hoping to speak with Lieutenant Lark. Is he in today?"

The woman—Chavez, per her nametag—frowned deeper. "You got an appointment?"

"I do not."

"You'll have to wait."

"Of course," James said. "We'll be right here whenever he's available."

"What's your name?"

"James Pinter."

"You can't bring kids in here," she said, scribbling something down. Maybe James's name.

"Oh no," James said. "Molly here is a professional sketch artist. And my notetaker."

The woman pursed her lips. "Is that so?"

"That is so," James said. "In fact, if you'd like, she could sketch you right now. You'd be impressed."

The woman rolled her eyes. "That won't be necessary. Have a seat."

James and Molly sat on chairs across from the annoyed woman's desk. There were only three, made of hard metal. Clearly the state police didn't want anyone waiting around.

"She seems lovely," Molly whispered.

"A real charmer," James agreed.

They sat for fifteen minutes. Twenty. Thirty. Molly shifted positions about a hundred times.

James thought about this Lieutenant Lark. Cops typically only came in a handful of personalities, and even fewer at this level—head of criminal investigations for the northwest region of New Mexico. Hard-assed. Smart. Someone who had an uncanny ability to understand people on a very deep level.

Finally, grumpy Chavez called, "James Pinter!" very loudly, even though no one had moved and she must have been well aware of that fact. She stood and glowered at them. "Lieutenant Lark will see you now." James and Molly followed her down a hallway.

"He's only got about ten minutes," she said over her shoulder. "So get to the point."

"Got it. Thanks for the heads-up."

Lieutenant Lark was shorter than James and had a buzz cut and sharp eyes. He shook James's hand first, then Molly's, and looked her right in the eye when he said hello. His office smelled of peppermint and chalk.

"How can I help you folks today?"

"I appreciate you seein' us on such short notice," James started. "My name's James Pinter, and I'm a private investigator. This here is my daughter and my assistant, Molly Pinter."

Lieutenant Lark nodded at each of them in turn.

"I've got a new client as of yesterday," James went on. "A Mr. Isaiah Winters. His parents were found dead about a week ago. A Judge Bartholomew Winters and his wife, Cathy Winters. Are you familiar with the case?"

"Yes," Lieutenant Lark answered immediately. "I've got

one of my senior investigators on it. The suspect is still miss-ing. An Indian man."

"That's right," James said.

"And why has Mr. Winters decided to bring on a P.I.?"

"I work closely with the Navajo Nation Police Depart-ment. My office is up there on the reservation. I have an established relationship with the Shiprock police, which is the region the suspect is from. Mr. Winters wanted someone with some connections to the Navajo."

Lieutenant Lark nodded. "Makes sense, I suppose." He took a moment to study James. "I haven't seen you around."

"I'm new to the area. Was living in Oklahoma for the past five or six years. I used to investigate all sorts. Drugs. Homicides."

"Oklahoma State Police?" Lieutenant Lark asked.

"No, sir. Army. CID."

Lieutenant Lark cracked a smile. "CID during Vietnam. Y'all did a lot of heavy work over there. Smuggling, drugs, rape, war crimes. We could use a guy with that type of experience."

"Working my own contracts suits me now. I don't have to answer to some general behind a desk in DC," James said.

"Huh," Lieutenant Lark said. James could feel the scru-tiny behind his stare. Like he couldn't possibly believe that James had fallen so far from being a cog in the big govern-ment machine.

"I was hoping I could get copies of the reports from the murders. Evidence findings. Crime scene photographs."

Lieutenant Lark's jaw worked. "Unlikely we can release everything," he finally said. "I'll have Sue at the front desk help you file a request. I have to be honest with you, Mr.

Pinter: I haven't had the chance to really comb through the case myself. But once you get the stuff, if there's anything else you need from me, please don't hesitate to call with any questions."

He pulled out his top drawer and groped around for a moment before handing James his business card.

"Thank you, sir," James said. "I do appreciate it."

James and Molly stood. So did Lieutenant Lark. They all shook hands once more.

"It was nice to meet you, Mr. Pinter," Lieutenant Lark said. "You too, Molly."

James watched Molly blush a little, duck her head. She smiled at the man. "Nice to meet you, too, sir."

They left the office, and Lark did not follow them to the door. When they got to the front desk, James leaned on it just a little. Put on his most charming smile.

"Sue, I hate to bother you again, but the lieutenant promised you would help me fill out a request for copies of a case file."

The desk phone rang, and Sue answered it, holding up a finger. "Uh huh. Yes," she said, then hung up.

She sighed loudly, stood, and said, "Come with me."

16

ADRIEL

ADRIEL MISSED how easy it had been to talk to his mom. He knew "talk" wasn't the right word. He couldn't do that. But with her, it felt like he could. Sometimes he wouldn't even have to point or do anything with his hands. Sometimes, just the look on his face would tell her everything she needed to know. But with his dad, George, it had always been harder. Adriel needed to write things down and draw much more often now. It exhausted him.

He was having fun with his dad, though. He was. Things had gotten much better after that first day. That first day was scary. And sad. He missed Sunny. But he wasn't scared anymore; he just wanted to know what they were doing. Where were they? How long would they be there? When would they go back to Sanostee? Back to Aunt Kay and Mrs. Long and that nice girl, Molly, who seemed to somehow understand him better than the grown-ups? If George understood what Adriel wanted to know, he didn't show it.

Finally, Adriel wrote, *Go hom?* and shoved it in front of George's breakfast one day. George stared at it for a long time with crinkled eyebrows and pursed lips. Had Adriel spelled it wrong?

George sighed. He shook his head. "Not yet." And that was all.

Wer ar we? Adriel wrote next.

"Somewhere safe. Mr. Tallsalt will keep us safe."

Adriel bit his lip. He wished his dad would tell him more, but he did like Mr. Tallsalt. He was an older man who didn't smile much, but when he did, his whole face changed. It reminded Adriel of a clown he saw once at the fair, who could change his face from a frown to a big happy smile behind his hand. He wondered if Mr. Tallsalt had ever been a clown. Adriel didn't think so, because Mr. Tallsalt was a serious guy. But he had told Adriel one joke, and Adriel giggled so much he almost peed his pants.

Even after Adriel stopped giggling and Mr. Tallsalt went back to being serious, Adriel could still see the kindness behind his eyes. He was a good person, Adriel could tell. And Adriel wanted him to smile more. To tell more jokes.

One day, when Mr. Tallsalt put him to work gathering firewood, he tapped Adriel on the shoulder.

"Follow," Mr. Tallsalt said. He made a gesture with his hands. Adriel nodded.

"No," Mr. Tallsalt said. "This means 'follow.' Do you see what I'm doing with my hands?"

Adriel watched the gesture again. Mr. Tallsalt had his hands in fists, thumbs on top. His arms were bent. Then he moved both fists together to one side.

"You do it," he said to Adriel. Adriel squatted down, put his wood on the ground, and did the same thing with his arms and hands.

"Good." Mr. Tallsalt nodded. "This is sign language. We'll keep learning more."

Adriel just stared at him for a moment. Mr. Tallsalt sighed and looked softly back at him.

"Sign language is how some deaf people talk. You know, deaf? They can't hear. They talk with their hands."

Adriel tried to slow his brain down. His thoughts were going too fast. He started to nod. He wanted Mr. Tallsalt to tell him more.

"It's a language. Like English or Diné."

Adriel kept nodding. He felt himself balancing on his toes. Like his body might explode. Take off into the air at any moment.

"Maybe we can teach your father, too," Mr. Tallsalt said.

Suddenly, Adriel felt tears at the backs of his eyes, and he didn't know why. He wasn't sad. He wasn't sad at all. He didn't know what to call this feeling. Happy? Exited? Surprised? He swallowed three times. Mr. Tallsalt didn't seem like the kind of guy who cried, and so Adriel tried not to, either.

He bent down and picked up the wood again. When he stood, Mr. Tallsalt was at his side. He patted Adriel's shoulder but said nothing else. They walked the winding path back to the house in silence. But Adriel's mind was not silent. Not silent at all.

17

KAY

JEFF NATONABAH LIVED EVEN FARTHER AWAY from anything resembling a town than Kay did. After a nice, greasy burger at a diner in Kayenta and a stop at the district offices for a detailed map, Wayne and Kay were heading west on a two-lane highway. She hadn't seen a building, a shed, or a trailer in two miles. Finally, Wayne turned onto a dirt road, and Kay could smell something burning.

They parked next to a trailer with a purple door. Smoke billowed from behind it. They circled around back and found a man tossing cardboard and tree branches into a fire.

"Hello?" Kay called over the crackle of the fire. "Mr. Natonabah?"

The man turned and waved. He was almost the same height as Kay. As they walked closer, she could make out the details of his face through the parting smoke. He had a wide nose and round eyes. A small, wrinkled mouth. He was wearing overalls and sandals.

He threw another piece of cardboard on the fire. "How can I help you folks?"

Wayne stuck out his hand. "I'm Lieutenant Wayne Tully."

Jeff turned his head to spit and then gripped Wayne's hand so tight his knuckles turned almost white.

"I'm Kay Benally," Kay said. Jeff gave her the same tight shake.

"We're looking for a guy from around here," Wayne went on. "He went missing with his eight-year-old son."

Jeff put his hands on his hips. "George Morris, right?"

"That's right," Wayne said.

"We've had quite a few people around here looking for George Morris. After he was all over the news." Jeff stepped closer. "Well now, let me get us some chairs."

He disappeared into a shed, emerging with three folding chairs. He set them up around the fire.

He smiled at Kay as he unfolded her chair, and something about the whole situation felt familiar. It made her miss her dad. Maybe because of all the times she'd sat next to him by a fire. Or maybe there was something fatherly about Jeff's smile. Or maybe it was a unique combination of smells and sights and feelings that couldn't easily be replicated. But at that moment, Kay felt like she could reach out and touch her father. Like if she buried her hands into the dirt just a little, she would find him there.

She was grateful for the beat of silence when they all sat. She watched the embers fall at her feet.

"Who else has been looking for George?" Wayne asked.

"There were some reporters at first. They're quick to descend on a town. Like a swarm of bees." Jeff chuckled. "Saw them up at the old trading post. But then I had a man come all the way out here. Definitely not a reporter, I can tell you that much. When I asked who he was, he gave me some story about working with George. Or working for a woman who worked with George. I think that was it. But he was from Albuquerque, he said, and I knew George lived over in Sanostee. The whole thing was strange. He scooted off, though, when I brought out the shotgun."

Jeff grinned, and that made Kay grin, too.

"What'd this guy look like?" Wayne asked.

"Pale. Freckles. Fiery red hair. Looked like bad news, to be honest. I didn't like the looks of him."

"Did he give you a name?"

Jeff looked deep in thought for a moment. He scratched his chin and looked up at the sky. "Can't say he did."

"Hm," Wayne answered.

"Can't imagine how the man found me, other than maybe by talking to Pastor Hogue."

"That's who sent us," Kay said. "He told us you were the youth director at the church in town."

Jeff nodded. "That's right. It's just like the pastor to send everyone to me. He never did like taking responsibility for things. Wouldn't want to be associated with a suspected killer." Jeff sighed. "Not that I mind you all coming by. I'm happy to help law enforcement."

"So, what can you tell us about your time with George?" Wayne asked.

"That family." Jeff shook his head, crossed his arms. Stared into the fire. "I felt for those kids. If any of us saw them around, we tried to help. Bought them a sandwich or a soda. Gave them spare change. Offered a ride. They were polite, too. Respectful. That always surprised me. You'd expect them to be feral with the way their parents were. For

George's upbringing? He was a good kid. A good kid. The George I knew wouldn't hurt a fly."

"When did you leave the church?" Wayne asked. "Was it while George was still around?"

Jeff shook his head. "George was long gone. I retired a few years ago. Hung in there as long as I could, but Pastor Hogue was wearing on me." He paused and scratched the back of his head. "You know, when I found Christianity, there was a different pastor at the church. I was looking for something that I hadn't found in the old teaching. The spirituality I grew up with." He paused and looked up at Kay. "No disrespect if you practice."

Kay wondered how he knew. She shook her head. "It's all right. Go on."

"I was looking for peace. For comfort. I was a fearful young man. As a boy, I was always seeing signs of skinwalkers. Was always convinced someone had cursed me and my family. The evil was too much. I never felt like I could defeat it. But the Bible's New Testament. Jesus. He brought me peace."

Jeff stopped again. He went to stand up. "Would you all like something to drink? I'm thirsty, myself. Been standing here all morning breathing in this smoke."

"Sure," Kay said.

"I'd appreciate it," Wayne said.

"What are you burning?" Kay jumped in, before Jeff could walk away. He frowned and swatted at the air.

"Just trash. My mother died recently. I'm slowly going through her things."

"I'm sorry to hear that," Kay said.

Jeff smiled. "She was old. Very old. But I still miss her."

Kay thought about George, then, after Jeff walked away. About his siblings. Their parents. What that must have been like. Kay and Linda had been poor, but they had been loved. Maybe George hadn't been loved. Maybe Linda's love felt like a gift to him. Kay felt a small tug of sympathy for George but pushed it away. He had stolen Adriel, she reminded herself. Possibly killed two people. She had no time for explanations or pity.

Jeff came back out and passed them bottles of Sprite.

"Where was I?" he asked, sitting back down.

"Jesus brought you peace," Wayne said.

Jeff nodded. "That's right. He did. I suppose we all come looking for different things. I'm not sure what brought Pastor Hogue, but if I had to guess, it might have been something like what brought me. Except he didn't find peace. Didn't seem like it to me, at least. He found anger. Maybe even hatred."

"What do you mean?" Kay asked.

"He railed against the old ways. Pure evil, he called them. We all must turn away completely. Repent. It never sat right with me how he used fear. I'd had enough of that. It wasn't what I went there to hear. Maybe it was the Old Testament that spoke to Pastor Hogue. A vengeful God. A punishing God."

Kay stared into the fire, feeling the bubbles from the soda in the back of her throat. "Maybe our people respond to that because it's something we understand. Suffering."

Jeff made a whistling sound as he sucked through his teeth. "Well now, isn't that the truth?" he asked. "I think sometimes our people are looking for an explanation. Why we went through what we went through. Why we're still going through it. Maybe we're all evil and we deserve it."

A quietness settled over the three of them. Kay took another sip. She didn't think Diné were inherently evil. She wondered what Wayne thought. She didn't know much about his spiritual beliefs other than the fact that he and Barbara attended a Catholic church.

"The kids, though," Jeff went on. "He was teaching them to hate themselves. Their families. Their culture. Everything they knew. It seemed to me Pastor Hogue wanted to tear them down to nothing."

"Is that why you stayed as long as you did?" Kay asked. "To counteract that?"

Jeff smiled a sad smile but didn't look at her. "I sure tried."

"Did George Morris believe that?" Wayne asked. "That he was no good?"

"George didn't need Pastor Hogue to tell him he was no good. He believed it in every fiber of his being before he ever set foot in that church. Pastor Hogue was speaking George's language. George already knew something was wrong with the world. His parents in particular. He ate those sermons up."

"Was he close with George?" Wayne asked.

"No," Jeff said. "Pastor Hogue is a little removed from his people. They're a little afraid of him, I think, and he doesn't mind that."

"Reverence," Kay said, softly.

Jeff nodded. "Reverence."

[18]

TAMMY

TAMMY MORRIS TAPPED the end of her cigarette into her ashtray, watching the black burnt parts crumble into a pile of ashes. She still expected the shrieks of children. Their annoying, incessant pleas for one thing or another. Money. Food. A ride. She had to remind herself constantly that the children were grown. Gone. The grandchildren didn't want to see her. And that was her fault, apparently.

But when Tammy tore through her memories trying to find what she could have done differently, all she felt was exhaustion. Not regret. Not longing.

Sunlight leaked into her kitchen—a corner of the third-floor apartment—and just as she was standing to pull the curtain closed, to give her aching head some peace, there was a knock at her door.

She stood still and waited. It was probably one of her neighbors. Edgar or Pearl. She didn't have the stomach for either of them this morning. Complainers. Thieves. Addicts. Pathetic people all around her.

She quieted her breath. More knocks. Then a voice.

"Mrs. Morris? Are you home?"

She didn't recognize this voice. A man, but not any of the neighbors she knew. Not the building's superintendent. None of them would call her "Mrs. Morris," anyway. She crept to the front door. Pressed her ear against it. She could hear two voices. One a man and one a woman. Who the hell were they? She flung the door open.

The woman was pretty. Much younger than Tammy. Probably around one of her children's age. Sandra's maybe. Tall and thin. The man, quite handsome in a rugged way. She liked the scar across his face. Too bad he was wearing a pig's uniform.

"Yes?" she asked, her voice lower and raspier than she'd expected. She tried to clear it.

"Hi, Mrs. Morris. My name is Wayne Tully. And this is Kay Benally. We were hoping we could have just a few minutes of your time."

Tammy chewed on the inside of her cheek and stared at the woman, who stared boldly back. She didn't even know this bitch. Who did she think she was?

"For what?" Tammy asked. She felt it coming. The blinding anger.

"George? Your son? He's missing. We were wondering if you've seen or heard from him."

George. One of those ones in the middle. Not born early enough for her to have raw, crisp, brand-new memories from back when her brain still produced happy chemicals all on its own. And not born late enough that she'd been almost done with this kid stuff. She'd had more than enough of it by kid eight, nine, ten. *Maybe the next one will kill me*, she'd some-times thought wistfully. *Maybe this will be it.*

But George was just another one. Another mouth to feed. Bottom to smack. Another one to get under her feet. Until he started going to that damn church and trying to tell her what to do and how to live her life. Trying to save her soul. Acting like he knew better than she did. Little brat.

"Good riddance, then," she said.

The woman eyed Tammy more carefully now.

"What are you looking at?" Tammy spat.

She watched the woman swallow her words. Could see how hard that was for her, and it made Tammy laugh. A throaty laugh that always ended with a cough.

"Say it," Tammy said, once she had gained control over herself. "Say what you want to say."

The cop jumped in. "We need to find George. He has his little boy with him. He's wanted for murder."

Tammy squinted. "Murder?" she asked. "George?" She grinned. "He doesn't have it in him. That little pussy. Cowardly little shit."

"So you haven't seen them?" the woman asked.

"Last time I saw George was a long time ago. He called me the devil, and I told him to get the hell out of here. Didn't even know he had a son."

"Let's go, Wayne," the woman muttered, as she turned slightly to leave. But the cop stayed where he was.

It was times like these that Tammy actually missed Samuel. If Samuel had been there, he would have told these people that George was a grown-ass man. He could take care of himself by now. Why the hell would they care where he was?

The man—the pig—was glancing over Tammy's shoulder

now, into her apartment. He couldn't mind his own fuckin' business, this guy. Typical.

"You see something in there?" she asked him. "You want to come in and pick through my things?"

His face reddened, and it pleased her. But then she looked back and saw what he would see. Stacks of bills. Ashtrays everywhere. Yellowing walls. Mouse shit. Why were these people still here? She told them she hadn't seen George since she kicked him out.

"Get the fuck out," she said, quietly.

"Told you," the woman said to the cop.

"Told him what? That you'd find a crazy lady here? Wahoo! You were right! I'm a real cunt! But *I* didn't show up at *your* doorstep judging your shit. Who do you think you are?"

Tammy felt hot fire down her arms, in her head, through her chest. She knew this was when things got bad.

"Okay, Mrs. Morris," he said. "We're leaving. Thank you for your time."

"You're not fuckin' welcome!" she shouted. "Get the fuck out!" She watched them scurry off down the hall. She laughed again, her throaty laugh. Then she slammed the door behind her and raced to the window. She opened it and waited until she saw them below. They were walking through the parking lot, looking over their shoulders as they left. Tammy laughed at them there, too.

"And don't fuckin' come back!" she yelled. "I'll kill you both for trespassing!"

She watched them get into a car. Tammy sat at that window and laughed at them until tears soaked her face.

19

WAYNE

WAYNE AND KAY sat silently in the parking lot of Tammy's apartment complex. It wasn't because he had nothing to say. He had plenty. Too much. He was sorting his thoughts. Organizing them. Deciding what he ought to tell Kay and what he ought to keep to himself. He watched a tiny lizard hop onto the light pole next to where they had parked.

Finally, Kay spoke. "Do you think he did it? Do you think he killed those people? If that's his mother, then . . ." She didn't have to finish the thought.

Wayne didn't respond at first. Neither he nor James had told Kay about Sunny the Gila monster and how it had been logged into evidence with the state police. All Kay knew was that the case was "off." That James had been hired because something wasn't "right." They didn't want her to know that the stuffed lizard was no longer in Adriel's possession. That he was no longer under its protection—something Kay probably didn't truly believe, anyway. And yet, the reality of it would likely be too much for her to handle.

"We know there are holes in the case. Things that don't

add up. Inconsistencies that both Sanchez and Isaiah Winters have reported," Wayne finally said.

Kay nodded. "Why did he take Adriel? Why couldn't he have left him with us?"

Wayne didn't respond to that at first, either.

"It's because he believes exactly what the pastor told him. That we're all evil," Kay said, answering her own question. Her voice was strained and quiet, and for the first time since they had gotten back in the car, Wayne looked at her face. There were tears.

What Wayne didn't say was that it was awfully generous for Kay to assume that George's intentions were good. If he had done what Kay was accusing him of, it meant he loved Adriel. It meant that wherever they had gone, maybe he could take good care of Adriel. Maybe he would. It was a thought that reassured Wayne. The same thought was causing tears in Kay, though, and he could understand that, too. Kay had no children. It was her responsibility to pass on what her father had taught her. And now, maybe, George was refusing to let her do that. Because George thought it was all evil.

"I'm not sure I even blame him after seeing that woman," Kay said. Wayne sighed.

Tammy Morris was clearly a troubled woman and most likely not fit to be a mother, but Wayne had seen worse. Tammy wasn't unique. Neither was George.

Wayne didn't know if Kay was still crying, because she had turned away from him. A moment later, she huffed a little and pointed to the corner of the lot, where a group of people huddled together, passing something around. "A needle," Kay said. "Real nice."

But Wayne wasn't looking at the needle. He was looking at something else. He didn't even shut off the cruiser as he got out and walked past the group. Didn't notice as they all pulled down their sleeves and shoved their belongings under their legs.

He heard Kay slam her door and scamper up behind him.

In the back of the lot, past the pavement, a truck was parked. A truck with no license plate. A truck that had been spray-painted. A half-assed cover-up.

"Shit," Kay hissed. "It's George's."

20

JAMES

FLOWERS HAD GROWN past the windows of the Winters'
historic Victorian home. Flowers James had never seen in
New Mexico. Molly cupped one in her hand and sniffed it.

The inside of the house was cold and musty. Molly
looked creeped out—shoulders raised, arms crossed. Her
Polaroid was slung around her neck, notebook clutched in her
hand. The kitchen was still blood-stained. James needed to
put her to work before she started to shut down. Crime
scenes could be tricky places, even though this one was long
abandoned.

"Medicine cabinets," he said.

"What?" Molly asked.

"Go find all the bathrooms and take photos of what's in
the medicine cabinets. Underneath the sinks. In towel clos-
ets. They're intimate places. They can tell us more than you
would think."

Molly nodded, heading off through the house like it was a
minefield.

James started in the kitchen. Emptied out drawers. Took

bills and grocery lists and notes left next to the phone and bagged them.

Next was the home study. It looked barely used. Serious, leather-bound law books lined the walls, but James found little in the drawers and cabinets other than notepads and letterhead and a bottle of whiskey with dusty glasses. Probably more of a social room than a workroom. It sounded like the judge had spent his work hours at the office.

He went down to the finished basement. Laundry, a guest room, an exercise room with a treadmill. Very tidy. He heard Molly sifting around upstairs and guessed she was at the half bath on the main level. He wasn't finished with his search yet but went up to meet her anyway.

"Anything good?" he asked, standing in the doorframe, arms crossed.

"I have no idea," Molly said, crouching in front of the sink cabinets. "Some prescription medication upstairs. But it didn't seem like too much. A normal amount, maybe, for people their age."

"Anything else?"

"Regular stuff. First aid. Aspirin."

She stood now, shook out each leg.

"So." James leaned against the frame. "Maybe you can help with this woman question I've got."

Molly put her hands on her hips. Cocked her head to the side. A little Dorothy. It made James smile. When he thought about it, he did miss Dorothy. Their good times, at least.

"We're kinda just like you guys, you know. Human beings?" Molly said.

"Sure. But women have foresight, for example. Which one could argue would make them better criminals."

Molly kept her hands on her hips, but her scowl softened. Her eyes widened a little. "You think Mrs. Winters was a criminal?"

James shrugged. "Isaiah said she had secrets."

"You're right. He did," Molly said. "So, what do you need my expert opinion on?"

"If you were Cathy Winters, where would you hide things from your husband?"

"Makeup kit?" Molly asked. "A box of tampons? Nothing there, though."

"Bigger things," James clarified.

Molly nodded and chewed her lip. "I don't know. A closet he didn't really use? Or the attic?"

"Let's check the attic, then," James said.

They went upstairs and then went from room to room, studying the ceiling for a hatch. Finally, in the big bedroom's closet, they found it.

The attic was smaller than James had expected but still big enough that they both could stand upright. James powered up his flashlight. Boxes of clothing were pushed against the walls. Isaiah's old school things. Report cards. Awards. A photo of him grinning with a baseball bat over his shoulder, ready to swing. A chest of old quilts. Family photo albums—a few of which James took.

An hour of searching and nothing obviously suspicious. He and Molly sat cross-legged on the floor, old coats strewn across their laps. Molly held up an old photo of a couple with a baby.

"Maybe she was squeaky clean," she said. "Maybe they were just a sweet couple. Good people. In love still after all these years. Maybe Isaiah is wrong."

There was a wistfulness to her voice. James sighed. He would visit the judge's office later with Isaiah. But the wife didn't have an office. If she had skeletons, they would be here. Not in the attic, clearly. But in the house. He guessed he ought to resume his basement search, maybe even pop open the ceiling tiles. It was then that Molly gasped.

"The shed!"

"There's a shed?" James asked. They had quickly peeked into the backyard before entering the house. He hadn't seen a shed, but they hadn't exactly been looking for one, either.

"I don't know, but we should check. She was a gardener. You saw the flowers."

"Excellent point," James said. He stood and brushed off his jeans. Offered Molly a hand. "To the backyard."

There was no freestanding shed, but one had been built under the deck. It had white doors that opened out.

It was locked, of course, and the front door key didn't open it, but the doors were weak enough that when James pulled harder, they popped open.

It was nice inside. For a shed. A roof had been built under the deck slats to keep everything dry. Shelves lined the walls, and wood panels were under their feet. It was neat, too. Labeled jars and bags of mulch or seed. A few binders, and when he opened one up, he saw they'd been used to keep track of weather and temperature.

Seemed like they'd struck out. James was about to tell Molly that this had been smart thinking nevertheless, when he noticed a floorboard in the far corner sticking up just a hair. He grabbed a trowel, got down on his knees, and started to pry the board up.

It creaked and resisted at first, but as he slid the trowel

along the wall, the board popped right off. The next three were easy to remove, and buried underneath them were shoeboxes.

James pulled each one out of the dirt, and Molly ripped off the tops. James suspected more photos. Maybe even love letters. Maybe the woman was having an affair. But rather, there were memos. Financial statements. Handwritten math problems and vague notes along the edges. Things like, *State fund 223* and *Federal grant money*. It looked like a woman's handwriting.

"Why would she hide these from her husband?" Molly asked, squinting at the papers.

"I don't know. Maybe she wasn't," James said. "Maybe she was hiding them from someone else."

21

MOLLY

EVEN THOUGH JAMES had been adamant that Molly needed to be back at school by Monday morning, here they still were, in Albuquerque, three and a half hours away from home. They were waiting in the dark before the sun rose halfway down a street that ended in a cul-de-sac.

They sipped their coffees. The car lights were off. Their bags packed. The shoeboxes and photo albums and other randoms items from the Winters' house loaded into the trunk, along with the court cases Molly had copied. They weren't staying another night. They were only staying long enough to follow Janice Stone to wherever she went on Monday mornings.

Molly watched a man a few houses down roll his trash can to the curb. He wore a robe and slippers. Farther down the street, a car roared to life in a driveaway, and what Molly guessed was a skunk scurried across the road.

James had said stakeouts normally required binoculars but that he stupidly hadn't brought any. He hadn't been expecting a stakeout. She assured him they'd get a pair to leave in the car for next time.

Last night, as they packed their bags after Molly's shower, James had finally told her about his oddly eventful meeting with Janice Stone. While her hair was still damp on her back, he said, "We've got one more thing to do before heading home."

Molly wanted to stay in Albuquerque longer. She had begged James to let her miss just a few days of school. And then, when he wouldn't relent, she begged for just one. If they were going to follow Janice, they probably wouldn't make it back in time for any of Monday's school day, anyway. They could go to Judge Winter's office in the afternoon. Make it back home late that night.

She'd had him almost convinced. Watched his certainty waver. But then he shook his head.

"I can't get into that habit. We've got to make this work with school. School is important." He swore he'd have her back at school by fifth period. Algebra. He told her algebra was important for investigators. Molly groaned. She had lost.

Now, they waited silently. James unwrapped his blueberry muffin, and Molly let herself think about what had happened that morning when they'd left the hotel.

They'd found a piece of paper tucked under their windshield wipers, fluttering in the wind. There was nothing on the cars to either side of theirs.

James read the paper in deep concentration, and then Molly thought she saw some surprise.

"Huh," he said, folding it up and slipping it in his back pocket.

"What did it say?" she asked, loading up the trunk and wishing she'd gotten to the paper first.

"A warning," James said. "Someone isn't too keen on us bein' here.'"

"Can I read it?"

But James didn't answer that. He just said, "Where to for coffee?"

Molly was a little annoyed, but she figured she could probably get it out of him once they were back on the reservation. Far away from Albuquerque.

Still, the thought sat in her stomach like a sticky piece of chewed-up bubble gum. Who was threatening them?

The taillights of Janice's car flashed on. The engine started up, and Molly sat up straighter. "Janice," she said. James blew on his coffee as he watched, even though it must have been cool enough by now.

He didn't turn his head when she drove past, and so Molly didn't, either—though she was very curious to see the woman. James waited until Janice reached the end of the street before he switched on their own headlights and turned the car around.

Even though she didn't have her license yet, Molly wished she were driving. They needed to go faster or they would lose her.

But then she reminded herself that James had probably been trained to do this. Surely he'd followed criminals before. Not that Janice was a criminal. Or maybe she was. James had described her as an older woman. It was hard to imagine someone like that as a criminal. But, of course, Molly had learned during their last case that no one could be dismissed.

Besides, if Janice was talking with George, maybe she was the key to finding Adriel.

James and Molly followed her through the suburbs, through the outskirts of the city filled with warehouses and big-box stores, toward the inner part of the city of Albuquerque. She pulled into the parking lot of a building next to a church. There were three names on the sign outside: Alvarez & Sons, Bright Smile Dental, and Forever Families Adoption Agency.

Janice Stone got out of her car and walked quickly toward the building's front door.

"Come on," James said, unbuckling his seatbelt.

"We're following her inside?" Molly asked. "What if she recognizes you?"

Sometimes it unnerved Molly how self-assured James was. Sometimes it comforted her. She couldn't tell which she felt this morning.

James paused. "You're right. You go in without me."

Molly swallowed. She was definitely unnerved. But she nodded anyway and realized she didn't have time to ask him how to do this sort of thing.

"Go," he urged her. But he was smiling. "Just find out which office she goes into. That's all we need to know today."

Molly got out and entered the building. Janice turned down a hallway to the left and then opened a door on the left. Molly couldn't yet read the sign on the door, so she approached. She looked up just as Janice glanced back into the hallway, and the two locked eyes. Chills ran up her spine, but she forced herself to smile. The woman seemed frightening. But then, quickly, her expression softened.

"Are you looking for something, sweetie?" she asked Molly.

Molly's mouth was dry. "Ummm, dentist," she mumbled.

Janice pointed back the way they had come.

"You just went down the wrong hallway, darling. Back where you came from, but it's straight ahead."

"Thank you," Molly said. Janice watched her from the door, so Molly did what she was supposed to and walked back toward the dentist's office. When she looked back over her shoulder, Janice was still standing there. Molly waved and rounded the corner, down the hallway leading to the dentist, and wondered how long she would need to wait. She stood very still and listened. After about a full minute, Molly thought she heard a door clicking closed. She counted to thirty. And then again. Then, she peeked around the corner. The hallway was empty now. She had to be quick. At the very end of the hallway was another exit. She would keep going, out that door.

She was walking so fast she almost hopped. She had to slow down. Stop herself from breaking into a run. That would be noisy. Even the swish of her pant legs brushing together seemed too loud.

She was almost at the door. As the pounding in her ears got louder, she glanced up. Saw the sign. She did not look back but kept going down the hall and out the door.

Once outside, she rounded the corner back to the front of the building. She stopped for moment, putting her hands on her head and catching her breath.

James grinned when he saw her. Molly sped over to him, relief washing over her. She got into the car and let out a big breath.

"Well?" he asked.

"She totally saw me!" Molly blurted. "We looked at each other, and I couldn't even see the name on the door because she was blocking it, and then she asked me if I was lost, and I said I was going to the dentist, and then she pointed to where the dentist was, and then she watched me! And then I had to pretend like I was going there, and it was so freaky!"

James's grin widened. "And?"

"And then I listened till the door closed and went back and practically had to run outside after I looked at the sign."

"So, what'd you find out?"

"The adoption agency." Molly breathed heavily.

"The adoption agency?"

"Yep." The implications slowly started to come over her. What did it mean that George was talking to some lady from an adoption agency?

"Were Linda and George trying to adopt?" Molly asked.

"I can't say I know," James said. "But it looks like that's a possibility, doesn't it?"

"Why?" Molly felt her cheeks redden. "Wasn't Adriel good enough? If they wanted more kids, why not just have some . . . the regular way?"

"Maybe they tried and couldn't. Or maybe they wanted to help a kid who needed a family," James said. "Or maybe they were afraid that Linda might only be able to have handicapped kids. You know. With her history of drug abuse."

"So what?" Molly was angry now. She was getting louder but couldn't help it. "Adriel is a wonderful kid! They would've been lucky to have another kid just like him!"

"You're right," he said. "But Mrs. Long is very old. And she's pretty much the only help they had with him."

"So George was just . . . looking for a perfect child instead?"

"Or maybe he needed help with Adriel. It's possible he was speaking with Janice to see what Adriel's options were."

Molly flushed. She could feel the sting of tears behind her eyes. "No. Linda would never have allowed that. His mom loved him. I don't believe that."

"All right." Molly's dad touched her arm gently. "But we can't get tunnel vision during an investigation. Everything is a possibility until we eliminate it. We don't know what George was doin' when he called Janice Stone."

Molly hadn't thought it possible to be any angrier with George. But now she was.

"I'll promise you this," James went on. "I will find out everything I possibly can about Janice Stone and what George wanted from her. Wayne and I will get to the bottom of this."

"Don't you have too much to do with the Winters case?"

"I never have too much to do. That's what coffee and cigarettes are for."

Molly took a deep breath. "How can I help?"

James took his hand back and put the car into gear. "You like talkin' on the phone. You and Paula are on it for hours and hours."

Molly laughed. That was not true. Maybe just one hour at a time. "Yeah, I guess," she said.

James smirked. "We've got plenty of phone calls to make this week."

22

SANCHEZ

BEFORE TRANSFERRING to the narcotics division, Agent Sanchez had been assigned to the Gallup barracks for five years. Gallup was surrounded by reservation land. Navajo and Zuni. It was an island, and not one aspect of life in Gallup was independent from the reservations. His fellow officers would claim that they couldn't throw a rock in Gallup without hitting an Indian, and yet the town could have operated on a different planet as far as the law was concerned.

Sanchez learned a whole hell of a lot about operating bare-bones while in Gallup. He learned about poverty and drugs and how many good people needed to fight for even the slightest change. It was depressing. But he'd pushed through because his father hadn't lived long enough to be taken seriously. To make detective. Albuquerque was Sanchez's opportunity to make it happen for himself.

Today, he was meeting with Lieutenant Lark, and though he didn't know for sure what this was about, he could guess. James had told him about his own meeting with Lark. So,

Sanchez assumed the lieutenant had taken an interest in the case.

When Sanchez pulled into the station, he took a moment to prepare himself. He had to assume the worst. That this really was a larger cover-up. He didn't think it was. Certainly, he hoped it wasn't. But he had to behave as if it were. He popped a mint into his mouth, took a deep breath through his nose, and got out of the car.

Lark's office door was open. He looked up at Sanchez and smiled, and Sanchez felt the urge to bolt. Instead, he smiled back and shook Lark's hand as he sat across from him.

"Gabriel Sanchez. I don't believe we've yet had the pleasure of meeting."

"I don't believe so, sir."

"How are you liking it down here in Albuquerque?"

"So far, so good, sir."

"You were called to the scene for one of my men's newest case. Two murders. Husband and wife. What did you think?"

Sanchez didn't know what he meant by that. What had he thought of the call? The crime scene? The way Duncan had handled it?

"Seemed pretty obvious what had happened, sir. Gunshot wounds. No weapon recovered. The Navajo man's papers right there on the desk and his son's plush toy left at the house. Puts the suspect at both crime scenes."

Lark nodded. Leaned over his desk and touched his fingertips together.

"Strange thing happened this weekend. A guy came in with his daughter. Says he's a P.I. James Pinter. He's interested in the Winters case. He says the murdered couple's son hired him because he works out on the reservation. Has connections there."

Sanchez tried to keep his expression neutral. His breath steady. Lark went on.

"Normal enough. Still, I like to know what I'm getting into when I work with P.I.s. So, I have Sue look through our records. See if a James Pinter pops up anywhere. Weirdly enough, it seems the two of you have worked together before."

"Yes, sir. Just a few months ago," Sanchez said. "He was working with Wayne Tully on the reservation. I've known Wayne for years, back when I was in Gallup."

Lark nodded once. Waited for Sanchez to continue.

"They called me up. Believed they had a murder on their hands."

"And did they?"

"I made the arrest. The woman confessed."

"Any idea why they called you up?"

"I suppose it's because Tully and I worked together before. He trusts me."

"And he doesn't trust the rest of us?"

Sanchez shifted a bit in his seat. "Well, he knew I would come."

Lark nodded again. Slowly this time. "And have you heard from this James Pinter since?"

"No, sir."

"What can you tell me about him? Was he really Army CID?"

"I believe so, sir. He's a smart man. He's the one that got the confession out of the woman. Without that, there would never have been enough evidence for a conviction."

"Has she been convicted?" Lark asked.

Sanchez was sure that Lark knew the answer. This whole conversation felt like a test.

"She will be, sir."

"That happen on the reservation? Was that why James Pinter was working with Tully?"

"No, sir. Off the reservation."

"So why weren't our people on it?"

"We were," Sanchez said. "We ruled it an overdose on-site."

Lark's eyebrows went up. He sat back and crossed his arms. "Not you, specifically, though. You were in Albuquerque by then."

So, Lark had been researching Sanchez, too. Not just James.

"Correct," Sanchez said.

"Which means this James Pinter already thinks the New Mexico State Police are incompetent. A bunch of fuckups."

Sanchez paused. He most certainly did at this point, if he hadn't before.

"I'm not sure what he thinks, sir. Like I said, I haven't spoken to him since the arrest. And he didn't say anything like that at the time."

"Not to you, he wouldn't. But we can assume that's exactly what he thinks," Lark said. He sighed.

"I'm going to have to take a good look at this case now. Make sure we're crossing all our Ts and dotting our Is. What did you see at the scene?"

"I'm not homicide, and I'm not lead on the case, sir."

"No. But you're a trained officer of the law and your

informant's parents are dead. You don't have a professional opinion?"

Every ounce of Sanchez's being shouted for him to tell the lieutenant the truth. He wanted so badly for this all to be a blunder on Duncan's part. But he couldn't be sure. He couldn't trust Lark.

"Detective Duncan seemed to be working diligently at both crime scenes. I think you'll find his report to be thorough."

Lark stared at him, and he couldn't tell what was behind that stare. Curiosity? Suspicion? Annoyance?

Lark finally stood and held out his hand. Sanchez shook it.

"Thank you for your time, Agent. I'll be looking into the case, like I said. Don't be surprised if you get another call from me."

"Yes, sir."

Sanchez left with a full day's work still ahead of him and wishing badly that he could go straight to the bar instead. If Lark hadn't already figured out the evidence log was fucked up, he would soon enough.

23

TONY

THE MECHANIC SHOP was right on Highway 160 just before the desert turned into a town and the cluster of gas stations signaled that life did, in fact, exist there.

If one turned down Highway 163, they'd soon find more signs of life. A laundromat. A drive-in burger place. Sidewalks with teenagers on bikes. The fire department. A church. The social security office.

But when Tony Morris drove home from a day's work at the shop, he did not turn at the cluster of gas stations. He kept going through to the other side of so-called civilization and back into the nothingness. The hugeness. The emptiness. His home. He turned right off the highway eventually. And then left. Right again.

He was thinking about his kid's fourth birthday coming up. He didn't live with the boy's mom anymore, but she was still close enough. They were on good enough terms.

They were even planning their son's birthday party together. Her whole family would be there. Parents, grandparents, aunts, uncles, cousins, brothers, sisters, their kids. Tony loved that about her. That she had a big family that actually liked each other. Or at least loved each other enough to always show up. Which wasn't exactly the same thing, but it was more than Tony could say about his own family.

His sister Sandra was coming with her kids. They lived close enough, too. And even though Tony and George had never been close, he wished now that George could come. He hadn't known until recently that George had a son. He seemed to still be the same tight-ass religious weirdo that he had been when he left home for good. But Tony was over it. Family was important.

He supposed it had been good timing, then, when George showed up a week ago—after all those years—looking for a car. He tried to tell Tony he'd just been passing through town when his truck started acting up. But George was full of crap and hadn't thought his lie through. So much for the Ten Commandments. Tony, a mechanic and an ex-con, knew both a perfectly good truck and a man on the run when he saw them.

He told George he'd be happy to take a look at his truck, but George declined. They did that back-and-forth for just a little bit before Tony said, "Look, man. I'm not gonna ask you any questions. You tell me what you need, and I'll hook you up."

George breathed a sigh of relief. "A car. That no one will be looking for."

The mechanic shop always had an extra car or two. Barely running, but enough to get George where he needed to go.

Tony said he'd leave the truck at their mom's for a while and sell it later, if George didn't want it back. "I love you, man," Tony said. "But I can't keep it here at the shop and I can't torch it. That sounds like something that could send me back to the slammer."

George had left his boy—Adriel, he said his name was—at Sandra's with his cousins, and Tony was sad about that. He would've liked to have met him.

Now, he imagined both of them coming to Tony's boy's birthday party. Slapping George on the back and handing him a beer. Or hell, a root beer if that was more his thing.

What Tony wasn't expecting was to come home to a Shiprock cop car sitting in his driveway. He knew now, of course, that George was wanted for murder. He wouldn't have guessed that, either. Didn't think he had it in him. But if he had killed those two people, it was probably because they had it coming. As Tony got out of his car, he was glad that George hadn't told him where he was going.

The cop stepped out of the car with a woman. A beautiful woman. Older than Tony, but beautiful. He almost ran his fingers through his hair but remembered they were still covered in grease.

The cop waved.

"Let me rinse off," Tony said, as he got close. "I'll be right back."

The woman did not smile at Tony. *Probably a bitch*, he thought. Most of the beautiful ones were.

He turned on the spigot out back behind his trailer and rinsed his hands. Then, he scrubbed them on the towel hanging on the fence. Good enough.

Tony strode back to the front. Shook both their hands.

"This about my brother?" he asked.

"Sure is," the cop said. "How'd you know?"

Tony couldn't tell if he was joking. The Shiprock cruiser seemed obvious enough. "Well, I know he lived up that way," he said. "And Shonto police have already been by to talk to me." He shrugged. "I'm smarter than I look."

The cop smirked. He'd probably already looked up Tony's record.

"Have you seen him lately?" the cop asked.

"No, sir."

"Any idea what he's driving these days?"

"Can't say I know much at all about my brother these days."

The cop nodded.

"We found his truck," the woman said. Tony wasn't surprised. He'd known someone would eventually.

"All right," Tony said.

"Here," she clarified. "In Kayenta."

"Really?" Tony did his best surprised face, which he knew was pretty good but maybe not good enough depending on what kind of cop this one was. Without waiting for an answer, he asked the woman, "What's your name?"

"Kay. Kay Benally. My sister was married to George."

"Huh. Didn't know George had a wife."

"He doesn't. Not anymore," Kay said. "She's dead."

"Oh. Well, um. I'm sorry. That's a real bummer." He could tell by Kay's face that "bummer" was probably not the right word.

"He kill her, too? Along with those other two?"

Kay's eyes grew fierce. It kinda turned him on.

"No. Someone else killed Linda," she said. "And we aren't sure George killed those two people. Maybe he did. Maybe he didn't. But he did steal my nephew."

"Stole his own kid?" Tony asked. "That isn't a thing."

Kay rolled her eyes and then said, "We . . . uh . . . met your mother."

"That couldn't have been fun," Tony said.

Finally, a smile. "She wasn't the most pleasant."

"So, can I assume you don't spend much time with her?" the cop asked.

"I've got a kid," Tony said. He crossed his arms. Tucked his hands under his armpits. "I don't want him anywhere near her."

"Understandable," the cop said. "You work at the mechanic shop." It wasn't a question, but Tony nodded anyway. "Does George know that?"

"I couldn't tell you," Tony said.

"Any cars go missing there recently?"

"Nope." Technically, that car had been abandoned months before.

"All right, son," the cop said. "I'm going to give you two phone numbers. One is the hotel we're staying at. We'll be there for a bit longer. The other is the number to the station here in Kayenta. If you think of anything important, if you get any surprise visits, you give me a call."

He handed Tony a piece of paper. Tony read it, stuffed it in his pocket, then grinned at the cop.

"You got it, Officer."

"Lieutenant," the woman, Kay, said. "He's a lieutenant."

"Right. Well, good for him. It was nice to meet you both."

Tony stared at them. The woman first, then the cop, waiting for them to leave.

As he watched their car finally pull away, Tony had an idea. A guess where George might have gone. Maybe, after the birthday party, he would go and see.

24

JAMES

JAMES CLOSED his eyes and rubbed his temples. He had spent the last four hours reading through Cathy Winters's shoeboxes.

He tapped his pen on the desk. Stared at the name he had circled. The day before, when he and Molly arrived back at the reservation, James had made some calls. To the Winters' family members, colleagues, neighbors. Not all of them were available to chat on a Monday afternoon, but those who were had nothing particularly enlightening to say about the couple. A neighbor called them a "charming family." Bartholomew's sister said they'd been happy. A fellow judge called Bartholomew a workaholic. But Cathy would often visit him during those long hours, bringing him dinner, coffee. He would hear the two of them laughing together. Bart, the judge said, was a warm man. Firm in his beliefs. He echoed much of what Isaiah had said: Bart had made enemies among those with conflicting goals and motivations. Some of the decision-makers in child services. Adoption agencies.

Upon picking up Cathy's boxes that morning, James had

found financial statements of people and companies that meant nothing to him. Names he'd have to run by Barbara. He did recognize one of them, though: the attorney general of New Mexico. At the bottom of the first box was a photocopied letter to him from Cathy. *Best not to tell Bart quite yet*, it read. *Let's keep it between the two of us.* She had clearly been hard at work, and her husband had no idea.

She was sending these financial statements to the AG. This one guy whose name James had circled, this Donald Andrews, had a lot of accounts. Owned a few companies. They were typed in blocky abbreviations: *FF AD AGENCY, COG HOME*, and *NMCA*.

SNAFU, James thought. Situation normal: all fucked up.

Barbara's Shiprock office was at the end of a street lined with government buildings. The BIA, Veterans Affairs, engineering and construction, Indian Health Services. And at the end, the Shiprock Chapter of the Navajo Nation. The trees lining the parking lot had started to lose their leaves. James stepped on a few as he crossed the lot.

The building was unique. All one story, rectangular at one end, round at the other. Lots of windows, and below them, purple stripes painted horizontally around the whole structure.

It was a thirty-minute drive from Barbara and Wayne's house to Shiprock, with not one town along the way. Just desert. James's eyes always needed a minute to adjust to the sight of buildings again. The man-made structures looked unnatural when they reappeared.

James walked in to an empty front desk. Helen, the secretary, must have been out for lunch. A sign behind her desk announced, It's a New Day. Another, sitting on her desk, said, Ring Bell for Help.

James didn't ring the bell. Instead, he walked straight down the hall to Barbara's office. The door was just a few inches ajar, and he knocked lightly.

"Come in," Barbara said, even though she had no idea who it was. That was the kind of councilwoman she was.

She looked up from her work, pen poised midair. She said, "So. Did my list help?"

James sat down. Ran his fingers through his hair and let out a deep breath. "What's your hourly rate?"

She chuckled. "You can't afford me."

"Well then, the Shiprock Police Department thanks you for your generosity with your time, because I'm gonna need some of it. What do you know about Donald Andrews? He wasn't on your list."

Barbara's eyebrows went up. "I can't say I know of a Donald Andrews. Why?"

"Cathy Winters. The judge's wife who was murdered. She was investigating Donald Andrews's finances. Sending her findings to the AG."

"Did she find dirt on him?"

"Looks that way to me. Problem is, it's all hidden in different accounts and businesses."

"What're the businesses?"

"FF AD AGENCY, COG HOME, and NMCA."

"So, some sort of advertising agency?"

"Possibly. But I'm wondering if it's an adoption agency.

Molly and I happened to follow a woman straight to a Forever Families Adoption Agency, which would fit."

"Children of God," Barbara said, snapping her fingers. "Children of God Home. They're the largest home for orphaned children in the state."

"Well, shit. Both owned by the same man? I suppose it makes sense if you're in the business of children. How about NMCA? Ring any bells?"

Barbara shook her head. "New Mexico something, I would assume."

"Interesting." James put both feet on the floor and slapped his knees. "When can I get on that calendar of yours? Believe it or not, that wasn't all. I've got some court cases I'd like you to take a look at."

"Just come over for dinner tonight. Bring Molly. Bring the cases. With Wayne out of town, I'm no good at cooking only for myself, anyway."

"You got it, ma'am." James stood up. Gave her a two-finger wave on the way out, then stuffed his hands in his pockets. Now he had a whole shitload of work to do.

25

GEORGE

THE CLOSEST PAYPHONE was miles away at the gas station, and George needed to come up with some excuse to go there. So, he told Mr. Tallsalt he had to get medicine in case Adriel got sick. Mr. Tallsalt never questioned anything George did for Adriel, and this was no exception. Tallsalt nodded once and went back to his newspaper and eggs.

At the gas station, George stared at the payphone. This might be a bad idea, he knew. But he also needed help. As long as he was wanted for murder, he wouldn't be able to protect Adriel. Until his name was clear, it wouldn't matter much what Tallsalt did.

He picked up the phone and dialed. Asked the operator to call Pinter P.I. James picked up on the second ring.

"Pinter P.I. This is James."

George swallowed his doubts. "James. This is George Morris."

The line was quiet for only a beat. "George. Nice to hear from you. Where you at?"

"I can't tell you that. And tracing this call won't help,

either. I needed to tell you that I didn't kill those people. I need your help. Please. I need you to find out who really did it."

"Believe it or not, I'm workin' on that as we speak. But I've got to be honest, George. It's not lookin' good for you. They recovered paperwork of yours right on the judge's desk and Adriel's stuffed lizard at the woman's house where she was murdered."

"What? Adriel's stuffed lizard?"

"That's right."

George's head swam. He tried to remember where he'd dropped it. He had thought it was at Janice Stone's office, but maybe it had been at the judge's. That whole day was a blur. A nightmare.

"It wasn't me. It wasn't us."

"Were you at Cathy's house?"

"I don't even know Cathy."

"The judge's office?" James asked.

George thought of what Tallsalt had told him. Don't talk to anyone. Don't admit to *anything* related to *any* of this.

"Yes, we were at the judge's office. Maybe Adriel left Sunny there. I can't remember. But the judge was alive then. We saw him. I spoke to him."

"What about?" James asked.

"I can't tell you. I can't tell you anything else. I'm not supposed to be talking to you."

"Who told you that?" James asked.

"I have to go. But, James . . . I need you to clear my name. Please."

"More information would help, George. Where can I call you if I need to talk to you?"

"You can't call me. I'll call you again. Sometime soon."

"Is Adriel safe?" James asked.

"Yes, Adriel is safe." George hung up quickly before James could say anything else. His heart hammered in his chest. He hoped he hadn't just made a mistake.

When George pulled back into the driveway and saw Tony's car sitting there, he forced himself to take deep breaths. He dug his fingernails into his palms to snap himself out of it. Had Tony seen him at the gas station? If he had, how had he gotten here first?

But it didn't really matter how Tony had found him. It would only be a matter of time now before someone else found him, too. George moved one leg and then another to get out of the car. Shut the door behind him. Tony got out of his car, too, and put his hands up in surrender.

"Brother!" Tony called and, when they were close enough, shook his hand.

"How did you find me?" George asked, quietly.

"I didn't tell anyone," Tony said. "Especially not them cops that came asking. Or your boy's aunt. You didn't tell me you were married."

Were, George thought, grief blanketing him for a moment. He still wasn't used to thinking of Linda in the past tense. "So, Kay told you she died."

"Murdered, she said." Tony crossed his arms. "But not by you."

George's jaw clenched. "I would never have." He felt his

breath catch. "I loved Linda." He looked away from Tony. "I miss her."

"I'm not going to ask if you killed those other two people. I don't want to know. I just want to know that you and your boy are safe." Tony craned his neck to look past George.

"Huh," George huffed. "Well, I *didn't* kill those people, and I don't know if we're safe. If *you* found me here . . ." He trailed off. Shrugged. Tried not to feel the weight of what it meant that Tony was here in front of him.

Tony uncrossed his arms. He looked down at the dirt road beneath his feet. Toed a rock. The gesture made him look younger for a moment. Maybe even embarrassed.

"You know how I've got a son, too? Well, when me and his mom were at our worst, she threatened me with a lot of shit. Tallsalt—" Tony jerked his head toward the house. "Everybody told me to come see him. He handled that kind of thing. Maybe he could help me keep my boy. Luckily, we made nice before it came to that."

George was still quiet. Wondering how Tony had made the connection between someone who helped people gain custody of their children and George.

"The news said that's why they think you did it. That there were some things you left for the judge. About being Adriel's dad. You were the last person to see the judge alive."

George wanted to laugh. What a poorly timed visit. Talk about some luck.

"I could help you, you know," Tony said.

George didn't want help from a criminal. He was in enough trouble. Maybe Tony could see it on his face, because he put his hands up again. George couldn't remember him ever being humble like this. Acting like George was the one to be afraid of. It made him feel upside down.

"I just mean I could keep an eye out around town," Tony went on. "Let you know if I hear about anyone looking for you. Make sure that cop gets off your ass. I want to help you keep your boy safe."

Just then, almost as if he had been summoned, George could hear Adriel's quick, light footsteps behind him. George hated this part. And he hated himself for hating this part. George loved Adriel with all his heart. Otherwise, he wouldn't be doing any of this. And George knew God loved Adriel even more than he did, somehow. Other people's judgment shouldn't matter. Still. He couldn't help the little bit of shame that washed over him, then. It didn't always happen when new people met Adriel. But it often did. This feeling. This need to explain to new people about the way Adriel was. To explain that it wasn't George's fault. Adriel didn't actually have any of George's genes.

But he knew that Adriel was exactly the way God intended him to be. It was this conviction now—this conviction always—that allowed George to cast away those feelings of shame at the last minute. To stand tall next to Adriel. To say, "This is my son. He can't speak, but he's smart. And he can love. Boy, can he love. You'll see."

Tears came to George's eyes. Why had he done it? Why had he gotten them into this mess?

26

BARBARA

BARBARA KNEW of both organizations from all the work she had done over the years. When she went home that evening, she went back through her own files to see if she could find any mention of an NMCA. Some of the stuff she had kept was a painful reminder of a time when she had been hopeful about becoming a foster parent. After she had given up on having children of her own. She sat on her closet floor, brochures from the state of New Mexico on her lap. As she read over them, she allowed the memories and the anger that accompanied them to pass through her. She had done everything right. She and Wayne had both had steady jobs by then, steady paychecks. She had finished law school. She had been elected to the council. They had bought a new trailer with an extra bedroom.

The state had sent a woman for a home check. Barbara had been polite and welcoming and had even made the woman a fresh plate of fry bread. They sat at Barbara's table as the woman praised the smells coming from the kitchen.

"And tell me, where is the closest hospital?" the woman had asked. "Closest elementary school?"

Barbara told her and watched the woman purse her lips and nod her head. She didn't think much of it at the time, but Barbara remembered now, when she watched the woman leave, how the woman had looked around her, down the road. Had squinted her eyes. Had brought her hand up to her forehead as a shield from the afternoon sun.

"You don't have neighbors," the woman had said.

"Oh, we do," Barbara had said, smiling. "A bike ride away."

"A bit isolated, isn't it?" the woman had asked.

Barbara had shrugged. "It's home."

She had never heard from the woman or from anyone else from the state ever again about being a foster parent. Despite the phone calls she had made and the letters she had written. That's when Barbara had refocused her efforts on passing the Indian Child Welfare Act.

Barbara put the boxes away after finding nothing regarding NMCA. She steeled herself for the evening ahead.

Molly showed up first, before James, with a Tupperware full of cupcakes. She kissed Barbara's cheek and strode into the house.

"What is this?" Barbara asked, accepting the cupcakes.

"Dad's bringing the files. He's been obnoxiously busy all day. Hasn't even stopped long enough to give me something to do." Molly shrugged. "So I thought I'd make dessert. Mom and I used to bake together."

Her face fell a little, and Barbara touched her arm. Her heart ached for the girl. Such a delicate age to lose the only parent she had ever known.

Barbara had never imagined Kay Benally as a mom, but she and Molly were filling space for one another in surprising ways. It wasn't a mother-daughter relationship. It was something else. Something special. Barbara knew that even with a missing piece, Molly could fill up on love from others. Love from Kay. From Barbara and Wayne. The Navajo had always believed—had always known—that family was just another word for people who loved you. People who cared.

"I can't wait to try them," Barbara said about the cupcakes.

Molly shrugged again but looked more unsure this time. "It's been a while. I hope they're all right." Then, she plopped down on the armchair. Barbara left for just a moment and returned with a bag of chips. She handed them to Molly with a smile. "While we wait for your dad."

Molly popped one in her mouth. "Thank you." She licked the salt from her fingers. "Tell me about your day, Barb."

Barbara sat down on the couch opposite her. "Well, your dad came to visit me. He wanted to know about Donald Andrews."

"Who's that?"

"He's . . . a businessman, I guess you could call him. But his business is children who need parents. Apparently, he owns both an orphanage and an adoption agency. And some other company that we don't know much about yet."

"What'd my dad want to know about him for?" Molly asked, popping another chip into her mouth.

"Remember all those papers you two found in that shed at the Winters' house?"

Molly nodded. Sat forward a little.

"It seems as if Cathy Winters was trying to find some dirt on the man."

Molly's eyebrows went up. "So what . . . ? Maybe . . . maybe he had someone kill her? And the judge, too?"

Barbara smiled. "Figuring that out is your dad's job."

Just then, there was a knock at the front door, and Molly grinned. Then she stood up, rushed to the door, and swung it open.

"You're a creep!" she shrieked. "We were just talking about you. It's like you knew!"

James had a box under his arm. He wiped his boots on the rug and hung his hat on a hook next to the door.

"She just loves her dad so much, doesn't she?" James said to Barbara. "Can't stop singing my praises."

Molly rolled her eyes and shut the door behind him. "Hardly. You didn't tell me about Donald Andrews! You think he had her killed?"

James chuckled. "Woah, woah. Slow down there. All we know is that Cathy was digging into his finances. Why? We don't know. Who, if anyone, knew she was doin' it? We don't know that, either." He set the box on the floor next to the dining room table. "In fact, the only thing we do know is that Cathy was hiding these findings from her husband. Or at least trying to."

"What?" Molly gasped. "How do you know that? Do you think he *did* know?"

"I found some letters between Cathy and the AG saying they ought not to tell Bart. It was recent. Maybe the judge really wasn't aware."

"Or maybe he *was*, and he killed his own wife!"

James shook his head but smiled. "Not possible. The judge was killed first."

"What's an AG?" Molly asked.

"Attorney general," Barbara answered. "The head prosecutor for the state."

Molly's eyes got wide. "Woah," she whispered. "Cathy was in deep!"

Barbara got up from the couch and waved toward the kitchen. "Let's eat before it gets cold."

27

MOLLY

MOLLY WAS SO full and content it was hard to concentrate on the conversation. She yawned. Barbara looked at her, surprised, and James tried to suppress a grin.

"Sorry," Molly said. "I just need a minute. Some fresh air."

She stood and walked outside. She sat on the top step and let the cool air wake her up as she stared into the blackness of the desert, listening to the noises of the animals. An owl. A coyote in the distance. The scurrying of something smaller. She could hear the soft drone of her dad's voice from inside. Music, maybe, coming from somewhere far away. She closed her eyes and thought of Adriel.

Two days before he disappeared, he had taken Molly to find ripe juniper berries. She hadn't known what they were doing or where they were going when they left that morning, but Adriel had been grinning, holding his bucket.

"Have fun!" Kay called after them.

"Where are we going?" Molly called back.

"You'll see!"

Adriel grabbed her hand as they walked. Sometimes, when they were alone, Molly really talked to him. About school. About the new P.I. business. About missing her mom. Molly was one of the few people who could understand Adriel's grief and he, hers. They had lost their mothers within weeks of one another. It was still so recent for them both.

Sometimes when Molly spoke, Adriel drew. She never asked to see the drawings and would never think of snooping, but one day, he showed her one. It was a picture of two smiling women, holding hands. Underneath, he'd written *Adriel Mom* and *Molly Mom*. It made her smile. She had never met Linda, Adriel's mom, but she had seen her once. When Adriel brought Molly to the woman's body. She had sketched her after that, too. She liked to think that her sketch had helped her dad solve the case. But now that she knew Adriel better, she didn't like to think about *that* Linda. The one with flies all around her, legs and arms at unnatural angles. She liked to imagine how Linda might have been when she was alive and happy. If she was anything like her son, Molly knew she'd been a good woman. She liked to picture their two moms together in some sort of heaven. No longer suffering in any way.

But that morning of the berry picking, Molly was quiet. It was getting cooler during the days now, too—not just at night —and that surprised her. Kay even said they would get snow come winter. Molly hadn't seen snow in years.

She enjoyed the quiet sometimes, and that morning was perfect for it. They walked toward the hills, up a dusty path from Kay's corral.

Finally, they stopped at a row of squat, bushy trees. Adriel set his bucket down, grabbed hold of a branch, and started to shake it. Small blue berries fell one at a time. He did it to another, and another, until about fifty berries dotted the ground. Adriel picked up a few and placed them in the bucket, then looked up at Molly and nodded. So, Molly squatted down and scooped a handful herself. She went to do it again, but Adriel touched her hand gently and shook his head.

"Leave the rest?" she asked. He nodded. They walked down the row, shaking and picking up for a while until the bucket was almost full.

When they got back, Molly brought the bucket to Kay in the kitchen.

"We've got some berries!" Molly exclaimed.

"Juniper," Kay said. "Good for tea." She squeezed one gently between her fingers before popping it into her mouth.

"Adriel left a bunch on the ground, though," Molly said.

"For the ants. They'll eat the good stuff and leave the inner shell. He'll take you out again in a month or two to collect them. Then, we can use them to make jewelry."

Now, Molly opened her eyes again to the night sky. It was probably almost time to gather the shells. A heaviness fell over her. Adriel wasn't here to make the jewelry. Neither was Kay.

"Please bring him home," she whispered into the air. She swallowed the sting at the back of her throat and stood up.

Molly could smell the coffee as soon as she went back inside. Apparently, she hadn't been the only one getting sleepy. She went into the kitchen and poured herself a cup, then sat next to Barbara, who was nodding and biting her bottom lip as she read one of the cases.

"This here," Barbara said to James, pointing to something. "Judge Winters is saying it violates the Indian Child Welfare Act."

"What's that?" Molly asked.

"It's a law that gives special protections to Indian children," Barbara said. "It's designed to keep them in the tribe if their family members can no longer care for them. You see, if the parents are deemed unfit to care for the child, the state's child services are supposed to try to find another family member. If they can't find a family member willing and able to take the child in, they're supposed to find another member of the same tribe before looking outside of the tribe. We fought a long time to have ICWA passed. To keep these kids on the reservation. And we won. It passed just last year."

"What happened with this case?" Molly asked.

Barbara pointed at the page again. "You see here that this adoption attorney is arguing that this little boy's foster parents—good people perhaps, but not part of the Navajo Nation—ought to be able to adopt this Navajo boy, even though a Navajo couple has been found that wants to care for him. Judge Winters is saying that this white couple adopting this boy would violate ICWA."

Barbara sat back in her chair and sighed. "It's what he argues in every case with a Navajo child. Or any other Indian child for that matter." Molly thought she looked sad just then. Tired.

"This law is so new. These kinds of judges who know it and enforce it . . ." She shook her head. "They're rare. Judge

Winters was one of the good ones. Maybe the only one in the state doing this."

"I didn't realize you knew him," James said.

"Knew of him, at least," Barbara said.

Molly had so many questions swirling around her head. But for some reason, the loudest thought wasn't about the murder or what this had to do with it. It was about how George and Adriel fit into all of this.

28

KAY

THE KAYENTA POLICE station was smaller than the one in Shiprock. Wayne walked back toward where Kay waited near the front door. He tossed her a set of car keys.

"Got us each a discreet vehicle. Thanks to two kind officers who are willing to let us use their personal vehicles for a bit."

Kay flipped the keys over in her palm and looked at the emblem. A Chevy. Wayne was also insisting she keep her pistol on her at all times now that the plan was to separate. The story that Kay was only here for a "personal visit" was quickly crumbling, but she didn't care to point that out.

"Yours is a pickup. An orange C10 in the lot out back." Wayne jerked his thumb behind him.

"And I can use their phone?" Kay asked.

"Sure." He took her down the hallway to the back. Maybe this was the phone they let the criminals use. He turned the dial for her. The receiver felt clammy in her hand.

"Tell him I miss him." Wayne grinned and winked. Kay

rolled her eyes but cracked a small smile. She didn't doubt that he did.

James picked up on the second ring. "Pinter P.I. This is James." The warmth of his voice flowed through her.

"It's Kay," she said.

"Hey there, bumblebee. How's it goin'?"

James knew Kay hated pet names. So, he made up the weirdest, corniest, most annoying ones. She would never tell him, but it was starting to grow on her.

"I miss you," she breathed. She closed her eyes. Suddenly, she felt exhausted. She wanted to curl up next to him in bed and sleep for days. But she forced her eyes back open. "We've talked to George's sister and mother and brother. We found his truck."

"Hey, nice job!"

"His mother is a real piece of work," Kay said. "It almost makes me feel sorry for him."

"What about the church? Have you gone there?"

"First day. Hated the pastor. No doubt *he* did a number on George, too."

"What about his siblings?"

Kay wrapped the telephone cord around her finger until it was so tight her finger started to turn white.

"Both suspicious. Which is why Wayne and I are at the station now. Wayne got each of us a vehicle. He wants us to watch the two of them. Follow them. I've got the sister; he's got the brother. We tried talking to the kids, too. Adriel's cousins. But they wouldn't say anything."

"A stakeout, huh? Damn, I wish I were there. Love a good stakeout. You got something to take notes with?"

"Of course."

"Sunglasses? Hat? Binoculars? Gun?"

"Check on all accounts."

"Camera?"

"Not that fancy here."

"Snacks?"

Kay smiled. "Not yet."

"Tell Wayne to get on it. Snacks are priority. And coffee. First things first."

"You got it, boss man."

James groaned. "You know I love it when you call me that."

Kay laughed. "*You* stay focused, too."

"I uh . . ." James hesitated. Kay knew what he wanted to say, because she wanted to say it, too. But they hadn't yet. And she knew he wouldn't now. Not while they were apart. "I can't wait to see you again," he finished.

"Me too," Kay said and hoped he knew what she meant.

[29]
TONY

PICKLE JUICE RAN down Tony's arm as he ate his sandwich in the shop, mixing with the oil that constantly stained his fingers. He leaned against the bumper of a truck he and his buddy Barry were working on.

Barry made a sound like "Oh!" with his mouth full, and his eyes got wide. Tony waited for him to swallow.

"Weirdest thing," Barry said, wiping his mouth with his forearm. "I was at Cal's the other day having a milkshake."

Tony grinned a little. Most guys would leave that part out. Having a milkshake. Barry didn't give a shit what anyone thought.

"This guy's sitting at the bar next to me. Not from around here. Red hair. Freckles all over. Starts talking to me. Asks me if I'm from around here. Asks me if I know a George Morris."

Tony stopped chewing. He looked sideways at his friend. "What did you say?"

"Figured this guy must be from the papers. Didn't look like it, though. Looked like a dirtbag. I say, 'Buddy, I haven't seen George Morris since he was shitting his pants.'"

Tony swallowed his bite. "You get this guy's name?"

Barry nodded. "He gave me his name and number in case I saw George."

"You got it with you?"

Barry went into his back pocket and pulled out his whole wallet. He handed it over to Tony. Tony put his sandwich down inside the truck bed. He flipped Barry's wallet open.

"Behind the picture of my mom," Barry said as he chewed.

Tony pulled out the scrap of paper. *Charlie Glover*, it said, with a phone number.

"Can I keep it?" he asked.

"Sure. Can't imagine George'll be showing up here again after all these years. Not with all these people who could ID him."

Tony grunted. He slid the paper into the pocket of his flannel vest. He wasn't wearing anything underneath. It was getting a little cold in the mornings, but he was still working up a sweat in the shop. Would be most of the winter.

"You going to call him?" Barry asked, nodding at Tony's pocket.

"Maybe. I don't like people poking around my family's business, you know? Whatever George did or didn't do, doesn't matter. Especially if this guy is here to cause trouble."

"I hear that," Barry said. "You let me know if you need my help."

Tony guessed Barry was right that this guy was no reporter. Maybe George hadn't actually killed those people. But maybe he knew who had, and now, this man was here to make sure he kept his mouth shut. Or maybe this man was here to make sure George disappeared. If George was tied to two murders, he was probably into some bad shit.

Tony considered going to George and telling him, but there were two problems with that. The first was that George wouldn't be able to do a damn thing about it. And Tony doubted George could outrun this man. Not with a kid in tow.

The other problem was the cop that had been following Tony for a couple of days. If he went to George, he'd lead the cop right to him.

He leaned over the truck bed, balled up the rest of his sandwich, and headed to the trashcan.

No, Tony would have to take care of this Charlie himself. Tell him George would never come back to these parts. That no one in his family could even stand George. That they'd rather shoot their own foot off than help him at all.

JAMES

JAMES HADN'T DREAMED about Vietnam in years. But that night, he was back there. Listening to those men in that dark restaurant in Danang, his back to them.

"The kids are cheaper," one man said in English. "It's fucked up, I know. But there's a reason I don't go to church anymore."

The two men chuckled, and James remembered vividly how much restraint it took for him to stay seated in that moment. The smell of the fish and the marijuana. The realization of whose voice he was hearing and what James would have to do.

He thought, then, in his dream, *I shouldn't be here. I already left. I don't have to be here anymore.* And then he woke up. His head was pounding. He breathed in slowly through his nose. He wasn't in Vietnam. He was in New Mexico. On the reservation. Molly was sleeping in the room next to his. That memory was from a lifetime ago.

James looked at the alarm clock: 5:42 a.m. He sat up and

sipped from the glass of water on the bedside table. He blinked a few times in the dark and let the memories fall away. He had a task to focus on. Today, he was meeting Isaiah at his father's office in Albuquerque.

He hoped there was still evidence left. The cops—or whoever had killed the judge—had probably taken most of it. But maybe they'd been careless. Maybe there'd still be something for him to find.

He stood and stretched his neck from side to side. Then, he went to the kitchen to make coffee. He stood at the window, hands on his hips, waiting for it to brew. The kitchen window faced Shiprock, and even though he couldn't see the rock Shiprock was named for, he could picture it. He'd always thought it looked more like a castle than a ship, and he wondered if there was a Castlerock somewhere. There were lots of towns around here named after rocks.

The coffee started to drip, and James could hear Molly stirring. The smell of coffee did that, he had learned. Slowly pulled her out of sleep. Damn high school started so early, it was almost time for her to get in the shower anyway.

James tried to switch his brain on while he sipped. He thought of the important names to look out for today. Donald Andrews, Attorney General Curtis Vasco, adoption attorney Bobby Tate. And all the things he didn't know that he was looking for. Things the police had overlooked. There was a possibility he would find something still lingering. He knew what Cathy had been hiding. But what about her husband?

James turned on the stove and took out a pan. Molly was banging around now. He took out the eggs, and the bread and butter for toast.

The drive to Albuquerque was frustratingly slow, even though James had left with plenty of time to make it to Judge Winters's office before Isaiah got there. There had been lanes closed for construction. Two accidents. He missed being high up in his rig. Able to see the whole highway stretched before him.

Isaiah was waiting for him in the parking lot and swore he had only been there a few minutes. James didn't like being late but plastered on a grin anyway.

The man who greeted them inside seemed to be busy. He showed them to the dead judge's office, pointed in the general direction of where he would be if they needed anything, and left them alone.

Isaiah looked a little confused. Maybe even disappointed. "This is it?" he asked.

"You haven't been here before?"

Isaiah shook his head. "Downstairs to meet up. But not this actual office. He used to work for another district. I've been to that office. This one is . . . a little sad."

James wasn't surprised by it. He'd seen the crime scene photographs. Standing here with Isaiah, though, he had to admit it looked more like an accountant's office than a judge's.

A framed law degree hung in the corner. A few other recognitions were on display. It was tidy, too, which disappointed James. It would have been too easy for the killer—or the police—to find and take whatever they needed. He was picking at bones now.

The government hadn't done much to the office since the

judge's death. Blood still stained the floor, and they hadn't replaced the blood-stained chair either. James wondered how long it would take to replace the judge himself, if it took weeks just to replace a chair. How many people out there could do what the judge had? Who would want to?

Isaiah looked uncomfortable. He had his hands in his pockets, then at his hips, then arms crossed. Gaze darting like a cornered rabbit.

There was an armchair in the corner. James gestured toward it. "Why don't you take a seat for a bit?"

Isaiah rubbed the back of his neck. "You don't need my help?"

"I might. I'll ask for it when I need it."

Isaiah stared expressionlessly at James for a moment before slowly nodding and sitting.

James started with the filing cabinets, and even though he doubted there would be much of interest, he set aside some things anyway. Memos from the AG that seemed to have nothing to do with much. Same for Bobby Tate. But he knew that sometimes just a date on a correspondence could prove important down the road.

He went through desk drawers next, any knickknacks on the judge's shelf that may have had small compartments. He opened the backs of picture frames. He found nothing. The sun was blaring into the office now, and just as he crossed the room to close the blinds, he spotted a jacket hanging on the back of the office door. It seemed too obvious, but he checked the pockets anyway, and in the inside right breast pocket, he found a folded letter.

James read it to himself, muttering in a tone Isaiah probably couldn't decipher.

"Well shit," he said, loudly and clearly.

Isaiah scooched to the edge of his chair. Leaned forward. "What is it?"

"Well, it's the answer to a question I've had about a company."

"A company?" Isaiah furrowed his eyebrows.

"We found some documents at your parents' house," James said. "Some financial statements for some mystery companies."

Isaiah's face went white, and James knew then that Isaiah knew exactly what he was talking about. Interesting.

"And that." Isaiah nodded at the letter. "It's related?"

"Would be a strange coincidence if it's not."

He didn't share with Isaiah the other thing that interested him about the letter. He would've let Isaiah read it if he asked, but he didn't ask, he just gripped his hands together tighter, his knuckles turning white.

James tucked the letter in his own breast pocket and let Isaiah think whatever he was thinking. He hoped Isaiah might say something more, but he didn't.

Next, James sat at the judge's desk. In the blood-stained chair. He wanted to see what the judge had seen. He looked straight ahead at a bookshelf. To his left was the window. His right, the door where the judge's jacket hung. Where the killer had probably entered. The direction from which the bullet had come. The judge's right side. Right hand.

He looked at the desk in front of him. Telephone. Rolodex. Coaster. Pen holder. Word processor. A stamp and some ink.

James opened the Rolodex. He took Bobby Tate's card and the AG's. No sign of Donald Andrews, though he was certain the two men would've needed to chat occasionally. Especially after what James had just learned from that letter.

Then, another name caught his eye. One he hadn't come across before. It was another judge. A judge with a Navajo name. Judge Tallsalt. James took that card, too.

[31]

ADRIEL

WHEN ADRIEL REACHED for the little pot to boil tea, he
noticed something on the other, bigger pot. It was an old
piece of crusted-on rice. He didn't judge Mr. Tallsalt for it.
He was old and used to being alone. He probably didn't care
about a small piece of old rice. Not everyone was as particular
as Adriel. He knew that. His mom had loved it about him.
Aunt Kay made good use of it. Sometimes he wondered if his
dad was annoyed by it.

Adriel picked at the rice with his fingernail, and even
when it came off, he still reached for the soapy rag to scrub
the pot some more. That was when the phone rang.

It was an old phone. Maybe one of the first ones ever
invented, Adriel guessed. It was close to him, just over the
carpet line that crossed from the kitchen into the living room.
He spun around to see if Mr. Tallsalt had heard.

The old man took a moment to get up from his chair.
Adriel wished he could help, answer it for him. But Mr. Tallsalt moved quickly enough once he was up.

"Hello?" he said into the phone.

Adriel put his head down again and focused on the pot. He didn't want to eavesdrop. But then, Mr. Tallsalt said something that made Adriel stop cold.

"Pinter, you said?" He saw Mr. Tallsalt's eyes dart to him. "Questions about what?"

Adriel stood frozen. Maybe James knew they were here. Maybe he was calling to check on them. Maybe Aunt Kay was with him.

Adriel almost reached for the phone, but Mr. Tallsalt gave him a cold stare and slowly shook his head. Adriel didn't understand. He stood rooted in place.

"Yes, I was a judge for the Navajo Nation for a while. But no longer."

Adriel tried to sign to him, "Is it James?" But midway through spelling James's name, Mr. Tallsalt turned away.

"Yes, I knew Bartholomew Winters." He stepped away, didn't look back at Adriel. "I handled adoptions of Navajo children to parents outside of the Nation."

Adriel's mind raced. He had heard that name before. He remembered he liked it. Being named after a season. His favorite season, too. Why was Mr. Tallsalt talking to James about that man?

"I don't anymore," Mr. Tallsalt said. He sighed. Looked up at the tiled ceiling. Then out the window. "I have nothing else to share, Mr. Pinter. Goodbye." And then, Mr. Tallsalt hung up the phone.

Adriel waited for Mr. Tallsalt to look at him. To offer some sort of explanation. But he didn't. The old man left the room. Walked right out the back door.

Adriel was still holding the soapy rag. Water dripped down his wrists, soaking his sleeves. At first, he thought he would cry. It wasn't until his fingers started to ache from gripping the pot's handle so tight that he realized what he felt was anger. Worse than anger. Adriel was furious. What was the point of sign language lessons—of waiting for his dad, who was so slow to learn that it drove Adriel crazy—if no one told him anything, anyway? He was sick of it. He was sick of the secrets.

32

SANCHEZ

SANCHEZ WATCHED two men shaking hands beneath the streetlight on the corner. He sipped his coffee. He was tired and jittery. Both from the coffee and his general state since he'd been called back to Lark's office just two days prior.

Lark had finally noticed the one-day delay in logging the plush lizard into evidence. But why he'd called Sanchez back in about it was a mystery. It was Duncan's case. Sanchez was not a homicide detective. Lark was not his boss. But damn it, he still had to please the man if he ever wanted to join Lark's team.

Sanchez shoved his free hand into his pocket and walked back to his cruiser. He told himself he'd keep an eye on these two brothers who were of interest in his most recent armed robbery case, but his mind wandered.

Lark had grilled him on it. Was the lizard at the scene? Had he seen it? Wasn't it possible he'd missed it? Sanchez had grit his teeth through the whole thing. How could he have missed a bright-fucking-orange lizard? But of course he'd said that maybe it *was* possible. What else was he supposed to say? Now, he felt like the whole meeting had been a setup, just to have some law enforcement officer admit that the toy *might* have been at the crime scene. Despite no photographic evidence.

He sighed as he turned up the heat. It was getting colder. He wiggled his toes and took another sip of his still-too-hot coffee. It didn't matter *why* Lark had called him back into his office. Sanchez knew that. Because if he didn't work with Lark on this—say what Lark wanted him to say—he could kiss a future as a homicide detective goodbye.

He watched the digital clock on his dash turn from 11:59 to midnight. End of shift. The men were long gone. He had to admit that he wasn't doing shit. He started up the cruiser. He'd call James in the morning. They needed to find out where the hell that lizard had come from.

33

MOLLY

MOLLY ERASED one last thing on her sketch of Janice Stone before feeding it through the copier in the corner of the office/living room. It was Janice's eyebrow. It curved a little too much on one end, making her look more sinister than Molly remembered. It was better now. Straighter.

She watched the twenty copies spit out slowly and funneled them into a stack. She carefully slid them into her bag, took a long gulp of water, and stomped her feet into her Vans sneakers.

The church was a twenty-minute bike ride away, and halfway there, Molly wished she had worn a hat. Her jean jacket wasn't enough protection from the October wind.

The parking lot was empty when she propped her bike up against the side of the church. She was early. Good. She wanted to catch people on their way into the meeting. While there was still a little daylight left.

James had gone to Albuquerque without her again. Officer Sanchez had said he needed to see James ASAP. Since it was the middle of the school week, James said Molly couldn't come. But he left her with a job this time: find out if anyone on the reservation knew Janice Stone and why George would be calling her. The sketch was Molly's idea. In case people knew her face but didn't recognize her name.

The church's heavy oak door was locked, so she knocked loudly. Someone was in there. She could see lights on, could hear muffled movement.

Fred answered and smiled warmly at her. "Molly, come in."

"Hi," Molly said, stepping softly inside. She found it strange to admit how much she liked to be inside this church. It felt both welcoming and hallowed at the same time. *Just as a church should be*, she thought. She reached for her bag and the sketch.

"We have a lead on George and Adriel," she told Fred. "I just wanted to ask some people if they know anything about this woman."

She handed Fred a copy and watched his face. She didn't see any kind of recognition there.

"Her name is Janice Stone," she offered.

"Janice Stone, Janice Stone," Fred muttered to himself. "I don't think I know a Janice Stone."

Molly slumped a little. Of course the first person she asked might not know. Still, Fred knew a lot of people. He greeted basically everyone who came through these doors. He was an assistant pastor.

Molly forced a smile. "That's okay. Maybe someone else does."

"You're welcome to ask around." Fred put a hand out, inviting her into the chapel. "We're just putting out drinks and snacks now."

"Thanks!" Molly walked past him to where volunteers were setting up folding tables with white tablecloths. Someone passed her with a plate of fry bread that smelled so good that she didn't immediately realize who was holding it.

But then she did. The most popular girl at school. Molly ducked her head. How embarrassing. Of all the places to be seen. She looked at her feet and tried to think of what to do. Surely, there was no way Julie Whitethorne even knew Molly existed.

Swallowing her anxiety, Molly walked up to a table, grabbing the opposite end of the tablecloth to help an older woman smooth it down. She was straightening the corners when she felt a hand on her shoulder.

"I know you," Julie Whitethorne said. Molly's breath caught. She looked over her shoulder.

"Oh right." She tried to sound unbothered. "We go to the same school, don't we?" She immediately felt stupid, pretending like everyone in that school didn't know exactly who Julie was. But Julie smiled a radiant, white, and straight smile.

"You're friends with Paula," Julie said.

"Yeah, my name's Molly."

"I'm Julie."

"Nice to meet you, Julie."

"Isn't your dad that white guy who's always at the police station?"

Molly felt her cheeks turn pink. If Julie had seen him there, she probably knew he was the same guy who'd brought Kay a coffee at school. The heartthrob of Shiprock High.

"That's him. He's a private investigator."

"Stellar! That's, like, amazing."

She sounded sincerely impressed, but since Molly didn't really know her, she couldn't tell for sure.

"And your dad is head of DNA legal services?" Molly asked.

"Yup!"

"And you volunteer here?"

Julie shrugged. "We come sometimes and bring snacks. Not every week." She leaned closer and lowered her voice. "My mom used to be an addict."

"Oh." Molly didn't know what to say to that. It seemed like an oddly intimate thing to tell someone you didn't know.

"*She's* not embarrassed." Julie tipped her head to the side, and Molly looked at a woman across the room. "She's proud. Twelve years clean."

The woman glanced up and gave a little wave.

"That's great," Molly said. Julie tucked her hair behind her ear.

"Are you . . . volunteering?"

"Actually, I'm here to ask people a few things." She fumbled with her bag's latch for a moment before pulling out a sketch. "Have you ever seen or heard of this woman? Her name is Janice Stone."

Julie scrunched her nose and moved her mouth to the side. Molly wondered if that was one of the looks that made all the boys at school go crazy for her.

"I don't think so," Julie said. "Why? Who is she?"

"We think she might be connected to Adriel's disappearance. The little boy who disappeared with his dad."

Julie's eyes grew wide, and she gripped Molly's forearm.

"Oh my gosh, I heard about him! Are you and your dad working on that?"

"Yeah," Molly said. "With the police."

Julie shook her head and put her other hand to her chest. "I hope you find him. That's so scary that his dad might be a killer!"

Molly swallowed. She found it hard to speak. "Yeah," she finally said. "It's pretty scary."

"Well, good luck," Julie said, releasing her. "I've got to run, but I'll see you at school."

Molly's heart fluttered at the thought of Julie Whitethorne acknowledging her at school in front of everyone. Of Paula's reaction.

"Great!" Molly forced a grin. She waved as Julie and her mom left and then lowered herself into a pew to wait for the meeting attendees to arrive. She felt a little giddy.

When Molly locked eyes with Willa Yazzie, she gave a small smile and a wave. She expected Willa to look away. The last time they'd spoken, Willa had insisted that Molly leave her alone. But now, Willa actually approached Molly.

She had gained weight. Her face had filled out a little, grown a little rounder. Her skin looked a little clearer. She still didn't smile, though.

"Hello," Willa said.

Molly stood. "It's good to see you, Willa."

"You still looking for George and Linda's boy?"

"Yes," Molly said. "We may have a new lead. A woman named Janice Stone. Have you heard of her?"

"With a crusty name like that?" Willa shook her head. "I wouldn't remember."

Molly brought out a sketch. "This is what she looks like."

Willa's eyes widened in recognition. Then her jaw tightened. "Yeah, I know that bitch," Willa said.

"Really?"

Willa nodded and then took a deep breath. "So, it turns out I lied to you all about a couple other things, too." She looked around the church. "In the interest of all of this . . ." She trailed off, tucked her hands under her arms. "Honesty. Living with my mistakes. Whatever. I should probably tell you the truth now."

"Okay," Molly said, afraid to break the spell. Willa grabbed Molly's arm and pulled her into the corner behind the pews, away from the door.

"It just . . . wouldn't have looked good for me at the time," Willa said.

"Can I write this down?" Molly asked.

"Sure."

Molly pulled out a paper and a pen. "Okay, keep going."

"I *did* see Linda right before the last time she and I spoke. I saw her about a week before, when I showed up at her house seeing stars I was so angry. Ready to kill her."

Willa's eyes darted to Molly's. Molly kept her expression neutral. She nodded.

"And I saw her a few weeks before that, too. When I told her I was pregnant."

Molly scribbled it all down. The vague timeline, the anger.

"I knew who the father was," Willa went on. "A real piece of shit. And me." She snorted. "Maybe a bigger piece of shit. Neither one of us could take care of ourselves. A child was a definite no. I knew what I had to do, but I was sad.

Disappointed in myself. For not being more careful. For not being the type of woman who could even consider keeping it."

She shook her head again. Looked down at the floor.

"Anyway, Linda is the only person I told. Which seems dumb, right? Like, if anyone was going to try to talk me out of it, it'd be her. She saw good in me when there wasn't any. She had found Jesus. But she was also the best friend I ever had. The people I had been hanging out with at the time were not friends. Drug friends aren't real friends. We all know it. Any one of them would have understood why I needed to get rid of the baby. But I didn't tell them. I told Linda. I guess I trusted her."

"What did she say?"

"She was surprisingly cool. She said kids were hard. A huge responsibility. Yes, she turned her life around for Adriel, but it was the hardest thing she'd ever done. I thought maybe she understood. It felt good to talk to her."

"But then . . . a few weeks later, you were angry at her?"

"Well." Willa pointed at the sketch of Janice. "*That* bitch shows up at my house. Tells me Jesus loves my baby. Tries to make me feel real guilty. Asks if I wouldn't like to give it to a nice Christian family in the suburbs of Albuquerque instead. No, I fucking wouldn't. That would mean I'd still have to get clean, and I wasn't ready for that."

"She works at an adoption agency," Molly said. "Janice Stone does."

"Figures."

"She said she didn't know Linda. She only knows George."

"So, she's lying," Willa said.

"Or maybe Linda told George, and George told Janice."
Willa shrugged.

"So, you went to Linda's house after that? When you were angry?"

"Furious," Willa said. "Linda acted all surprised. She kept telling me to slow down. She didn't understand. I was just so pissed that she'd told someone. After she promised she wouldn't. It seemed like she was making plans for me. It's *my* life. It wasn't her place to do that."

"That makes sense."

Willa bit her lip. "How does George know this woman, anyway?"

"We don't actually know."

"You can see how I wouldn't have looked so great if I'd told you all of this before. You all would've thought I'd been mad enough to kill her."

"Probably," Molly conceded. "Did you ever remember anything else about that last conversation with Linda?"

"No. I try not to think about it."

"Were you still mad at her?"

"I don't know. I was high. I didn't feel much of anything."

"We found him, you know. Assman."

Willa nodded. "Wayne told me."

"Do you still want me to leave you alone? Or can I come see you if I have more questions?"

Willa shrugged again. "You can come see me."

"Can I bring my dad?"

"Bring Wayne."

Molly couldn't bring Wayne. Not until he got back. Still, she nodded. "Okay."

JAMES

JUDGE WINTERS SEEMED convinced in his drafted letter to the US attorney that Forever Families Adoption Agency was purposefully violating ICWA. But it seemed as though he was struggling with how exactly to prove that.

James thought he understood the process. A child was taken away from unfit, neglectful, or abusive parents by New Mexico's child services. The child was then put into a foster home or a group home—like Children of God—until an adoption could be arranged. If Donald Andrews was violating ICWA, it meant that child services had not done their due diligence in looking for an Indian home for these children. And so, though James was scheduled to have dinner with Sanchez, he'd left for Albuquerque early in the morning to pay a visit to child services.

It was a typical two-story government building. Ugly as hell to look at. James arrived early enough that he wasn't interrupting anyone's lunch hour. And yet, the office was eerily quiet. There was a woman at the front desk, though, so he stopped to check in with her first.

"Hey there." He smiled at her. She was young with a round face and wide eyes. Her brown hair was cropped in a severe line just below her jaw and her bangs hung just past her eyebrows.

"Yes?" she asked. "Can I help you?"

"I'd like to speak with the person who handles foster cases."

"Like, all of them?"

"Sure," James said. The young woman shook her head. "Joan is out today."

"All right, so who *is* here?"

The woman bit her bottom lip. "Mr. Turner is here, I think."

"Great, and what does Mr. Turner do?"

"Accounting."

"How about the folks who go into the field? Agents, maybe? You know, whoever you've got that goes into the homes of the kids."

The woman blinked. "Most of that is done by our partner agency."

"Partner agency? Isn't this New Mexico's Children and Family Services Protective Division?"

The woman nodded.

"But you don't have agents who go out and visit people's homes?"

"Well, I think we used to. I'm kinda new here. We do a ton of paperwork. Mr. Turner and Mr. Howard handle that."

"All right, so this partner agency, do they also work with Joan on the foster side?"

The woman smiled and nodded vigorously, probably pleased that James was finally absorbing into his thick skull what she was trying to tell him. "That's right. It's been real nice, because they don't have all this red tape that we have. We kinda just pass off the money and the work, and they get things done real quick. We're able to help, like, way more kids this way."

"And the partner agency's name is . . . ?"

"New Mexico Children's Agency."

"Huh," James said. "Well, there ya go. You know, maybe I will talk to Mr. Turner."

The woman smiled again. "Second door on the left."

"Thanks."

James walked the full length of the hallway, noting all the empty desks in all the empty rooms before turning back around to find Mr. Turner's office.

He knocked on the doorframe. Mr. Turner was an older, balding man wearing thick glasses. He peered over them to size James up.

"Can I help you?" he asked.

"I hope so," James said. "You see, I'm down from Santa Fe today, from the state house. Name's James Smith."

He walked into the office and stuck out his hand. Mr. Turner shook it.

"Please take a seat," Mr. Turner said. "What can I help you with today?"

"We think this spending bill allocating money to y'all and to NMCA has been working well. Real well, in fact. I'd like to see some numbers. How much the state's savin' with this, uh, relationship. Bring those numbers back to the committee, so we can put together a bill for next year."

Mr. Turner nodded. "They're certainly doing an excellent job keeping track of spending. Makes my job easier than it was when I had to wrangle all these cases myself."

"Can you show me an example?" James asked. "Maybe last month's reports?"

Mr. Turner got up and rummaged through a filing cabinet for a moment, muttering to himself. He sat back down and placed a stack of papers in front of James. "So, this first sheet reports salaries," he said. "Field agents, case managers, foster families." He paused. "The number of which has gone down drastically. The Children of God home takes the bulk of our cases now—they do a lovely job—and everyone seems to be pleased with that. Well, except maybe the foster parents, who used to receive a check for their services. But not all those families were good families, and it was a headache to check up on them."

James nodded. "Makes sense."

"So that's what you see here." He pointed farther down the page. "The money that gets allocated to Children of God Home. That's a large number, but still significantly less than it was when we had to pay separate foster families."

"I can see that."

Mr. Turner flipped to the next sheet. "Here's the break-down of the Children of God Home's expenses, which is also incredibly helpful. We don't get this sort of thing with foster families. Foster families get a check, and how they spend it is unknown to us."

"Huh. Helpful," James said. He pointed to a line item that said SN. "What's this designation?"

"Special needs," Mr. Turner said. "The state allocates a certain amount of money toward caring for special needs fosters. And we get grant money from the federal government for that, as well."

"Seems like a high number."

Mr. Turner frowned. "You can imagine that special needs children are already difficult to care for with the best parents and the greatest resources. Now imagine the families we deal with here in Child Protective Services. Some of these kids check multiple special needs boxes. Each one of those boxes gets additional funding."

"I see," James said. "So, if a special needs kid has multiple issues, y'all get funds for each issue."

"Correct."

Mr. Turner showed him a few more expense sheets. Lawyer fees was another large number. James didn't see any money going to Forever Families Adoption Agency, which he supposed made sense. He remembered from the financials that it was the only entity of Andrews's designated as for-profit. Parents interested in adopting paid big money.

"Thank you for your time, Mr. Turner," James said on his way out. He had copies of the expenses in hand. "This sheds a light on the important work NMCA is doin'. It'll help us pass that bill."

Mr. Turner shook his hand again. "Happy to help."

———————————

Sanchez's backyard chairs were the fold-up kind with aluminum frames made from woven strips of brown and white plastic. He and James sat next to one another on the small patch of concrete, sipping beers and thinking their own thoughts about what they needed from each other.

"So, updates on the case," James said. "Seems that both the judge and his wife made enemies of a man named Donald Andrews. You know him?"

"Can't say I do," Sanchez said.

"Donald Andrews has got the biggest operation in the state concerning children without parents. He's got a group home, an adoption agency, and a so-called nonprofit that supposedly assists where the state's child services fall short."

"Supposedly?" Sanchez asked.

"It seems Andrews has got a whole bunch of state politicians in his back pocket. He'd have to in order to pull off what he's doing. Everything child services *ought* to be doing has been transferred to his organizations. Federal grants are going straight to Andrews. In return, I can assume he helps to fund these politicians' campaigns and most likely endorses them publicly, too—something that goes a long way coming from a guy who seems to be savin' the state a hell of a lot of money while also saving children. New Mexico Child Services is operating bare bones, but only because Donald Andrews has made it that way. And Cathy was on to him. She was diggin' through his financials."

"Well, shit, Pinter."

"Add to that, the judge was ready to tell the US attorney for the state of New Mexico that Andrews was violatin' a federal law through a system Andrews himself created. I found a draft of a letter Judge Winters wrote. Never sent it, though."

"They were attacking him in a concerted effort," Sanchez said.

"Not exactly. Found a recent correspondence between Cathy and the AG. She says, 'Best not tell Bart quite yet.'"

"Yeah, but he still could've known she was looking into it. Maybe he just didn't know what she had concluded."

"Fair enough."

"Shit, Pinter," Sanchez said again. "That's pretty damning."

"The judge knew Andrews was violating a federal law. He was considering telling the US attorney that Andrews was doin' it on purpose. But I can tell from the letter he drafted that he didn't think he had enough evidence. Which is why I don't think Cathy told him what she had found. Her findings would have supported his theory."

"What law is this?" Sanchez asked.

"The Indian Child Welfare Act."

"Don't know anything about that," Sanchez said, taking a sip of his beer.

"Well, if you get a chance, read up on it. Let's just say Andrews shouldn't be adopting out as many Indian children as he is." James sipped his beer, too. It was Sanchez's turn to share now. They both knew it.

"So, ah . . ." Sanchez began. "Lark came to me about the lizard. He noticed it was late going into evidence and then couldn't find it in the photos."

James raised his eyebrows. "What did he want with you?"

"He wanted to know if I saw it there. I said no, of course. But he kept pushing. He wanted me to admit I might have missed it, but there's no way."

"You think he's gone to Duncan about it?"

"Hell if I know." Sanchez spread his palms out over his knees. "You think Lark is setting me up to fail? Getting me to admit that I saw something that wasn't there?"

"Why?"

"Maybe he doesn't trust me. He thinks I lied about working with you."

"Maybe. Lark doesn't strike me as a dumb man."

"Fuck," Sanchez muttered, looking down at his shoes. And then he started to laugh. It started as a chuckle, but then he was grabbing his stomach, throwing his head back. Tears glistened on his face.

"Pinter," he finally said, catching his breath. He wiped his face. "I'm in way over my head. This shit goes deep. I can't take down this Andrews. And I definitely can't take down the head of homicide investigations. Neither can you."

"You're gettin' ahead of yourself," James said. "For all we know Lark just doesn't trust Duncan. As far as Andrews goes, it could all be a damned unfortunate coincidence. We still need more."

"And how are we going to get more?"

"I'm tryna figure that out. We got some key players we haven't even spoken to yet. The AG, for one. And for two, a lawyer who showed up frequently in adoption cases that Judge Winters presided over *and* who represented parents who wanted to adopt Indian kids. I'd bet my hat he's got a relationship with Donald Andrews's adoption agency. It's the biggest in the state, and he seems to be the go-to lawyer."

"I might be able to help with one of those players."

"Oh yeah?"

"Vasco. The AG. I grew up playing baseball with his son."

"No shit. Think you can set somethin' up?"

Sanchez rubbed the back of his neck. "I'm sure he'd talk to me."

"And me?" James asked.

"He might. Either way, if Lark finds out . . ."

"Don't worry 'bout that now."

"Easy for you to say. It's not your job," Sanchez said.

"I'll take the fall for diggin' too deep," James said. "It'll be on me. I promise you that."

35

GEORGE

"Pinter P.I. This is James."

George was cold. The wind struck his face, and he pressed closer to the payphone, hoping the plastic siding would protect him.

"It's George again."

"Hello, George."

"Did you get my package? I mailed you something."

"No, I haven't. When did you send it?"

"You'll get it soon. Janice Stone did it." George didn't want to waste any time. "That's where Adriel left his lizard. Janice's office. She killed them and framed me. She was always complaining about the judge."

"And why were you at Janice Stone's office?"

"She was trying to take Adriel from me. He dropped Sunny, and there was no time to pick it back up. We had to get out of there quickly."

"I see. But why did you bring Adriel to her office in the first place?"

George ignored that question. "After that, we went to

Judge Winters's office for help. I knew he helped parents like me. I left him the legal documentation that proved Adriel is my son."

"What did the judge tell you?"

"He told me where to go."

"Which you still won't tell me," James said. George thought it was supposed to be a question. One they both knew the answer to.

"If you need me, you can call my brother Tony. He'll pass along the message." He gave James the number.

"I'm doing what I can, George, but more information is always appreciated."

"I know." George hung up. He couldn't give James more information. He couldn't tell James anything that would make him look guilty.

36

BARBARA

ON HER WAY home that day, Barbara had picked up a burger and some fries at a drive-thru. She placed them on the kitchen counter and hung her purse on the back of the chair. She was frustrated and tired. She popped a French fry in her mouth right as the phone rang. She stared at the phone for a moment as she chewed and swallowed. Then she picked it up.

"Hello, this is Barbara Tully."

"Hey, Barb," James said.

"Hey, James. Are you back home?"

"Sure am."

"I checked on Molly yesterday, like you asked. She was just bursting with updates on Adriel's case. Have you seen her yet?"

"I have not. I got back here in the middle of the night, and then, by the time I was up, she was already gone for school. Now, she's out with Paula. She opened the door and shouted that at me." James chuckled. "Life with a teenager, I guess."

"Ask her as soon as you see her tonight. She's got an earful for you."

"Thanks for checkin' in on her. You know I appreciate that."

"I told her she can always stay here if she doesn't like being alone."

"You seen that girl eat?" James asked.

Barbara smiled to herself. "Have you seen me cook?"

"Y'all are just made for one another. Hey, I've got a question for you, Barb. Do you happen to know a judge on the reservation named Tallsalt?"

"Tallsalt," Barbara repeated, thinking.

"Retired, he says. A couple years. Wouldn't talk to me much, though. Hung up real quick."

"Hmmm. Don't know if I know a Tallsalt."

"I found his contact in Judge Winters's Rolodex."

"His home phone number?" Barbara asked.

"Office and home."

"Hmmm, personal relationship, then."

"Mr. Tallsalt said he used to handle adoptions of Navajo children to outside parents," James said.

A vague memory of a tired, somewhat wrinkled face came to Barbara, then.

"Wait," she said. "Tallsalt. He was part of the ICWA talks."

"What'd you think of him?"

"Very helpful. Very supportive of having ICWA passed."

"Huh," James said. The line was quiet for a moment. "You happen to know who does that now? Who puts that stamp on those adoption papers?"

"That's a good question. I'm not sure. I haven't been as involved since ICWA passed."

"You think you could find out?"

"Sure."

"Thanks, Barb." There was another pause. Barbara could hear the coffee machine in the background dripping. "How about Tallsalt? You think he'd talk to you? Since y'all know each other?"

"It's been a few years, but I could try him."

Barbara wrote down the number.

"You hear from Wayne recently?" James asked.

"Earlier today."

"He still trailin' George's brother?"

"He sure is," Barbara said.

"I've got to call him."

"Actually," Barbara said, drawing a small flower next to the phone number. "He'll know."

"He'll know what?"

"The judge who handles the adoptions. Well, he should."

"Really?"

"Sometimes the families ask him to speak to the judge on their behalf. I can't remember the last time that happened, but I imagine it was within the last year."

"Perfect. I'll ask him. Thanks again, Barb."

After she hung up, she looked at Tallsalt's number, trying to remember more about the man. He wasn't from Shiprock. He was only at the larger meetings. But she couldn't remember which district he *was* from. Supportive, yes. But also quiet. She scribbled herself a note. Then, she plopped down on the couch and ate her burger.

37

WAYNE

THEY DID NOT FIND any blood in George's truck, but they did find hair. It was bagged and logged and sent to the lab in Albuquerque for further analysis.

Now, both Wayne and Kay were on a coffee break at the station, and Wayne was growing increasingly anxious about how much time they had been away from their posts. Part of Wayne, the part he was most familiar with, was reluctant to leave Kay to her own devices. Even though she hadn't done anything drastic yet, he still knew she was a liability.

Another part of Wayne, a part he didn't quite recognize, wondered if Kay's way was more effective. This was a kid they were looking for. A kid Wayne knew and loved. He had never worked a case so intimate, had never felt this sense of urgency tugging at his insides, screaming at him to do more, to do anything, damned the consequences. They didn't have time. The red tape that Wayne thought he had learned to live with felt like a noose around his neck. He stood and threw away his cup.

"Back to babysitting, then?" Kay asked, still seated.

"They could lead us to him," Wayne said. "Either one." He could hear the weariness in his own voice and assumed Kay could, too. But she didn't argue. She stood up.

They were almost out the door when the young man working the front desk called out, "Lieutenant Tully!"

Wayne turned around. The man held up the phone. "Phone call."

Wayne went back and took the call.

"Glad I caught ya, Wayne," James said on the other line. "I've got a question for you."

"What's up?"

"Do you know the name of the judge on the reservation who handles adoptions? Specifically for kids going to families outside of the Nation?"

"Sure," Wayne said. "There's more than one. The judge I work with is Robert John. But there are a couple. Why?"

"Guess I didn't realize that was part of the process until I found a Mr. Tallsalt in Judge Winters's Rolodex. Your wife vaguely remembers him. He used to approve or deny those adoptions. Retired now."

"The Navajo Nation requires all outside adoptions to be approved officially. Wasn't always that way. We had to fight for it. But . . ." Wayne paused and looked out the window at Kay. She was leaning on her borrowed pickup, apparently deep in thought. "It isn't foolproof. These judges are busy. Some are assholes. Like John. Too politically motivated to spend much time on each family. Not something that's going to get them reelected."

"That John, then? Politically motivated?"

"Oh yeah," Wayne said. "He's on Jackson's new Supreme Judicial Council."

"What's that?"

"A court created to make sure the other courts—the real Navajo courts—don't make any decisions Jackson disapproves of. If they do, the council can overturn it."

James whistled softly. "I don't think it's supposed to work like that."

"You said it, not me."

"Thanks, Wayne."

Wayne opened his mouth to say adios, when James interrupted him.

"Oh yeah. News for you. Remember Janice Stone, who works for the adoption agency and knows George?"

"Sure do."

"Well, Willa Yazzie recognized her from a sketch Molly did. Apparently, Willa was pregnant. Told Linda, and a few weeks later, Janice Stone was on her doorstep trying to get her to put that baby up for adoption."

"So, Linda told George and George called up Janice Stone? Why? He want to adopt the baby?"

"If he did, that message did not get relayed to Miss Stone. According to Willa, Miss Stone specifically mentioned a nice Christian family off the reservation."

"Can we trust Willa?"

James didn't say anything at first. Wayne knew Willa was a good person, but she was also a drug addict.

"She's lied to us before," James finally said. "But she also gave us Assman. Molly seems to think her memory on this is lucid."

"Interesting."

"Tell Kay to call me the next time her hardass boss lets her take a break."

"No can do. She's busy. No lovey-dovey distractions."

James snorted. "Keep up the good work, LT."

38

TONY

AFTER A COUPLE of days debating how to approach this "Charlie," Tony decided on the dumbest option: He'd pick a fight.

Of course, he made sure the cop was following him first. He might get arrested, but he knew what this cop wanted, and as cocky as it sounded, he also knew he was smarter than the cop. Tony had a plan and that plan involved talking shit and throwing down.

Charlie's motel was shitty but still not the shittiest option in the area, and Tony lucked out as far as front desk workers went. A teenage girl. With the perfect mix of charm and intimidation and a story about a friend he was meeting, Tony got the room number. He didn't need a key. Didn't want one, either.

He could've just walked to the other side of the motel, but instead, he got in his car and drove so he could be sure the cop would follow him. Room 226. Perfect height to throw rocks at. A gravel walkway from one side of the motel to the other, with—who could've guessed—plenty of rocks. Everything was going to plan.

Tony picked up some pebbles and started throwing them at the window of 226. "Hey!" he yelled. "Charlie!"

The cop's stare was hot on the back of his neck. He threw a few more stones. *Come out, come out*, he begged inside his head. "Hey!" he yelled again. The pebbles left indentations in his palms.

Tony was about to go up and bang on the door when this pasty dude in a track jacket and jeans opened the door, squinting into the sunlight.

"The fuck?" the guy asked, barely loud enough for Tony to hear.

"Charlie, right?" Tony yelled to him.

"Who's askin'?"

"*I'm* asking, obviously. You've been talking shit about my brother."

"Man, I don't know you or your brother or anyone else in this fuckin' town."

"George Morris," Tony yelled back, louder than necessary to make sure the cop heard.

The Charlie guy still stared at him.

"You want to come down here and fucking say it to my face?" Tony shouted.

"I'm just lookin' for him, man. I've got somethin' to tell him."

"Come tell me, then. I'll pass along the message." Tony chuckled a little. He willed the man to hurry up and get his ass down there. He didn't know how patient the cop would be.

Charlie muttered under his breath and then said, "Hold on a second." He disappeared into the room before reemerging with sneakers and a striped ski hat topped with a red pompom.

Tony listened as Charlie shuffled down the stairs. He ought to provoke him more, hope Charlie started shoving. But he didn't know how much the cop would tolerate.

He started to laugh as Charlie approached. "You've got balls going around *my* town talking shit about my brother."

"Look, I don't know what someone told you—"

"No one's gotta tell me nothing. I can see for myself you're a little bitch."

"What's your deal, man? I'm just tryin' to have a conversation with your little bro."

"And I'm trying to tell you to fuck off."

Finally, the pasty man smiled and not in a friendly way. He smiled in the way a fellow prisoner might in the prison yard. The forthcoming pleasure of fucking someone up creeping onto his face.

Tony smiled back. "Go ahead," he goaded.

Charlie stepped closer. "Fine. Why don't you tell little Georgey that he's got somethin' she needs? Something that's hers. He knows what I'm talkin' about. He'll bring it back if he cares about his boy."

There it was. A threat toward the boy. Tony's fists were shaking now. He had no idea how he managed to keep them by his side.

"What did you say about his boy?" he asked. It was almost a whisper.

Charlie stepped closer. "You heard me."

"What are you going to do with the little boy? You going to diddle him? You into that?"

Fire flashed in Charlie's eyes. He pushed Tony's chest. "You fuckin' sick?"

Tony hoped the cop saw that, because he wasn't waiting another second. Tony punched him so hard and so fast that the only thing he could see in Charlie's eyes as he fell back—arms reaching forward, grabbing nothing—was surprise.

But Charlie recovered quick, scrambling to his feet just as Tony heard the cop close his car door behind them. He had to let Charlie get a good one in now, so he put his hands up and beckoned him closer with his fingers. "Come on," he growled. Charlie hit him. A right hook across the jaw. It landed perfectly, and in that moment, a part of Tony missed all of this. He missed this feeling that anything might happen. That this man's life was in his hands. He missed getting hit that hard.

Tony turned and hit Charlie again, this time landing his punch right in Charlie's stomach. He backed up. What the hell was that cop waiting for? Charlie spat and groaned.

Tony laughed. "That all you got?"

Charlie stood up straight, breathed deeply, and then ran at Tony, full speed, knocking him onto his back. Tony gasped for air, but Charlie was on top of him now. He punched Tony's face again, and for a second, everything went black. Finally, Tony heard a voice.

"All right, all right. Knock it off. Police."

About fucking time.

"Fuck," Charlie muttered. He got up to run away but kicked Tony between the legs first.

"Shit," Tony groaned, curling onto his side. He could taste the pavement now. Could feel the blood dripping from his nose. He heard the cop getting closer. Then, his shadow was blocking the sun, and Tony looked up at him.

"What in the hell was that about?" the cop asked.

"Go," Tony tried to yell, but it came out more like a squeak. The cop knelt down, his face close to Tony's, looking annoyed.

"Go after him," Tony managed to get out. "He knows." He had to stop for a breath before finishing. "He knows about George."

The cop was clearly irritated, but he stood up anyway and ran to his car. Tony closed his eyes. The cop must have had one of those little portable lights for the top of his unmarked car, because Tony could hear the siren as he lay on the pavement in the fetal position, bleeding.

39

ADRIEL

Mr. Tallsalt and George were out front talking with Uncle Tony, and Adriel wanted to hear what they were saying. But he was still so angry at his dad and Mr. Tallsalt. He had been angry for days. He wouldn't do what they asked. Adriel had always been a good kid, but he had also never felt lied to like this before. Even after Mr. Tallsalt tried to explain.

He had told Adriel that he and George were trying to protect him. They were doing what was best for him. That his father loved him very much and that Mr. Tallsalt had the power to help Adriel. He signed this to Adriel as he spoke.

Adriel signed back as best he could, asking why James couldn't help them, too.

"We don't know him. We can't trust him. We can't make any mistakes," Mr. Tallsalt said.

"What about Aunt Kay?" Adriel signed, again trying his best with what he had learned so far.

"Your dad is a little . . . afraid of your aunt Kay."

Adriel knew his aunt Kay could get angry and be a little

scary. But he also knew how much she loved him. She would forgive his dad for anything if it meant helping Adriel. He knew it.

When he tried to ask more, Mr. Tallsalt said, "Please, Adriel. You have to trust us. You have to be patient."

But Adriel did not want to be patient. He wanted to go home. He kept being mad, and now, whenever the phone rang, he would watch the two grown-ups. Sometimes they just let it ring and ring. Sometimes they picked up, listened for a moment, said nothing, and then hung up again.

Adriel let his anger win that night and stayed away from the men. He decided he didn't care what they were saying. He didn't care about them at all. And he didn't think he *was* safe anymore. Maybe he would run away. But as soon as the idea came into his head, he knew it wouldn't work. He could see all around him and there was nothing. He couldn't even see a road from Mr. Tallsalt's house. He imagined finding one anyway. Making a sign that read Shonto and hitchhiking.

He sat on the couch next to the phone. He stared at it, wishing it would ring. He didn't know why. He couldn't talk to whoever would be on the other line.

And then, he noticed a blinking light on the answering machine. A new message. Had he been outside when it came? He looked toward the front door. Would someone hear if he played it? He decided to take the chance. His heart thumped against the inside of his chest as he pushed the play button.

"Hello there, Mr. Tallsalt. I'm not sure if you remember me. My name is Barbara Tully."

Adriel breathed in quick, still staring at the front door. Nobody opened it.

"We worked together on the ICWA bill," Barbara said in the message. "We realized you had worked with my father, David."

The warmth Adriel felt hearing Barbara's voice made him smile without realizing it.

"I believe you received a phone call from a James Pinter recently. He's investigating the murder of a Judge Winters. I'm sure you've heard about the case, but I think you could help. We're not so sure the police have got this right."

Adriel's mind raced. Winters. It was there again, that name.

"I would love to talk sometime about the judge. He was a supporter and defender of ICWA. Such a shame he was taken away so violently. I can't say it's all that surprising, though, that he was targeted. Anyway, please do give me a call when you have a chance. My number is . . ."

Adriel fumbled around, searching desperately for something to write with. He repeated the numbers back in his head over and over again. He couldn't find anything to write them on, so instead, he picked up the phone and dialed them.

The phone rang and rang, three times, maybe four, before he heard Barbara's voice. "Hello, this is Barbara," she said. "I'm not here right now to take your message, but please leave your name and number after the tone and I'll return your call as soon as possible."

Adriel didn't know why he was doing it. He listened to the beep. He stayed on the line. There was silence. He wanted so badly to be able to talk right then. To say, "Please help me!" or, "I miss you." Or even, "I'm safe. I think." But he couldn't. So, he did the only thing he could. He cried.

JAMES

A THICK ENVELOPE arrived that afternoon at the trailer. No return address. James ripped it open and found a cassette tape inside, along with a note that read, *I was working for her.* –G. He popped the tape into his own answering machine and listened for a little while before realizing it was time to pick up Molly from school. He hadn't come across anything suspicious yet—anything that might explain the note.

He leaned against a fence post near the school, far enough away that the other students wouldn't notice him. He took a deep breath and let the cool air fill his lungs. A moment later, the bell rang, and teenagers tumbled out the front doors, their laughs and groans and shouts piercing the quiet, peaceful afternoon.

James squinted, trying to find Molly in the crowd. Cars in the parking lot fired to life—some sounding like they were coming back from the dead. A boy jumped on the hood of one car as it slowly drove away. The car accelerated quickly and then stopped. The boy laughed, grabbing on to keep from falling off. James wondered if that boy—any of these boys—

had caught Molly's eye. He wondered how he would know when it happened. If she would tell him. He wondered what it would feel like to try to take any of these kids seriously, because he would. For Molly, he would.

A line of bikes sped toward him. The first three kids were older than Molly. Two girls and a boy. None of them smiled as they passed. In fact, they wouldn't even meet his eye. Molly always said he carried himself like a cop, which was why, when he picked her up from school, he hung back. He wasn't there to scare the kids. Then, in the distance he saw her. Right behind Paula.

As they got closer, he could see their grins. Paula let go of the handlebars to give him a little salute.

"Hey, Mr. P," she said, making a wide circle around him. "What's the news? Busy day cracking cases?"

"Gosh, Paula. These criminals had no idea what was comin' for them when the Pinters came to town."

Paula snapped her gum. "Poor bastards."

"Not the B-word, Paula."

"Sorry, Sergeant."

"Hey, Dad," Molly said, coming up on his right in a slow zigzag. "Paula's feeling feisty today."

"Oh yeah?"

"Yeah," Molly went on. "Julie Whitethorne spoke to us, and she's been having a fit ever since."

"Oh my God," Paula groaned. "I do not care about your girlfriend."

James grinned. "Jealous?"

"I know. Right, Dad?" Molly said, pedaling faster to keep up with Paula.

"I'm not jealous, Mr. P," Paula called behind her. "It's just that Molly is a traitor!"

"Hey!" Molly yelled, and then Paula took off with Molly on her heels. James watched them chase each other down the road and wondered what Paula had against who he assumed was Harold Whitethorne's kid. He had seemed like a decent enough fellow, the one time they had met.

The girls stopped at the next road, the way to Paula's house. He couldn't hear them, but he watched Molly cock her head to the side. Paula smiled. They hugged each other. And then James and Molly both watched Paula ride off down the road.

"Is Paula mad?" James asked when he caught up to Molly.

"Not really. She just has to act like it."

Molly swung her leg back over her bike and started to pedal slow enough that James could keep up.

"Why does she have to act like it?" he asked.

Molly shrugged. "Because she doesn't like Julie."

"Why not?"

"Jealous, I guess, like you said. Julie is beautiful and popular, and she has two nice parents and a cute little sister."

"How about you? Are you jealous of Julie?"

Molly shook her head. "It would be nice to be popular. But she never gets to do anything embarrassing, you know? Everyone is always, I don't know, looking at her. It's probably annoying."

"What did Julie say to you?" James was still trying to understand all this girl stuff. The rules. The moods.

"She said hi. I saw her at the church the night I was

asking around about Janice Stone. Her mom was bringing fry bread. She used to be an addict, too. Her mom, I mean. I was surprised Julie told me that."

"She sounds like a nice girl."

"I think she is."

A few cars drove past, blowing dust onto their legs.

"What'd you do today?" Molly asked.

"Left messages. For Kay and Wayne, for our lawyer friend, Bobby Tate. Turns out everyone was busy today except me."

"Do you think they'll call back?"

"Kay and Wayne better!"

"I wish I could be there with them," Molly said, quietly.

"I know you do," James said. "They're doin' good work."

"How about Isaiah?" Molly asked, straightening up a bit. "Have you heard from him since you went to the judge's office together?"

"I called him yesterday, actually. He's a nervous wreck every time I talk to him."

"Maybe he did it."

"Doesn't seem likely. He's got an alibi. A shaky one, though. Work. Grocery store."

"And you *know* he went to the grocery store?"

"Told him the police would need a witness or a receipt once we cracked this thing open. He says he's got both, but I haven't seen or looked into either. Don't want to scare him off. He *is* the client. But I might have to start diggin' around."

They turned off the main road. They could see the trailer now and, next to it, a scraggly stray dog that had started coming around. James had known after it showed up a few times, wagging its tail, licking Molly's hands, that they were probably stuck with it.

Molly hopped off her bike and held her hand out to the dog. It came over, its whole body wagging. Molly leaned over.

"Hey, cutest boy," she cooed. She scratched his ears and whispered more things in a silly voice. The dog licked James's hand as he passed, too.

"Good afternoon," he said to the dog.

It dutifully followed him up the steps and sat at attention next to the door, seemingly awaiting instructions.

"At ease, Private," James said. "We'll scrub you down another day."

"Dad!" Molly pleaded. "Can't we bring him inside?"

"You got flea shampoo?"

"Well, no."

"Sorry, kiddo. The dog stays outside tonight."

She gave the dog an apologetic look. "I'll find you a blanket," she said. The dog wagged its tail. Swish, swish. "And I'll bring you dinner."

The dog lay down and put his head on his paws. Molly gave the top of his head one last scratch. "Good boy," she said. "Private," she muttered as she went inside. "Like a soldier. Like our little guard. Like a private eye! Private . . . Private . . ."

"Private Fleabag," James finished for her.

"No! That's mean," Molly said, dropping her bookbag down on the couch.

"Private Slobber," he tried again.

Molly rolled her eyes, and then, the phone rang.

James picked it up. "Pinter P.I. This is James."

"James!" It was Kay, and she seemed a little worked up.

"Hey, muffin mix, what's the news?"

"We found a guy," Kay said. "Someone who's been looking for George, too. Wayne was following the brother, Tony, when he gets to this seedy motel. Tony starts yelling at this guy about George and then the two start fighting. Wayne goes to break it up, and the other guy runs off. Tony tells Wayne to go after the guy because the guy knows about George, so Wayne does. They arrest him, and he immediately starts talking. He says he's here to find George Morris, because George has something that's *hers*. Something that she needs. That George knows what it is . . ."

"But he didn't tell you what it is?" James asked.

"He doesn't know, apparently."

"Who is 'she'?"

"He doesn't know that, either. Or he won't say."

"Interesting. You and Wayne have any theories?"

"Maybe Janice Stone? I mean, she's the only woman we know George was in contact with."

"That'd be my guess, too."

"So that would mean Janice doesn't know where George is, either," Kay said.

"Sounds like that's the case."

"Oh, here. Wayne wants to talk to you." There was a pause. The muffled noises of a phone being handed off. Then Wayne's voice, but still distant. Like he was holding the phone away from his ear. "Can you go grab . . ." and then his voice trailed off, drowned out by what James assumed was his palm over the receiver. A moment later, Wayne spoke clearly into the phone.

"James. The man threatened Adriel. I didn't want Kay to hear that part. But when he was talking to Tony, he said that

George would give Janice back what was hers if he didn't want Adriel harmed."

"The man is in custody now, though, correct?" James asked.

"Yeah. We're going to keep him for as long as we can."

"Good." James could take a real good guess at what George had that Janice thought was hers. But he couldn't assume. That'd be foolish and possibly devastating for Adriel. He looked down at his answering machine with George's cassette tape inside. If he could only get Wayne alone for longer than a minute or two to bend his ear about George's phone calls. But Kay was always right by Wayne's side.

"I'll call you both soon," he told Wayne. "Keep up the good work."

After he hung up, he tucked George's note away and called Molly over. It was fair to ask her to keep some secrets. But not from the people she loved.

"I've got this tape to listen to," he told her. "Sent to me today anonymously. It's George's answering machine messages."

Her eyes grew wide and excited.

"I haven't found anything interesting yet. But I've still got a few minutes left. Pull up a chair and a pad of paper," James said. He went and grabbed her some Oreo cookies and milk to munch on while they listened. He knew how hungry she always was after school. He poured himself another coffee while he was at it.

"You ready?" he asked once they were all set up. She nodded, and he hit play. There was silence for a moment as the machine picked up the next message. Then it played.

"George, it's Janice. We might need to pause for a bit.

Just hold off. That judge I was telling you about—Judge Winters. He's becoming quite a problem for us. We're trying to figure out what to do. If you can think of anything, any solutions, call me back. Otherwise, we're going to need to wait. I'll be in touch again soon. All right, George. Goodbye."

BARBARA

BARBARA COULD NOT UNDERSTAND why in the hell no one was answering her calls. A kid had called her office phone, crying. Possibly a woman, but Barbara felt sure it was a child. She could hear the difference. Feel it in her bones. And what other child would leave a message without saying anything? Maybe, wherever he was, Adriel had access to a phone book. She couldn't imagine how else he would have known her office number.

She'd called Wayne twice. Once at the hotel, where the receptionist said there was no answer in his room, and then again at the Kayenta station, where the officer who answered thought at first that Wayne *was* there, but then said, no, in fact, he wasn't.

"Please make sure he understands this is an *emergency*. He needs to call me back *right away!*"

Then, she tried James, who didn't answer, either. It was right when Molly got off school and maybe they had plans.

She ought to go over there, she thought now. James could help her get a warrant. But then, as she went to grab her serape, she paused. What she needed was the Shiprock Chapter's phone bill. Maybe she didn't need a warrant to get that. Maybe she just needed Helen—the office secretary—to make a phone call. The phone company ought to be able to tell them what number the call had come from. Even though Barbara didn't even know what time Adriel had called. Sometime after she had left the office yesterday.

Barbara strode down the hall, and when she saw Helen at the front desk, concentrating on something in a three-ring binder, she rushed forward.

"Helen!" she called.

The young woman jumped a bit. Her bushy eyebrows furrowed right above her thick glasses.

"Everything okay, ma'am?"

"I need you to do something for me. Do you usually deal with the phone bill?"

"Sure. Yeah, I call them every month and pay on the phone. And then they probably put that call on our next phone bill." She smiled sideways at Barbara.

"I need to find out who called my office last night. Can you call them and see if they'll tell you?"

Helen picked up the phone and dialed, looking out the window while she waited. Barbara kept staring at her.

"Hello, this is Helen calling from the Navajo Nation. I'm looking for someone who can tell me the phone number of a call that came into one of our offices."

"Probably yesterday," Barbara interrupted.

"Probably yesterday," Helen repeated. She did not look back at Barbara. She nodded a few times before saying, "Mmmhmm," and a moment later, "I see. So you would need a court order, you're saying?"

She finally looked at Barbara and mouthed, "Court order." Barbara nodded, mouthed back, "Thank you," and left.

The last time Barbara remembered crying was the day she'd taken her last pregnancy test. She and Wayne had tried to get pregnant for years, and finally, when Barbara turned thirty-seven and got yet another negative, the doctor told her it was time to stop trying. Stop tracking and stressing and buying vitamins and taking the traditional medicine. It was probably too late. But in the car, on the way to James's house, Barbara felt like crying.

A dog greeted her when she arrived. The same one she had seen hanging around here a few days ago. The dog whined as she went to the door but must have recognized her because he wasn't aggressive.

Barbara banged on the door. "James!" she yelled. The dog's ears perked up. He stood and cocked his head to the side.

Molly swung open the door, a duffel bag in her hand.

"Are you coming or going?" Barbara asked.

"Both," Molly said. "We just got home from school a little while ago, but Dad wants to go to Albuquerque now."

"Then I'm glad I caught you. I got a call last night," Barbara said before Molly could elaborate. "From Adriel."

Molly gasped. "Are you sure?"

"No," Barbara said. "Of course not. I can't be. But someone called and left me a message. I'm certain it was a child. They were crying, but they said nothing. I think it was him."

Molly brought her hand to her mouth. Her eyes started to water. She sniffed and swallowed and then called, "Dad!"

James came around the corner, shrugging his shoulders into a jacket.

"Barbara got a call from Adriel," Molly said.

"Awww, hell," James said. "Well, come in, Barb."

They sat around James's desk as Barbara told him about the call and the phone company's insistence on a warrant.

"All right," James said. "All right. We'll get that warrant. Molly and I were on our way to Albuquerque, but we'll go to the station first. I'll make sure one of the officers takes it to the judge this evening."

Barbara breathed deeply. She rubbed her temples. "Tell me why you're going to Albuquerque," she said.

James glanced at Molly before speaking. "We've got quite a bit of evidence now that George was working with Janice Stone, who is the head of Forever Families Adoption Agency. With what Willa told Molly, we're guessing that George might have been doin' exactly what he did in Willa's case. Finding potential children on the reservation to put up for adoption through Donald Andrews's adoption agency. You see, Donald Andrews hasn't been going through child services at all. He's nearly cut them out of the equation entirely. The kids go from their home to the children's home, which Andrews runs, to a new family."

Barbara clenched her jaw. She thought of all the ICWA meetings. All the cases she had reviewed. The families she'd spoken to. The elders and her peers forced to slowly and in great detail relive the pain of the boarding schools, all so that

Barbara and her committee and the wider organization of Indians from tribes across the country could help draft ICWA. All the times Barbara had had to swallow her own tears while listening to accounts of loved, wanted children torn from their families and their tribes.

"Go on," Barbara said to James. Her voice was low and steady but only because she was trying her best to control it. To not lose her mind over this news.

"Molly and I were thinkin' that we ought to pay a visit to Donald Andrews's group home for children. We don't have any reason to believe that Adriel is there, but if George had a relationship with Janice, it's possible he left Adriel with her. We feel like we ought to check, just in case."

"Damn it, George," Barbara hissed through clenched teeth. She was on the edge of her seat now. "What the hell is wrong with him? Doesn't he get it? Doesn't he understand what these people really want?"

James leaned back in his chair, interlocked his fingers in his lap. Barbara understood he was letting her speak, say what she needed to. But for some reason, that only made her angrier.

"Ask me, James!" She was standing now. Her arms thrown up. "Ask me what they want!"

"They want your kids, Barbara," James said. "It's fucked up. But they want to take your kids from you."

Barbara shook her head, and a crazy kind of laugh escaped her lips. "If only it were that simple! They want us gone. Every last one of us. They don't want Indian reservations anymore. They don't want Indians at all! We're an outdated obligation to these people. If they take our kids away, we'll have nothing. We'll turn to dust. To wind. And that is *exactly* what they want."

Barbara put her hands on her hips. Threw her head back and glared at the ceiling. Tried to calm herself but couldn't. "George isn't the only one," she said. "He can't be." She looked forward again, at James. "How many more are there? How many of us have they convinced to do this? How stupid could I have been to think we won when ICWA was passed?"

"Not stupid, Barb. You know how important laws are. ICWA is damn important, and it'll be crucial if we need to fight to get Adriel back."

Barbara was only half listening, because while James was right about that, Barbara wasn't finished with her anger.

"And how easy would it have been for this Janice to convince George to give Adriel up?" she went on. "How easy would it have been for her to show George just how many wealthy families were lining up to give Adriel a better life? A better education. Better opportunities. Everything better! But it's *not* better just because it's their way! Our way is good for our people! Being here. On this sacred land. Learning from our elders. Understanding that we are all a small part of something much larger, something that goes back to the beginning. It's what Adriel needs. It's what we all need! They'll never understand that. They want everything that's ours. It's never enough! Why? Why isn't it enough?"

Barbara felt like her chest would explode. She needed to move, so she strode out of James's trailer and let out the yell that had been trapped inside of her. Even the dog backed away. She turned and looked at the mutt with his ears tucked into his head and his tail between his legs.

"I'm not crazy," she told him. He stared back at her. "It's our children. Our *children*." The dog almost seemed to understand her. Understand, at least, that she wasn't a threat. He sat down but kept his eyes on her. Finally, Barbara went back inside.

"I'm coming with you to that children's home," she said. "You'll need my help."

[42]

JAMES

THEY NEEDED TO GET INSIDE, that much was clear, and so James told Molly and Barbara that it was time for a little performance. They would be a family. He and Barbara were looking to adopt.

"Molly, I might have you stay in the car," James said. "Scope out the property first and then keep a lookout. See if Adriel comes in or out of any of the doors. If you're questioned, you can say your parents are inside."

"Barb," James said, turning to Barbara, who was adjusting her wig in the hotel room's bathroom. "If this sort of acting turns your stomach—and I understand if it does—you just let me do the talkin'."

Barbara didn't respond. Molly only nodded.

"You gals ready for this?"

Barbara turned to face him. "If Adriel is here, I will murder George Morris myself."

A smile crept onto Molly's face.

"Is that a confession?" James asked.

"Yes," Barbara said.

James sighed and ran his fingers through his hair. "Let me handle one murder case at a time, please."

The children's home did look quite nice. These people had money. No cracking cement. No peeling paint. It looked like a college campus with a full, brand-new playground snaking around the side of the main building.

James grabbed Barbara's hand as they walked up the steps, and she held her head a little higher. He could hear laughter inside. Happy sounds.

He rang the doorbell with his free hand. Barbara still did not look at him. She seemed to be concentrating, getting into character.

James rang a second time, and a moment later, a woman answered. She wore a casual blouse tucked into a pair of jeans. Her brown hair was pulled back by a scarf.

"Can I help you?"

"I sure hope so," James said with a wide grin. "My wife and I are lookin' to adopt!"

"Oh." The young woman brought a hand to her chest. "Well, you'll need to get in touch with our sister agency, then. This is the home for orphans."

"Yes! We would like to adopt an orphan! We'd like to see who's available."

"Sir, I'm sorry, but that's not usually how this works."

"Well, maybe not usually. But we spoke to Mr. Andrews. He's a friend of mine. He said to come by and check out the kids."

James stared intently at the young woman, who stammered an apology.

"I suppose I could show you around a little. But there are many factors in an adoption, and I can't exactly guarantee . . ."

"That's the spirit." James plastered on that grin again and brushed past the woman, pulling Barbara along with him.

The entrance to the house was grand, and he could hear feet pitter-pattering on the floor above.

"So, the children attend classes," the woman said, trying to scurry ahead. "But we can poke our heads into some of the classrooms if you would like."

"Sure, sure," James said. "That sounds good. We're lookin' for an Indian kid. You see, my wife here has got some Indian blood in her on her daddy's side." James paused here to lean into the young woman. He lowered his voice. "Indian princess, would you believe it? Anyhow, we'd love to ah . . . tap into that heritage."

The young woman smiled warmly at them. James didn't dare look at Barbara just then, but he hoped she wasn't rolling her eyes.

"I see. Well, there's certainly no shortage of Indian children here. It's a common request among our adopters, as well. Life is difficult for the Indian children. They come from poverty and broken homes, drug addiction and alcoholism. I believe God blesses the Indian children who find their way here. And the potential parents who have it in their hearts to give these children a better future."

"It's a damn shame what those kids have to deal with," James said, shaking his head. "A damn shame." He squeezed Barbara's hand to remind her this was all an act. He knew she would bite her tongue, but he also knew how much willpower that would take. In response, she gripped his hand tighter. Her nails jabbed into his skin.

"That certainly narrows our classrooms down, too! We put the Indian children together, because we have found them to be quite behind in their education. So, please be aware of that. In fact, the state classifies these children as 'special needs,' because it takes a bit of work for them to catch up in public school."

"And once we find an Indian child we like, what happens then?" he asked.

"Our adoption agency will get you the appropriate paperwork, but we like to make it as simple as possible for you all. We want these children to find homes, even though we love taking care of them here."

"No legal headaches, then?" James asked.

"Oh, no. Our lawyers have already done the work. Just show up on your court date to sign the papers."

"Wonderful."

The woman led them up the stairs and into a classroom to their right. She opened the door slowly. A male teacher stood at the front of a room full of Indian children at their desks. Everyone looked up.

"Sorry to interrupt," the young woman murmured to the teacher. Her face turned pink. "We have a friend of Mr. Andrews here today who is interested in adopting! He's just having a look around."

The teacher's gaze moved from the young woman to James and Barbara. He gave them a tight smile and a single nod. Then, he turned back to the class.

"Children! Please say hello to Mr. and Mrs. . . . ."

"Mulvaney!" James boomed.

"Hello, Mr. and Mrs. Mulvaney," the children said.

James scanned each child's face. Not Adriel. Not Adriel. Not Adriel. Not Adriel. He looked at Barbara. Her eyes were sharp. Her lips unmoving. James wondered if she recognized any of these kids.

"Looks like there's some learnin' happenin' here!" James said. "We'll leave you to it. Apologies for interrupting."

James turned to the young woman. "You got more classrooms?"

"Three more full classrooms. One of Indian children."

"Let's see it."

The woman took them to another classroom, where there was, once again, no Adriel.

"Do you want to, um, speak with any of the children? Meet them?" the woman asked.

"We'll be in touch with the agency," James said. "If you'll point me in the direction of the little boys' room, we'll be out of your hair."

MOLLY

MOLLY HAD EXPECTED lookout duty to be boring, so when a young man stepped out of a car, looked around nervously, and then darted to the side of the building—away from the playgrounds and toward the dumpsters—she had to convince herself that he was, in fact, who she thought he was.

She had only met Isaiah Winters that one time. But the nervous man in the parking lot was definitely the same guy who'd incessantly stirred his coffee that morning in the kitchen.

She could still see him, but barely. He stood at the top of a sloping hill, next to one of the building's side doors. One hand was slung across his body, clutching his side, while the other held a lit cigarette.

Molly waited, watching. A minute, two minutes, maybe five. Finally, another man emerged from the side door, and the two began to speak. Molly grabbed her sketchpad and pencil and tried to begin sketching the second man. But he was too far away.

Could she get closer? She spotted a bench not too far from them and wondered how suspicious it would be if she sat there. The men seemed engrossed in their conversation, so maybe if she was quiet and inconspicuous, she could manage it. Isaiah couldn't recognize her, though. She had a pair of sunglasses—and was grateful it was a sunny day—but thought she needed more. She looked in the back seat and found James's baseball cap. She scooped her hair up, twisted it on top of her head, and tucked it under the cap. *Good enough*, she thought. She grabbed her purse—with her pistol inside—and opened the door.

When she got out of the car, she hugged the building as she approached the walking path and bench. She hoped she could pass as a staff member, which she thought would be less suspicious. But then, maybe that would make the men stop talking. Maybe it was better to pass as a kid. A resident. She took her jacket from around her waist and put it on. She wasn't sure what she was trying to be, but she knew she needed a good look at the man's face. Catching a little of their conversation wouldn't hurt, either.

She walked slowly but deliberately toward the bench. When she sat, her back was to the men. She carefully opened her purse and brought out her pocket mirror. She opened it and looked through it at them. They didn't seem to have noticed her. She studied Isaiah's companion. Long, light-brown hair. Clean-shaven chin and lip. Purposeful, neatly trimmed sideburns. Clear skin. Lighter eyes, maybe green. A few freckles across his nose. Early twenties. Denim button-down.

"I thought you were done with this now they're gone," he said.

"I thought so, too, but maybe I shouldn't be. Maybe I should finish what we started."

"Isn't that dangerous?"

Molly didn't hear Isaiah's response.

The other man spoke again. "And so, just, what? Screw me and my job? Is that it?"

"You actually want to work for these monsters?" Isaiah asked.

"I want to pay my rent."

"We can find you another job." Isaiah lightly touched the other man's forearm, and the man's face relaxed.

"It's just . . . these are powerful people," the man said.

"You think I don't know this? My parents are dead. Murdered." Isaiah's voice cracked.

"So why keep going?"

Isaiah pulled away. He sighed. "If I'm losing sleep anyway, I might as well do some good."

There was silence. Molly kept still, studying them.

"This is the last thing, right?" the man asked.

"I promise."

The man looked at his wristwatch. "Give me five minutes."

Isaiah glanced around, and Molly lowered her mirror into her lap. "Take your time," he said, though Molly could tell he didn't mean it.

"I'll be right back," the other man said, and then he went back inside.

Molly didn't know what to do now. She wanted to leave, but that would draw attention. She also wanted to stay and find out why Isaiah was there. She slid down into herself, trying to hide most of her body as she sketched the other man.

Every so often, she would bring her mirror up to see if Isaiah was still there. To see if the other man had come back.

It felt like more than five minutes, but she couldn't be sure. James had bought her a watch, but she never wore it. She would need to start.

Finally, the other man came back out. She brought the mirror up. Papers.

They didn't say anything else. Isaiah left, and the other man went back inside. Molly sat on the bench for a while after, finishing her sketch.

[44]

ADRIEL

AFTER CALLING BARBARA, Adriel stayed where he was. He didn't want to. He wanted to leave. Run as far away as he could. But he thought maybe Barbara could find him now. Maybe Wayne or James knew how to find him through the phone wires.

He'd thought Mr. Tallsalt was a good person, but maybe he was wrong about that. He'd thought his dad loved him, but maybe he was wrong about that, too. Maybe Adriel had trusted them too much. Maybe no one was *really* good. Maybe all grownups had bad things inside them. Things that made them lie to kids.

Adriel wouldn't listen. He wouldn't cooperate. He spent his days in his bedroom or outside, ignoring everyone. Once, he'd even hit his dad when George got frustrated and tried to grab him. It made him a little sad to see his dad's face after that. Surprised. Confused. But Adriel was determined to stay mad. It wasn't okay what they were doing. It all felt wrong.

And then, one day, Mr. Tallsalt said, "We have somewhere important to go today, Adriel. And if you don't go willingly, we will drag you there. Do you understand?"

Adriel nodded.

45

SANCHEZ

CURTIS VASCO always carried himself as if his memories had been wiped clean the moment he crossed the border. And maybe, in a way, they had. Sanchez had no idea what the attorney general had experienced in Mexico as a teenager. He didn't know what needed forgetting. But Vasco was an American now, through and through.

The attorney general's son, Curtis Jr.—or CJ, as most kids called him—had embraced baseball, because it was one of the few places he was allowed to be himself. Brown and Mexican and also American. The baseball diamond didn't care. So, when he threw his shoulder out freshman year of college when the major league recruiters were already eying him, he took it particularly hard. He never played baseball again, never finished college, and bounced from job to job. He had not found peace as an adult.

Sanchez knew the senior Curtis would speak to him. They had, in some ways, kept in touch. Their families sent one another Christmas cards and invited each other to birthday and anniversary celebrations. Not surprisingly, the attorney general approved of Sanchez's career field. He never acted as though he was better than a police officer or the son of a police officer who now worked in narcotics. Curtis Vasco believed in law and order.

But Sanchez had never asked the attorney general for a work-related favor. Though it was understood that they respected one another's work, they never spoke of it beyond a simple, "How are things at the office?" and the standard reply, "Oh, they're going. You know how it is."

So, for Sanchez to call up Curtis Vasco and ask to meet, to ask to bring along a friend—a private detective poking around the business of government officials—it took some working up of courage. And some whiskey.

Curtis's wife answered. "Gabriel! So good to hear from you. How is your mother?"

"She's good. Keeping busy with the church. Making packages for the children's hospital right now."

"Oh, bless her. She's a good woman. You'll tell her I said hello, won't you?"

"Of course."

"And how about your sisters? Your father?"

"They're all doing well."

"That's good to hear. What can I help you with tonight, dear?"

"Is your husband home?"

"He is."

"I wanted to ask him something. I wanted to see if he has time to meet up with me and a friend."

"Oh, I'm sure he has time for you, Gabriel. Let me go get him."

"Thank you, Mrs. Vasco."

Sanchez took another sip of his whiskey as he waited, listening to how quiet the Vasco house was on the other end of the line.

Finally, he heard Curtis's voice. "Gabriel. How have you been?" Smooth and deep. Assured. The attorney general had also, of course, always intimidated Sanchez.

"Well, sir. And you?"

"Busy. Busy."

"I can imagine, sir. I was calling to see if I could grab just an hour or so of your time. Perhaps we can schedule time for coffee? Or I could buy you lunch." Sanchez cleared his throat. Why did his voice sound so high and shaky?

"I'm sure I could make that happen. Let me take a look at my calendar."

"Yes, sir."

"Next week. On Tuesday. An 8 a.m. coffee?"

"That would be perfect. I uh . . ." *Just get it done with,* Sanchez told himself. "Would you mind if I brought a buddy of mine? He's a private investigator working a case he thought you'd be interested in."

"James Pinter," the attorney general said.

Sanchez's mouth felt sticky. "Yes, that's right. How did you know?"

"Word gets around."

Sanchez waited. Swallowed too many times.

"He's working the Judge Winters case," Vasco said.

"I uh . . ." Still nothing was coming to Sanchez. The whiskey was supposed to give him courage, but now his thoughts were stuck.

"It's all right, Gabriel," the attorney general said. "He's welcome to come. I'd like to hear what he has to say."

"Excellent, sir. Thank you. We'll see you Tuesday."

"Please say hello to your family."

"Yes, sir." Sanchez hung up. His hand shook as he brought his glass to his lips and sipped. Lark was the one telling people about Pinter. That Sanchez was working with him. Probably warning them. Shit. He slammed his glass down. What a stupid decision. This would send him back to patrol.

46

ISAIAH

THE MOST RECENT reports Isaiah had gotten from Peter were probably the last piece of the puzzle his mother had needed. He knew his relationship with Peter was over. Had been for a while. Ever since Isaiah had started to use him.

He set down the reports and rubbed his eyes. Would she be proud? Why had Cathy really come to Isaiah? Because she wanted his help? Because she loved him? He wished it were that pure, but the truth was that she'd needed her son's boyfriend to fill in the gaps in her case. That was why she had come to him.

She had never voiced any disapproval of Isaiah's lifestyle, but they had kept it between the two of them, never telling his father. Maybe she'd thought it was just a phase. Maybe that was why she'd never taken Peter seriously.

Isaiah sighed, picked up the large envelope, slid the report inside, and addressed it to the attorney general. It was out of his hands now. He would try to repair his relationship with Peter, but it was probably too far gone. Isaiah felt it. He was sure Peter did, too, if not because of broken promises, then because of resentment.

Which was why Isaiah was so surprised when his phone rang at 10:45 p.m. Only Peter ever called at this hour. Maybe it wasn't too late for them. Maybe they could fix this. Isaiah could apologize and really mean it. Explain, somehow, the love he had for his mother.

But Isaiah knew as soon as he picked up that something was wrong.

"Zay," Peter said, breathless. It tugged on something inside of Isaiah. A loose knot. It had been so long since Peter had called him that.

"What is it?" Isaiah asked.

"I'm scared."

"What's happening?"

"Someone's following me."

"What?" Isaiah pushed forward on the couch. Leaned into the phone.

"A man is following me."

"What kind of man?"

"I haven't been able to get a look at his face. I thought I noticed him yesterday, but then he disappeared, and I realized I was being paranoid and have been paranoid for weeks now. But then he showed up again tonight. He was following my car. I took the long way home and stopped at two stores, and he followed me anyway."

"Shit."

"Yeah."

"You're sure?"

"I'm sure."

"Is he still there?" Isaiah asked.

"He's parked down the street. I'm looking at his car right now. He hasn't gotten out. He's just sitting there."

"Is he alone?"

"I think so. I don't see anyone in the passenger's seat."

"Stay there. I'm coming over."

"But, Zay . . ." Too late. He had hung up. Grabbed his jacket. He wished he wasn't afraid to use a gun. Because he had his mother's now. He could take it with him. But he didn't.

Isaiah waited in his car, watching Peter's doorstep, looking for the guy's car with no clue what he was driving or what he looked like. Peter lived in the heart of the city, so it could be any one of the cars around him. Isaiah couldn't exactly peek into every window.

He knew he should probably go in. Peter was expecting him. But his skin prickled. He felt like something was about to happen and that this was where he ought to be when it did. Watching.

Twenty minutes. Then thirty. And then, finally, when Isaiah was about to give up and go inside, something did happen. A man got out of a car on the opposite side of the street, crossed to Peter's mailbox, and put something in it. The man looked around, crossed the street again, got into his car, and pulled away.

Isaiah willed himself to walk to the mailbox. To open it. To not think about bombs. To only think about Peter and what this man might want from him. What Isaiah had gotten him into. This was Isaiah's responsibility.

When he felt a piece of paper in his hand—a note—he let out a shaky breath. He wanted to laugh at himself. Or cry. Instead, he pocketed the note and let himself into Peter's house.

He heard the TV on, and even though Peter didn't get up to greet him, as soon as Isaiah came through the door, he asked, "Where have you been?"

"I've been watching for him. He left something in your mailbox."

Isaiah held the paper out to Peter, an offering, and with that, Peter did get up off the couch. His eyes narrowed in the light of the flashing television as he unfolded the paper.

"It's just a telephone number," Peter said.

"So call it."

Peter said nothing. He stared at the number, so Isaiah snatched it back, walked to the telephone, and dialed. It rang and rang, and then, finally, an outgoing message played.

"You've reached Bobby Tate. Please leave a message with your name and number and I'll return your call at my earliest convenience. Goodbye."

Bobby Tate. Where had he heard that name before? Isaiah hung up just as the machine beeped.

47

JAMES

THE LIQUOR STORE was empty except for the clerk and Janice Stone. James sat in the parking lot with two stacks of files in the seat beside him. He watched Janice walk down the third aisle in that clipped manner of hers. She stopped, plucked a bottle from the shelf, and made her way to the counter.

James sighed and stepped out of the car. Locked the files in behind him. He leaned up against Janice's bumper, crossed his arms, and waited.

When she saw him, her face paled. She was about to turn on her heels and, he assumed, go back into the liquor store. Maybe ask the clerk to call the cops.

"The orange lizard," James said. "The child's toy. You had it first."

That stopped her. She narrowed her eyes but said nothing.

"And then, somehow, it ended up in the evidence locker at the New Mexico State Police headquarters in Albuquerque."

Janice took a deep breath, and James might have seen her bottom lip quiver. It was hard to tell in the dim light of the strip mall parking lot.

"We also recovered a voicemail from George Morris's answering machine," he went on. "'Judge Winters is becoming a problem.' Your exact words."

James uncrossed his arms and stood up straight.

"We can go back to your house now. Or to an all-night diner. Hell, wherever you'd like to chat, Janice. And we can talk about what George Morris was doin' for you. What you might've done for him. Or, when you go back into that liquor store and call the cops on me, I can tell them all about your connections to the dead judge."

Janice closed her eyes for a breath. "Come to my office. I'll show you the way."

"Don't think about speedin' off, now. I'm pretty damn good at keepin' a tail."

She stared hard at him. Maybe there was fury there. Good.

"I'm sure you are," she said.

James kept the radio low, barely audible, as he followed Janice's taillights back through the city streets to her empty office building.

When they arrived, James zipped up the coat that was too warm for the night, adjusted what was hidden underneath, and got out of the car. He kept a few feet between him and Janice. She didn't look back at him until she held her office door open for him.

It was organized in there. Sparse. A photo of a young Janice and a man sat on the shelf behind her desk. The only other thing in the room was a black-and-white poster on the wall. A wide-eyed cat hung from a branch. It said, *Hang in there, baby*.

Janice pulled the bottle out of the brown paper bag and set it on the desk. She retrieved two glasses from the bottom drawer.

"Not much of a brandy drinker," James said. "But I appreciate the gesture."

She put one of the glasses back but still didn't speak. Didn't even look at James. He waited for her to get comfortable, but instead of sitting, she walked to the other side of the office, shuffled through a file cabinet, and plopped a thick folder in front of him. Then, she sat.

"What's this?" he asked.

"That is the file on every single Indian in New Mexico who is doing for this organization what George is doing for me. So, before we get started, know that George is not unique."

"Well, he is in one sense. He disappeared the day before Judge Winters was killed and is accused of murdering two people. Don't know if we can say the same about any of these other . . . what would you call them? Scouts?"

Janice chuckled but without humor. "They're doing important work. They're finding children who need help."

"Do you pay these scouts to find children for you?"

"It's volunteer work. They feel they are called to do it."

James wasn't sure he believed that.

"So." He leaned back. Propped his ankle on his knee. Adjusted his jacket. "George helps out at addict meetings. Gets to know people on the reservation. He calls you up, tells you about these parents. You call someone from one of your sister organizations. An employee from New Mexico Children's Agency then goes to pay the family a visit. Sees signs of neglect at the home. Takes the child. Brings them to Children of God Home."

"Nothing wrong with any of that. Like I said, those kids need our help."

James nodded. "The way things are on the reservation. Would you say the situation is bleak for these children?"

"Would you?" Janice asked. "You've seen enough of it."

James tried not to smirk. "I would say you care very much about helping Indian children. Especially considering your earlier employment at the boarding school."

He could see he had alarmed her now. Her eyes grew a little wider. She swallowed. Maybe she thought she had buried that.

"I have a heart for them. These people," Janice practically whispered. "They've been left to live in poverty and addiction, and they don't know how to get themselves out. I'm helping to break the cycle."

"And you do that by finding them new homes," James clarified. "With adopted families."

"Yes, that's right."

"Any of those adopted families also Indians?"

Janice cleared her throat. "Not usually. The adoption process is quite expensive and there's very little we can do about that."

"I see. Does Mr. Andrews really have room for all of these children? Do you ever find yourself working with foster families?"

"There are select foster families that NMCA, our partner organization, has identified as reliable. Other foster families we have worked with in the past have gone on to adopt the children in their care and have declared their homes full."

"Any of those families Indians?"

Janice pursed her lips.

"The Navajo I work with, like George, have chosen to help in their own way. Like I've said, poverty and addiction are rampant on the reservation. Most homes are unfit for fostering."

James thumbed through the files in front of him.

"I understand you care for these children. The Indian ones, specifically. Any idea why Mr. Andrews has tasked you with this job? Finding these scouts? Does he share your, ah," James paused. "Your passion."

Janice shrugged. Put her hands out, palms up.

"My job is to create relationships with individuals on nearby reservations who are open to this sort of work. I've no idea Mr. Andrews's motivations."

"Do these scouts all come from churches?" James asked.

"Many. They recognize, from scripture, the importance of a home with both a stable mother and a stable father."

"George was certainly ripe for the pickin', then."

Janice took another sip of brandy and did not respond.

"When Linda died, George must've felt guilty," James went on. "For no longer having a stable mother for Adriel. Was he trying to get rid of him? Was he lookin' for a family to take Adriel?"

Janice's eyebrows inched up her forehead. "At first," she said, "it was understood that Adriel was not up for discussion. But then Adriel's mother died. Overdosed was the word on the reservation and what I thought had happened until you informed me otherwise. I knew George would understand that Adriel needed a mother. I left him some messages to let him know the type of services a wealthy family could provide for the boy. I wanted him to know his options."

She stood up again, walked to a different file cabinet, grabbed a stack of documents clipped together. She set those in front of James, too.

"George decided I was right. He couldn't handle the child by himself. Which is why he signed these adoption papers. The morning Judge Winters was killed."

James looked down at the papers. George's signature was there. He kept his face steady. Why the hell hadn't George told him about this?

"I assume," Janice went on, "that he went on to kill the judge after he left my office, just as the police claim. He knew Judge Winters would be an obstacle. George thought his son deserved better. A nice family. Hope for a future. The judge would stand in his way."

James held up the signed adoption papers. "But you haven't given these to the police."

"I'm not interested in punishing George for murdering Bartholomew Winters. God is the ultimate judge for us all. I'm interested in helping poor Adriel. He clearly needs someone stable to care for him. He is in danger. And all I want is to get the boy back and into a safe and loving home."

"That's why you sent that man. For Adriel. Adriel is the thing George has that's yours."

Janice Stone barely blinked. "I haven't a clue what you're talking about."

"Cathy is what doesn't add up so neatly," James said. "George hasn't got one reason to kill the woman. It would've been foolish. He should've been long gone. Out of Albuquerque. He didn't even know her."

"I don't know what to tell you," Janice said. "He's clearly unwell."

"Indeed." James waited a beat, then slapped his knees and leaned forward in his chair. "Well, Janice, this is what I know. When the state of New Mexico allocates money to children in the care of foster families or children's homes, any child that is designated 'special needs' is given more money by both the state and the federal government."

Janice's frown deepened and James went on.

"This alone would make Adriel a valuable find. But there's more. Adriel is also the member of an Indian tribe, which automatically checks off a separate special needs box. I can't say I've got any clue as to how Mr. Andrews pulled that off, but I do know that it sheds some light on why he's so intent on you working with these Indian scouts to identify Indian children for his organization. Hell, an Indian kid *with* a special need? You must've felt like you hit the jackpot, Janice. How long exactly have you had your eye on the boy?"

She sighed and her breath sounded shaky to James. She tucked a stray hair behind her ear.

"It wasn't like that at all."

"You can see how it might look that way to me," James said. "Care to set the record straight?"

"I've told you. This is my calling. I sleep well at night because I know these children will go on to have better lives. I'm changing their lives, Mr. Pinter. The rest is noise to me."

"Ever heard of the Indian Child Welfare Act?" James asked.

Janice closed her eyes for a brief moment. She looked tired.

"Of course. I wouldn't be very good at my job if I wasn't abreast these sorts of things."

"One more thing," James said, eyeing the files in front of him. "Would you mind if I ran these through the copier before I left? Our little secret."

"Of course I mind. It's my job to protect their identities."

"Well then." James stood. Put his hat back on. "I'll be seein' you around, Janice Stone."

48

BARBARA

BARBARA AND MOLLY had made two stops before this one. The first was at a pet store right outside of Albuquerque for dog food and flea shampoo.

"I know it'll be too dark to give him a bath tonight, but after school tomorrow, I want to. It's getting too cold for sleeping outside."

Barbara smiled and did not remind Molly that the dog had fur and an ability to find itself shelter. It had probably been sleeping outside its whole life. It didn't look like an old dog, but it wasn't a puppy, either.

The second stop had been to Barbara's office. She knew the phone company had not yet responded to the court order, but she felt the need to check anyway. Instead, she found a voice message. Her heartbeat quickened. Had Adriel called again?

But when Barbara pushed the button, it was James's voice that spoke to her.

"It's me, Barb. I know you just left, but I forgot to ask," he said. "Can you look into a judge for me? He's on the reservation. Wayne gave me the name of a guy who does now what Tallsalt used to do. Robert John. I want to see what we can find out about him. I'll see you tomorrow. Thanks, Barb."

Now, Barbara watched Molly speak to the dog, scratch his ears. The dog's mouth was open, his tongue lolling to the side. He looked so happy it made Barbara laugh.

Molly disappeared into the house for a few minutes and came back out with a bowl of the new dog food. She put it in front of him, and he didn't even stand up to start eating it. Just put his muzzle right into that bowl. Barbara shook her head. These rez dogs were something else.

Molly clambered back into the car. "You sure you don't mind if I use your washing machine tonight?"

"Honey, what's mine is yours."

Molly grinned and grabbed the files off the dash. They'd made copies at the Albuquerque library earlier that day before leaving James behind. "What are you gonna do with these?" she'd asked her dad.

James hadn't been concerned about stealing from the children's home. "They won't miss them for an afternoon," he'd said. "If anyone notices they're gone, it'll likely be a lower-level employee who would only suspect someone misplaced them. They won't report it right away."

"How will you get them back?" Barbara asked.

James shrugged. "Slip them into their mailbox, maybe. Like I said, Donald Andrews ain't checkin' it."

Barbara almost mentioned that the wrong person might take the blame. But why did she care what happened to those employees? What kind of people worked for kidnappers, anyway? They all knew what was going on there. They had to.

"I want to look through the intake list," Barbara said to Molly now as they drove away from James's trailer. The roads were empty. It was dark. They could only see the things Barbara's headlights reached.

"I want to find the Navajo kids," Barbara went on. "Learn their stories. See if any of this was done the way it ought to have been."

"And you'll recognize all the names?" Molly asked. "You'll know the families?"

"I know a lot of people on the reservation. But if there's anyone who knows more, it's my father."

"So, you'll show it to him?"

"Yes. I was going to do it tomorrow, but . . ." Barbara glanced at Molly. "Would you like to go with me now? He's a night owl. He'll be awake."

"Yes! I'd love to come."

But then Barbara checked her watch. "It's ten o'clock. You've got school tomorrow."

"I won't tell my dad," Molly said.

Barbara's mouth curled into a small smile. James wouldn't care. Not really.

"I've been wanting to meet your dad," Molly added.

"You'll like him," Barbara said. "Everyone does."

49

WAYNE

THERE WAS an empty bar stool next to Tony Morris, and Wayne was not surprised. He assumed it was for him and sat in it.

"Cool off for a minute, Chief, before you start talking," Tony said. "I ordered you a beer."

"Lieutenant," Wayne said, reaching for the Budweiser.

"Whatever."

"You dragged me more than an hour away out here."

Tony shrugged. "I knew you wanted to talk."

"So talk," Wayne said. "What was that all about?"

"I thought he might be able to help you find George. You were both looking for him."

"And you couldn't have just come to me and told me that?"

"What's the fun in that?" Tony grinned. "Besides, I didn't want to spook the guy. Maybe he would've been even quicker than me to figure out a cop was following him."

Wayne sighed loudly. Took another sip of beer.

"I won't say it was a waste of time talking to the guy,"

Wayne said. "It wasn't. But I will say I know for a fact that you've got a better idea of where George is than he does. You saw George when he dropped his truck off. I'm guessing you also found him another vehicle."

Tony shook his head. "I don't know where he is now."

Now. But he had known. Wayne felt violent for a moment. Like he wanted to slam this punk into the wall. He didn't like how clever Tony thought he was, and he didn't like how far behind he felt. Wayne had looked up Tony's rap sheet. A larceny charge. Tony had been stealing money—most likely collecting a drug debt, police had concluded—and had been arrested with a weapon on him. No criminal mastermind, just a regular, run-of-the-mill criminal.

"Why can't you just let him sort out whatever he needs to sort out?" Tony asked.

"Because he's got Adriel. And he's a suspect in a murder investigation."

"Which he didn't commit. He loves Adriel."

"Then why did he take him from the rest of his family?" Wayne asked.

"He's got his reasons."

Wayne probably should have swallowed his next words. "Do you know what George was doing before he disappeared?" He was sure that Tony was protecting a man he didn't even know.

Tony shook his head. "I don't want to."

"I think you do." Wayne held eye contact. "George was working for a woman at an adoption agency in Albuquerque. He was finding Diné children for them to take. Kids with parents addicted to drugs, alcohol, in jail."

He added that last one for fun and watched Tony's breath quicken.

"Parents who never saw their children again. George was a traitor. And a snitch."

Tony looked angry but not exactly surprised. So he'd known at least some of it already.

"No," Tony said. "Those people. They found him."

"It doesn't matter how he got involved, does it? He *was* involved. Janice Stone—the woman who sent the man you fought—she works for the agency. And George worked for her."

Tony shook his head. Tore pieces off the small cocktail napkin beneath his beer.

"He's running from those people," Tony said, almost to himself. "That's who he's running from."

"Did he tell you that?" Wayne asked.

Tony looked at his shredded napkin pile. "He told me they were coming for Adriel."

"And he's trying to protect Adriel?" Wayne asked. He didn't know if he could believe Tony. And he didn't know if Tony ought to believe George.

"Yeah," Tony said. "And it'd probably be easier to do that if you'd lay off him."

"We can protect Adriel," Wayne said. "You can tell him that. If he comes home, we can protect Adriel."

Tony laughed. A bitter laugh. "You're telling me that George was involved in this little operation of taking kids and that he doesn't know that you *can't* protect Adriel?"

He turned his whole body to face Wayne. "If you can protect this boy, then why are these other kids getting taken? What are you doing for them? Jack shit."

Wayne wanted to defend himself. He wanted to explain the impossible task that was his job. He wanted Tony to understand that most of police work was just staving off the inevitable—the disasters, the crisis—for another day. But he couldn't put it into words. He also knew that Tony was right. That someone, somewhere, *should* be doing something more. Who better than Wayne? These kids—the future of the Navajo Nation—were slipping through his fingers.

So instead, he said, "They will not take Adriel. I will lose my job before I allow that to happen. But I can't protect him if I don't know where he is."

Tony studied him for a moment.

"Sorry, boss," he finally said. "Even if I knew where he was, I wouldn't tell you. Because I just don't believe you."

50

MOLLY

"IT'S FOR YOUR OWN GOOD," Molly said, but the dog still looked at her like he was in pain as she hosed down his backside. "It's just water."

The dog was tied to the last rail at the bottom of the steps, and Molly had on gloves to protect her hands from the harsh shampoo. She lathered up again and scratched his butt. The dog hung his head in surrender.

"And now, you can sleep inside with me tonight. Protect me until Dad gets home."

The dog shook, flinging soapy water all over Molly. She gasped and then laughed. It was a little too cold for this, she knew, and she felt bad that the water wasn't warmer. But the dog deserved a warm home.

"Fair enough. You stinker." The dog wagged his tail low and slow at the sound of her playful tone. Maybe he forgave her.

When she finished, she dried him as best she could with an old beach towel and then let him in the house. He was cautious at first. Sniffing the floors, the trashcan, the toilet bowl. Then, he started to feel a little rowdy. He planted his feet and pressed his body up against the couch, drying off the rest of his dampness. Molly laughed again.

"Good thing that'll dry before tomorrow. My dad will never have to know. Until your next bath, I suppose."

She plopped down on the couch, and the dog did the same on the rug at her feet. She thought about the night before. About meeting Barbara's dad. Molly had not expected him to be so playful and funny. It brought light out of Barbara, too, and Molly could feel the love between them, like the warmth of an oven baking brownies.

Mr. Nakai's laugh was deep and loud and made Molly smile. "Not everyone gets to see that side of him," Barbara told her later. "He's so serious in public."

When they looked at the list of children, Molly had seen that seriousness. It was almost fierce. He and Barbara confirmed fifty-two children from the Navajo Nation on that list. Barbara set her jaw and rubbed her temples.

"After all that work," she said.

"You knew the fight wasn't over," her father said. "It might never be. But you're my daughter. You have plenty left to give to it."

"I know," she said.

"What will you do now?" Molly asked. "With those names?"

"Check in with the families, with the courts," Barbara said. "I think we can guess that things weren't done correctly knowing what we know about Donald Andrews's organizations. But like your dad said, the law was written for a reason. Now we start the long process of justice. Bringing those kids home, if we can."

"We used to hide from them, you know," Mr. Nakai said.

"Who?" Molly asked.

"The people that took us to the boarding schools. They would come onto the reservation and round up the kids. Most parents couldn't see a way around it. And it was free education for their kids. That's what many of them thought. They didn't want to send their kids so far away, but the schools around here weren't what they are now. There weren't very many at all on the reservation, and they were bad."

He paused and sipped his tea. "My parents, though. They would hide us. My mother said there wasn't anything the boarding schools could teach me that she couldn't teach me better."

Molly knew she hadn't seen the worst of it. She knew there was heartache and pain and struggle here. Especially with the poverty. But there was so much love, too. Molly had received it herself. And who had she been to them? A stranger.

Now, as Molly sat on the couch, she thought of Adriel. He wasn't at the children's home, so where was he? Was he with George? What was he doing right then? Was he safe? Comfortable? Cared for? Did he feel loved? Did he miss them?

There was a knock at the door, then. Molly opened it slowly and peeked her head out. Her heart pounded in her chest. It was Isaiah Winters. Had he seen her at the children's home? Was he coming here to threaten her? Or worse?

But when she looked at his face, he didn't look angry. He looked nervous. She remembered her dad saying that he always looked nervous.

"Isaiah, right?" Molly asked, opening the door a little

wider. The dog was standing next to her now. Alert. Ears up, tail out. Isaiah noticed, too, and took a step back.

"You're my P.I.'s daughter," Isaiah said. "Is he here?"

Molly considered what to say. She didn't necessarily want him to know she was alone, but she did want to know what he'd come all this way for. The dog was there. And by the looks of him, ready to defend her if need be.

"James isn't home right now," Molly said.

Isaiah nodded. Took another half step back. He was almost at the stairs now.

"I'll just wait for him here, then."

Molly bit her bottom lip. "Actually . . . he's in Albuquerque."

"What?"

"I know. I'm sorry you came all this way. But here. Why don't you come in? I'll make some coffee. Or tea. Which would you like?"

Isaiah looked at the dog. "Is he going to rip my face off?"

Molly looked at the dog, too. She patted the top of his head. Scratched behind one of his ears. "Not unless I tell him to."

"That's reassuring."

Isaiah flattened himself against the doorway and shuffled his way in. "Good doggie," he whispered.

Private—which was the name lodged into Molly's head—eyed Isaiah but didn't do much else. When Isaiah was finally inside, the dog looked up at Molly. Panted. Let his tongue loll out. Molly leaned down and whispered into his ear.

"He's okay, I think. But don't go too far."

Private licked Molly's face, and she straightened.

"So. What'll it be? Tea? Coffee?"

"Coffee, please," Isaiah said.

"Okay, you got it," Molly said. "You can sit."

Isaiah looked around and chose a folding chair in the corner next to James's desk. The dripping coffee and the dog's panting were the only sounds in the trailer for a couple of minutes. When the coffee was ready, Molly brought it out with sugar and milk.

"Sugar and a little milk, right?"

"Good memory," Isaiah said.

They sat and sipped for a moment—Isaiah on the folding chair, Molly on her swivel chair.

"You drove a ways to see my dad," she finally said.

Isaiah nodded. "My, um, friend is being followed. I wanted to let your dad know. Agent Sanchez wanted me to let your dad know."

Molly kept her expression neutral. "By who?"

"This lawyer, I think. His name is Bobby Tate."

Molly eyes widened. "Bobby Tate?"

"Do you know of him?"

Molly nodded. "He was a lawyer on a lot of your father's cases."

"Was he?"

"Yes. My dad and I noticed when we were going through your dad's cases. Bobby Tate kept showing up."

"Representing children?"

"I think he was representing the parents. The ones trying to adopt."

"What does he want with Peter?" Molly knew it wasn't a question for her. Isaiah stared into his coffee, and Molly felt like he knew exactly what Bobby Tate wanted with Peter. Dread was written all over Isaiah's face.

"Peter . . . is he like a childhood friend? Have you known him for a long time?"

Isaiah stared at Molly. Studying her, she thought. She was trying to be professional with all of this. Cool and relaxed. Trying to put Isaiah at ease.

"My boyfriend, actually," he said. "We've been together for about a year."

Boyfriend. Woah. Molly didn't know any gay people in real life. Still, she kept her expression the same. Or at least, she hoped she did.

"Oh," Molly said. "So, your parents knew him? A year is kind of a while."

"No," Isaiah said. "They never met. My dad didn't know."

Molly nodded. That must've been hard, she thought. But she didn't say anything. She was afraid of saying the wrong thing just then.

Isaiah stood. He put his hands in his pants pockets and started to pace.

"There are some things I should probably tell your dad," he said.

"I can write them down," Molly said. "Exactly. And then he'll know. Or . . . we have a tape recorder. I could record you. Or not. Whichever you prefer."

Isaiah stopped pacing.

"All right," he said. "Tape recorder is fine."

That surprised Molly, but she didn't sit there a second longer. At first, she couldn't find it. It wasn't where she knew they kept it. But then she found a different tape recorder. Interesting. She brought it out and set it up on James's desk.

"This is insurance, I guess," Isaiah said, as Molly replaced the cassette tape with a new one. "In case something happens to me."

"Do you think something is gonna happen to you?"

Isaiah shrugged. "You found my mom's shoeboxes, right? In the garden shed?"

"Yes." Molly pressed the record button.

"I was helping her."

"What was she doing?"

"She was investigating Donald Andrews. Specifically, she was looking for incorrect use of donations, profiting from his nonprofits, proof of bribery, things like that. Whatever she could find."

"And why were you helping her?"

"Because she asked me to. Peter could get us the documents she needed. Well, some of them."

"And your mom was sending what she found to the attorney general."

"Yes."

"But she didn't want your dad to know."

Isaiah pursed his lips.

"Would he have been angry if he found out what she was doing?"

"Probably."

"So how did your mom even start on this . . . project? If it wasn't for your dad?"

"She volunteers a lot. She used to, I mean. She used to give money to Donald Andrews's children's home. Money for orphans. What could be wrong with that? But then Dad started telling her what he knew about Donald Andrews and the ICWA law. How Andrews was in violation. How he thought Andrews was skipping steps. Not going through the proper channels."

Isaiah paused for a moment. He picked at his fingernail, then combed his fingers through his hair.

"My parents hated injustice. It brought them together. When they met, Mom was involved in those early civil rights protests. I think when she heard about Donald Andrews, she felt personally offended. Like she'd been tricked into supporting this person who was doing things that disgusted her. But she's been around this kind of stuff long enough to know that what people truly care about is financial crime. It gets their attention. She was set on bringing Andrews down."

"And what kind of things was your boyfriend getting for her?"

He looked sideways at the recorder, and Molly realized she probably should have just said "friend." But Isaiah went on anyway.

"Anything that might help. Peter coordinates between the children's home and the adoption agency. He has access to a lot of files. Like the backend financing."

"And now this lawyer, Bobby Tate, is following him. So, he must know?"

"I guess?" Isaiah had his hands open, his shoulders up.

"Has Peter worked with Bobby Tate before? The children's home has lawyers, right?"

"Sure, they have lawyers. It's not Peter's area, though. So, if he *has* worked with Tate, he doesn't remember. It would have been briefly."

"Maybe it has nothing to do with this, then. Maybe it's something else. How did you guys figure out the lawyer was following him?"

"He left a note in Peter's mailbox with just Tate's office number on it."

"Did Peter call?" Molly asked.

Isaiah shook his head. "I did. It was late at night. I got his answering machine."

"Maybe Peter should talk to the lawyer. Find out what he wants."

"I was hoping your dad would do that," Isaiah said. "I don't want Peter in any danger. Well, in any more danger than I've already put him in."

"I don't want to promise anything without my dad, but Bobby Tate is already part of our investigation. I'm sure he can go talk to him."

Isaiah slid his palms down his knees. "All right."

Molly pushed the button again to stop the recorder. Isaiah still seemed nervous but, Molly thought, maybe a little less so now.

"Try not to worry too much," Molly said. "My dad is really good at what he does."

Isaiah actually smiled, then. She thought she saw some pity behind it. But that was okay. Isaiah didn't know her dad like Molly did.

"Okay," Isaiah said. "Thank you for your help."

"It's Molly," she said, because she could tell he didn't remember her name.

"Right. Molly." He stood up. Stuck his hand out for her to shake. "Tell your dad he knows where to find me."

51

KAY

WAYNE HAD TRIED to prepare her before they left Kayenta. They knew now that Adriel had called Barbara from Lester Tallsalt's phone. Perhaps they'd find Tallsalt at his home, but after speaking with Tony, Wayne was sure George and Adriel would be long gone.

Still, Kay's heart raced as they drove to Tallsalt's place. She wanted to get out and run, which made no sense. Wayne was driving fast enough. She closed her eyes. She prayed.

When she opened them again, they were on a long, unpaved road between the buttes. She breathed deeply for several minutes, waiting for a house to come into view. Tallsalt's was the only house there, at the end of the road, and Wayne had to slam on the brakes because Kay had already flung open the door.

She tried to run to the house, but Wayne stopped her. Grabbed her by the shoulders before she could get more than a few steps from the car.

"Are you trained to enter a home with possible hostile and armed suspects?" he demanded. His eyes were piercing.

She rarely saw this side of Wayne and had forgotten how intimidating he could be.

"No," Kay said through gritted teeth. "But I'm armed, too."

"Let. Me. Go. First."

"Fine." Kay twisted her arms a little, and Wayne let go. He turned away from her and approached the house. She watched him knock on the front door. Stand to the side, gun pointed at the ground but gripped with two hands.

Wayne knocked two times. Three. Four. No answer.

"Tribal Police. Come to the door or make yourself known," he shouted.

Nothing. Kay's stomach dropped. It was silent out here. Nothing stirred. No noises came from the house or from anywhere else, either.

Wayne looked into the windows next, circling the house. Finally, he tried the back door. Kay waited outside as instructed, listening to him repeat what he had said at the front.

At last, from inside the house, Wayne opened the front door. "Don't touch anything," he said. "Stick by my side and let me know if you see any signs of Adriel."

Kay almost didn't want to. She didn't want to see another empty space where Adriel had been. She didn't want to see a left-behind comic book or a bed that Adriel's hands had recently made. But she went inside anyway, because she knew she had to keep looking. Maybe Adriel had left her something.

She breathed deeply as she crossed the threshold. The house was well enough taken care of, neat, and not as empty as she'd expected. Drying dishes, coats hung on the wall. A framed photo sat on a shelf. A younger man and a girl, taken a while ago. Was it Tallsalt? And who was the girl? She didn't look Indian to Kay, but the photo was that old brownish color, so it was hard to be sure.

"I'm going to check all the rooms now," Wayne said. "Stay behind me. If you see any signs of a person in distress, alert me."

Kay nodded. She walked down the hall carefully, quietly, almost tiptoeing. There were shelves, more framed photos. Tallsalt at different ages with different people. There were three bedrooms in the house and two full bathrooms. An ex-judge indeed. It reminded Kay of a lodge. Dark. Cool, some-how. She supposed it was in the shade of the butte most of the day.

The last door Wayne opened clearly led to the bedroom where Adriel had stayed. She closed her eyes after seeing the small bed, the baseball glove on the dresser. Not Adriel's, she didn't think. He didn't have one. But some little boy's. At some point. Or girl's, she supposed. The girl in the photograph?

The closet was empty. No clothes left on the floor.

"Can we see what's in the dresser drawers?" she asked.

"No," Wayne said. "We're looking for people right now, not things."

Then, something caught her eye. The mattress was askew. Just a little bit. But underneath, she could see some-thing. She crossed the room and lifted the mattress. She heard Wayne hiss something at her. She ignored him. There were loose papers there, folded in half. A stack of them. Kay unfolded them. They were drawings of hands. Fingers sticking up and out. Arrows motioning around them. Words beside them. What was this? Sign language? The hands were drawn a little too precisely to be done by Adriel. Had George learned sign language?

Kay brought her hand to her mouth and tried not to cry. She reminded herself of what she had learned about George. Of her rage. How dangerous he could be. And Tallsalt. She didn't know him at all. But this was a gift. This in her hand. Whatever the intentions behind it, the motivations, it was still a gift.

She would learn, too, she thought. Adriel could teach her. When she found him. An ache tugged at her chest. She missed him so much. If George gave him away, she would never forgive herself.

Kay looked down at the words on the paper. *Father. Mother. Family. Love.*

52

SANCHEZ

LARK SHUT the door and closed the blinds. Sanchez wasn't exactly sure why. It was dark outside by then, past dinnertime, and almost no one was at the station.

There were fresh, empty Styrofoam takeout boxes in Lark's trashcan. But his eyes were alert. Not at all tired. And he was starting to make Sanchez nervous.

Sanchez expected a tongue-lashing. For what, he wasn't sure. For secretly working with James? But instead, Lark handed Sanchez a coffee. Told him to make himself comfortable, which made Sanchez very uncomfortable.

Finally, Lark began to speak. Low. Quiet. But clear.

"Duncan has been placed on administrative leave for tampering with evidence," he began. Sanchez sat up straighter. "He admitted to logging the plush toy a day late. He claims to have accidentally slipped it into his pocket."

Sanchez breathed a sigh of relief. "That's . . . a bit strange, sir."

"Agreed. I'm going to ask you something unusual. You are

not a homicide detective, and you are not trained as such. However, I understand that your P.I. friend is quite experienced in the field. I would like you to work with him as an outside source and report to me."

"Yes. Yes, sir," Sanchez managed to say. "But with Duncan on leave, do you think those who were involved might suspect what we're doing?"

Lark leaned back in his chair. Tapped his pen on the desk.

"Mishandling of evidence is a serious offense. Anyone would expect to see consequences. Officially, I will take over the case and do very little with it. I will, of course, be investigating the evidence custodian to find out why he accepted and logged the evidence produced by Duncan. Aside from that, whoever is involved will see me treating it as Duncan did—waiting on George Morris to show up somewhere."

He pointed his pen at Sanchez. "In reality, you and James Pinter will continue to investigate. We'll meet weekly, at this same time, here in my office, and you will update me on the case."

Sanchez almost couldn't breathe. Holy shit. This was not how he'd imagined his first homicide case.

"This is a very delicate case," Lark went on. "You don't need me to tell you that. Politicians may be involved. You will need to be careful. You will speak of the case to no one else but me."

"Can I bring Pinter to our meetings, sir?" Sanchez knew James might not be able to come to every meeting. But some would be crucial.

"That will be fine."

"Thank you, sir."

"So," Lark said, sliding a notepad in front of him. "Catch me up. What have you got so far?"

53

JAMES

FROM HIS HOTEL ROOM, James had called the number George had given him for his brother, Tony Morris. No one picked up, but he left a voicemail asking why in the hell George hadn't told him about putting Adriel up for adoption. It sure didn't make George look like an innocent man.

Now, early on the morning of November 2, 1979, James and Sanchez were meeting the attorney general of New Mexico. The café was on the fourteenth floor of one of the tallest buildings in downtown Albuquerque. Vasco's office was next door.

James had dressed for the occasion. No hat, a pair of blue slacks, and his shirt buttoned up to the collar. Sanchez looked stiff in his shirt and tie.

"Loosen up," James said, slapping him on the back. "He's your friend, remember?"

"More like a second father who scares the shit out of me."

James chuckled. "At least you now know you're not gonna lose your job."

"Not because of *this* meeting. But maybe for some other

bullshit. Might turn out that Lark is actually setting me up to take the fall. Or maybe he's even involved! The possibilities . . ."

James grinned. "It's fun, isn't it?"

Sanchez tried not to laugh but did. Together, they walked toward the far window in the back, where the attorney general waited for them.

Vasco was nicely put together, freshly shaved, hair cut and styled, not a spot or stray hair on his jacket. Still, to James, he was any other politician. But he understood that for Sanchez, it was personal.

Vasco stood and embraced Sanchez. "So good to see you, Gabriel," he said as he pulled away.

"You too, sir," Sanchez said.

"I know the job is demanding these days," Vasco said. "I hope you're hanging in there."

Sanchez's smile didn't quite reach his eyes. "I am, sir. I am. This is the friend I told you about. James Pinter."

Vasco shook his hand. "It's nice to meet you, Mr. Pinter. Have a seat."

The three of them sat at the round table with a white tablecloth.

"I understand you're investigating the murder of Cathy Winters."

"Cathy and Bartholomew," James said. "That's correct."

"You don't believe it was George Morris, then."

It wasn't a question, but James answered anyway. "The evidence of that is questionable at best."

"You know that Cathy and I were corresponding."

Again, not a question. "About Donald Andrews's organizations and finances," James said.

Vasco nodded. "She did some good work."

"Do you know how she obtained that information?"

"I didn't ask. But it is all authentic. My special prosecutions people are following up."

"You're building a case?" James asked.

Vasco smiled and studied him. "You have to understand that I can't answer that."

James nodded. "The information came from a friend of Cathy's son, Isaiah. This friend works for one of Donald Andrews's organizations."

"Perhaps that is how I received another package after Cathy passed away. I thought it odd," Vasco said.

"That'd be Isaiah. This friend, though. He's being followed now. By a lawyer named Bobby Tate. You happen to know him?"

"Can't say I do."

"Huh," James responded.

"Who are your leads?" the attorney general asked.

"Donald Andrews is the main one," James answered. "You see, the judge also seemed to be pokin' around Mr. Andrews's affairs. I found a letter to the US attorney that Bart never sent."

"Is that so?" Vasco asked. James didn't think he sounded at all surprised.

"You got any guesses what it was about?" James asked.

Vasco smiled again. He was sure of himself. James could see that much.

"I'd rather you simply tell me."

"ICWA. The new federal law regarding Indian children. Andrews was skirtin' it, and the judge was tryin' to prove that he was doin' it on purpose."

"So, you think Andrews is involved," Vasco said.

"Appears to be," James said.

Vasco rested his arms on the table and touched his finger-tips together. "I suppose I ought to contact the US attorney. It seems our interests overlap."

"Your target does, at least. And maybe we can add a double homicide charge."

"Other than motive, do you have any hard evidence against him?" Vasco asked.

"Nothing," James admitted.

The waitress came just then. Dressed in a suit and heels. She was young. They each ordered a coffee, nothing else.

"I find it interesting that Cathy was keeping all this from her husband," James said.

"She was adamant about it," Vasco said. "Which makes me wonder if the judge hadn't already mentioned the ICWA violation."

James knew he had. "You and the judge. You had a good relationship?"

"We worked together many times in the interest of protecting our state's children."

"And you were comfortable keeping it from him, as well?"

"I didn't want any conflicts of interest, either. I didn't know about the ICWA violations or the judge's knowledge of it, but I thought Cathy was smart to be overly cautious. Truthfully, I thought she ought not to be wading into these waters at all, though I was grateful for the information."

"Can I ask you what this last document was? The one that recently came from Isaiah?"

The attorney general grinned this time. A large, toothy

smile. "I was hoping you would ask." The waitress returned with the coffee, and he thanked her. He stirred sugar into his, and James waited for him to continue.

"Evidence of transfers. Large amounts to a bank account on the Navajo reservation."

"Donald Andrews was payin' someone on the reservation?" James asked.

"That's right."

"Who?"

"We don't know, and we can't force a warrant." Vasco raised an eyebrow. "But maybe you can. Or a friend of yours?"

54

GEORGE

CROSSING that invisible line had made George feel only a little more at ease. He still wasn't convinced that Mr. Tallsalt could do what he had promised. George didn't want to have to trust a stranger with this. But now he had to.

The dreams still woke him at night. In this unfamiliar place, where at first, in the dark, he was convinced he had failed. Because everything still felt upside down in real life, like it often did in a dream. George hadn't had time to sort out what this meant for him. Who he was now. But it seemed his subconscious was trying to.

There was one dream he had over and over. He was back in Janice Stone's office. He was sweating and upset. He felt hot tears on his face. He had just signed the last adoption paper she had put in front of him. He looked up at her face. Her smile. She had something stuck between her teeth. A piece of pepper, maybe.

He hated her so much in that moment. He knew he ought not to hate anyone. They were all children of God. But Janice had asked so much of him the last couple of years. And now she was asking for the last thing he had. For Adriel.

How had she convinced him to do this? He tried to remember all the reasons she had given. He tried to remember what he had been thinking that morning. Or the day before that. How had he come to this decision? He'd told himself it was because of love. Adriel deserved better. George was trying his hardest to be a good dad, but he didn't really know how. What example did he have to draw from? Linda had been the good parent. The one who'd been raised with love. The one who understood Adriel easily. She'd barely had to try. They'd had a connection that George couldn't replicate. George's best just wasn't good enough.

In real life, George had decided in that moment, sitting in that chair in Janice's office, that it was all nonsense. Every reason Janice had given. Every reason George himself had given. It meant nothing. It didn't matter that he didn't always know what to do. He loved Adriel. He loved him more than anything. Adriel had always forgiven his mistakes. He was such a patient kid. Such a good kid. They would figure it out together. How to communicate. How to live life without Linda.

He had gotten up quickly. Grabbed Adriel by the arm, startling him. Adriel dropped Sunny. Fought a little. Tried to pick the lizard up, but George yanked him away from Janice —yanked him hard. They could get another stuffed lizard, but they needed to get away from that woman.

He should have taken the papers, he realized too late. He should've torn them up. Burned them. But he hadn't, and he was still furious with himself for that. What a stupid mistake. Adriel had cried, and Janice had shouted, "Hey! What are you doing? Get back here! Adriel is ours now! We need to take him to the home! Where are you going?"

But George didn't look back. "We have to run, now," he said to Adriel. There were tears in the boy's eyes. Tears for Sunny. Tears for the scary woman, probably. For everything Adriel didn't understand and yet, on some level, did. He understood the danger, because he ran with George. He ran down that hallway and down those stairs and to the truck like he was running for his life.

They went to Judge Winters's office after that, looking for help. And the judge sent them to Lester Tallsalt.

But in the dream, Janice snatched Adriel from George's side, and George froze. He couldn't speak. Couldn't move. He watched her drag Adriel away from him. He felt the hot tears that really had been there that day. He woke up breathing heavily. Forgetting where he was. Especially now, in this unfamiliar place.

And Adriel. Adriel—who wouldn't touch George during the day. Who had come to resent him. Who wouldn't listen to him. Wouldn't look at him, if he could avoid it. Adriel would burrow into him in the dark dead of the night, grab onto him, and George would think, *It's all worth it, after all.*

55

MOLLY

JAMES WAS HOME, and Molly was happy to be with him. They sat with the record player low, as the rays from the setting sun sliced into the living room and fell at their feet.

Private basked in the day's final pool of vitamin D. He looked so cute and content. It took Molly a lot of effort to resist the urge to go pet him and wake him up.

James was writing up a request for one of the Shiprock police officers to obtain another warrant. This one was a little complex, he'd said. He would have to get into all the Donald Andrews financial hullabaloo. Revealing the holder of a bank account was no small thing. James had spent a lot of the afternoon staring at nothing, eyebrows furrowed, occasionally muttering or shaking his head, followed by some scribbling.

He had tasked Molly with reviewing Bobby Tate's cases again. He was going to visit Tate in Albuquerque, and Molly tried not to think of how annoyed she was that she would once again be stuck at home. James hadn't set up a meeting. He wanted to show up unannounced, which meant during office hours—when Molly would most certainly be in school.

James assured her that what she was doing was critical. He hadn't even read through all the Bobby Tate cases himself. But now that Tate was following Peter, they needed information. Molly noticed that Tate hadn't been involved in a case in almost two years. She wondered about this. Maybe he'd switched areas of law. She made a note for her dad.

Molly got up to get a coffee, and Private lifted his head a bit, opened one eye, decided she would be in no danger in the kitchen, and went back to sleep. For a rez dog, he seemed to have made himself comfortable indoors pretty quickly.

She took three long, satisfying sips of coffee before picking up the next case. A custody case. She read through the transcript, willing her eyes and brain to slow down. To actually read and not just skim.

This one was much older—about twelve years ago—and strange. There were redactions. The father's entire name had been redacted, as well as the mother's surname. But her first name was still there. Janice. Molly sat up straighter, tried to make sense of what she was reading. Janice whoever had gained full custody of their daughter after Judge Winters found there was sufficient proof of abuse from the husband.

"Dad!" Molly was on her feet before James could respond. She waved the case above her head. "Janice!"

"Janice Stone?" James asked.

"I don't know," she said. James was up now, walking toward her. She handed him the case. "It's been redacted."

She watched his eyebrows go up as he read. "A daughter," he muttered. "Didn't see any signs of a daughter. Could be a coincidence."

"Could be," Molly agreed.

"But . . . it might connect Janice to this Bobby Tate fella.

If it is her. We need to find out what's redacted there. Maybe Mr. Tate will enlighten me."

Molly nodded seriously, wishing she could go with him.

"Hey," James said, putting his hand on her shoulder. "Great find, kid. Great find." He pulled her in for a hug.

56

RONNIE

RONNIE CODY HAD TASKED his most competent eyes and ears man to figure out what the fuck was going on down in Albuquerque. There had been way too many busts lately. Someone was snitching. Ronnie didn't wait for Cecil to notice the slowdown. Couldn't afford to. His dad had important shit to do, which had been made clear to Ronnie his whole life. This part was Ronnie's job, and if he fucked it up enough that Cecil needed to get involved, it wouldn't be his job for long.

When Ronnie's man came back to tell him that he had identified the informant, Ronnie was annoyed to find out it was the fag at the new fag bar. He'd known all along he shouldn't have trusted him. He could handle this one himself. He wanted to.

Ronnie wore a ski mask and gloves. He wouldn't be seen; he'd make sure of that. But he didn't want to be sloppy in any way. He waited outside, watched these men who might as well have been beat-up looking chicks go in and out of the bar. Ronnie hadn't been inside yet. They always met somewhere else. That place made Ronnie sick. But he kept watching anyway. Waited for the bar to clear out after last call.

Finally, Ronnie saw him. Isaiah Winters was alone. He shoved his hands in his pockets and put his head down.

Ronnie followed him for a couple of blocks before jumping him. He pulled him into an alleyway, covered the guy's mouth. The fag was pissing himself. Crying.

"Please," he said. It was muffled, but Ronnie knew it was what he'd said. It was what most people said in this situation. Isaiah tried to say something else, but Ronnie plunged the knife into his side and said, "Shut the fuck up."

Isaiah gasped as Ronnie untangled himself from the bleeding man and let him crumple to the ground.

"Bobby Tate," Isaiah panted.

"Who?" Ronnie asked.

"He sent you."

"No," Ronnie said. "*I* sent me. You're a fucking rat. This is what happens."

Tears streamed down Isaiah's face as he clutched his side.

"Who the fuck is Bobby Tate?" Ronnie asked.

But Isaiah was past talking. He was taking his last breaths now.

Damn it, Ronnie thought. *Should've let him talk.*

57

BARBARA

BARBARA HAD VISITED two of the families on the children's home intake list that morning and was drained. She needed a break, so she stopped at the Shiprock Chapter office to look into this Robert John's membership files.

As a councilwoman, Barbara had special privileges. Not just anyone had access to these files. Family members of the individual, sometimes. But this information was generally confidential.

What Barbara knew about Robert John from asking around was that there wasn't much to know. He was new to the reservation. Hadn't lived there for most of his life. She had managed to find a *Navajo Times* article from when he was appointed to Jackson's court last year. There was a small bio. Born on the reservation. Adopted out to a family from the suburbs outside of Albuquerque. Graduated from the University of New Mexico School of Law in 1965. But when Barbara called the University of New Mexico School of Law, they had no record of a Robert John graduating that year. No Robs or Robbies or Bobs or Bobbies, either. No Johns at all.

But in the Diné membership files, there *were* a fair number of Johns. Only one Robert John, though. Born in 1939 to Allison and Ernest John. Allison's parents were the Claws, who Barbara knew of, though not well. Ernest's parents were Darlene John (*née* King) and Jarvis John. There were death certificates for all six. She looked for any surviving relatives. Aunts, uncles, cousins, brothers, sisters. She found a Lorraine Claw, sister of Allison, and a Christopher King, cousin of Ernest.

Christopher lived in Phoenix now, but Lorraine was still close enough, over in Kirtland. She had no idea if Lorraine would remember her nephew—or if she even knew he existed. But perhaps she knew him well. Perhaps they had a relationship. The records didn't tell much of a story. Birth records, death records, marriage records, most recent known mailing address. A path, perhaps. But not the steps along the way. The relationships were a mystery. Who had left because they intended never to speak to their family again? Who had stayed and taken care of one another?

Most days, Barbara felt like a machine. Today, she felt like a person with real limits. She wasn't ready to go back to the list of children, so she ate her egg salad sandwich in the car and drove to Kirtland.

The town of Kirtland kissed the outermost edge of the reservation. Lorraine lived on the same road as a high school, in a yellow-painted, ranch-style brick home. As she approached the front door, Barbara could smell something cooking. Beans maybe. Or mushrooms. She knocked and listened for signs of Lorraine.

"You just wait one minute out there," a faint voice said. And then, a stooped woman maybe twenty years older than Barbara opened the door and frowned at her from behind the screen.

"If you're coming to talk about that election coming up, I'm not voting."

The woman turned to close the door when Barbara said, "I'm here about Allison."

The older woman stopped and turned back around. "Allison?"

"Your sister."

The old woman sighed, slow and deep, and it appeared to pain her.

"Allison is dead. Has been for some time."

"I know," Barbara said. "But I'd like to ask you a few questions about her."

The woman gave her a tired look, but said, "All right, then." She pushed the screen door open with one hand, and Barbara went in.

Lorraine gestured wordlessly to the couch before disappearing into the kitchen. Barbara took it as an invitation and sat. She looked around. The room was clean and warm, and there were various chairs and benches and sofas scattered around, each covered in pillows and folded blankets.

Lorraine came back in, cupping her hands around a mug of something hot. She handed it to Barbara, again without a word, and then went back to the kitchen. She came out with a mug for herself and sat across from Barbara. She stretched her short legs all the way out and pointed and flexed her feet a few times.

"At my age, you've got to keep your blood moving. It's funny. I never expected to outlast everyone."

Lorraine had a low, scratchy voice that was pleasant to listen to. There was a joke behind her words, it seemed, just by the way she said them. An expectation of a laugh. Barbara marveled in that moment at how she never took this for granted. Sitting in a fellow Diné's home, listening to their story.

"I should probably do more stretching," Barbara admitted. "I'm already starting to feel my age."

"Oh, honey, it's only just begun for you." At that, Lorraine did laugh, and Barbara liked the sound of that, too. It made her smile.

They sat quietly and sipped, staring into the fireplace.

"Allison was a curious little thing when we were young," Lorraine finally said. "The questions she would ask our elders!" Another chuckle. "Auntie, why do you have hairs above your lip like my father? Auntie, why is your tummy so fat? Auntie, do all boys have that weird thing between their legs?" Lorraine winked. "Even when she got a little older, she was still hard to embarrass or shock. She just wanted to know things."

Lorraine sipped her tea. "I wonder now if she lived that way because she somehow knew that her time here would be short. She needed to take it all in while she could. Collect as much knowledge as she could, damned what anyone else thought."

"What happened to her?" Barbara asked.

"Car accident. That husband of hers was nothing but

pain and suffering. She married too young to realize there was better out there. Much better. He was drunk, of course. Crashed right into a guardrail and sent them spinning. They both died." She shook her head. She hadn't mentioned a child yet.

"Did you know . . ." Barbara began. Her voice was quieter than she intended, but before she could continue, Lorraine finished the sentence for her.

"About the boy?"

"Yes," Barbara said. "About the little boy."

"Of course I did. Little Robert." Lorraine shook her head again. "I adored that baby."

"What happened to him?"

"That . . ." Lorraine lifted her eyebrows and pointed up at the air. "That was a bad year for Allison."

"The year Robert was born?"

"The year Robert was born. First, Ernest lost his job while Allison was pregnant. Then, Allison lost hers, too, when she had to leave to have the baby. It was a hard birth. It took her a long time to recover."

Lorraine stood up abruptly and left the room. Barbara wasn't sure if she should follow her, so she just waited. A few minutes later, Lorraine returned holding a framed photograph. It was a baby. He had round cheeks. A mischievous smile.

"This was him," Lorraine said. "And we all loved him. Oh, we loved him so much. We told Allison we'd take him. We'd raise him. But that was also the year that Ernest hit her for the first time. She didn't tell us. But the second time, when he threw her up against the wall while she was still recovering from childbirth, she couldn't hide it. She was bleeding a lot. We had to take her to the hospital."

"I'm sorry," Barbara said.

"Me too," Lorraine said. "That baby was gone before his first birthday. She said she wanted him somewhere Ernest couldn't find him."

Lorraine turned the photo back around and lovingly wiped the dust from the frame with her thumb.

"Maybe the adoption was a blessing," Lorraine said. "Maybe the car accident was, too. In its own way."

Barbara felt the weight of what she was about to say quicken her heart.

"Lorraine," Barbara said. "I have some news about Robert. Why don't you sit back down?"

58

KAY

OTHER THAN THE small lamp next to Kay's bed, the only light in the hotel room came from the television. Kay wasn't watching. She was reading Lester Tallsalt's Navajo enrollment and membership records. Tallsalt was wanted now for harboring a murder suspect, and Wayne had gathered what he could from the Kayenta Chapter records, the newspaper archives, and the police reports.

Kay set the records down on the bed and rubbed her eyes. She tried to imagine what it would be like to look at the world from First Woman's eyes. To watch humans make the same mistakes over and over, to hurt one another in the same way for thousands of years. For Kay, it was tiring enough for one lifetime.

Lester Tallsalt, it turned out, had gone to a boarding school as a child. No surprise there. He'd had a son in the 1940s who was also sent away—but this time, to a Mormon family in Utah as part of the LDS Indian Student Placement Program. Kay had heard of this. Back before the new high school opened in Shiprock, she'd known of parents who sent their children to live with Mormon families in Utah for nine months out of the year. She'd been skeptical of the program even before she saw the letters the program sent home, urging parents not to visit over the holidays, lest the children become homesick. That left her seriously disgusted.

It seemed that the program hadn't been any good for Lester's son, either, who had some arrest records and eventually disappeared from the reservation completely sometime in the last five years.

Kay remembered the photo of the adult Tallsalt with the young girl. Not his daughter, then. There was no record of a daughter. Perhaps she was a part of this Mormon family? Tallsalt had looked so happy with her. Kay couldn't make sense of it.

She picked up the records again, combing for more information about the LDS program. There it was. A family name. The Bensons. Betty and Thomas Benson.

Kay pushed the papers aside, got up, and knocked on the door to Wayne's adjoining room. She hoped he was still awake. It took a minute, but he answered, still seemingly as alert as Kay.

"They might be in Utah," she said. "We have to find this family. The Benson family."

Wayne crossed his arms. "Start over. What family? Why Utah?"

"Tallsalt's son lived with a family there nine months out of the year as part of that LDS Indian Student Program. There was a photograph of Tallsalt with a young girl back at the house. She looked white to me."

Wayne's eyebrows went up.

"They're going to give him away!" Kay was close to

shouting. She tried to lower her voice, but it didn't sound any quieter. "To a family who can speak to him in sign language!" Kay grabbed the sketches from the dresser and thrust them at Wayne.

"We don't know that," he said in his stupid, calming cop voice, making Kay feel manipulated. She wasn't some criminal he was about to arrest. She was trying to make him see what was right in front of his face.

"Look." Wayne uncrossed his arms and put his hands up either in surrender—which Kay knew he wasn't doing—or else pleadingly. "This is a great find. You're right that we do need to speak with this family. Tomorrow we'll get ourselves a phone number."

"I have an address," Kay said. "In the records. It's Monticello, Utah."

"We can start there," Wayne said, nodding. "When is the address from?"

"1952," Kay said. "The year Tallsalt's son started the program."

"It may be outdated. But we can try."

"Thank you," Kay said. She studied Wayne. He looked as beaten down as she felt.

"We will find him," Wayne said, though the conviction in his voice wasn't there anymore. "We will bring him home safe."

"All right, Wayne," Kay said. And though she wanted to find comfort in that, in the idea of finding Adriel and bringing him home—where she would see her students again, be with James again—she wasn't sure anywhere was safe for these kids. The system was designed to wipe them all away, and it was so complete that it was working from the inside out.

59

JAMES

JAMES ARRIVED at the parking lot for the Law Offices of White, Young, and Tate at 5:30 a.m. He sat in his car, drank his coffee, ate a bagel, and waited for Tate to show up. He had found photos of Tate from some Albuquerque newspaper articles. James knew who to look for.

At 6:32 a.m., with James's car still only one of three in the parking lot, he got out and threw his trash away. He waited near the front door. 7:00 a.m., no one who looked like Bobby Tate. 7:15, 7:30, 7:55, still no Tate. James waited another twenty minutes before going inside.

"Can I help you?" the man at the front desk asked as James approached.

"I'm looking for the Law Offices of White, Young, and Tate," James said.

"Second floor. Number 245."

"Thanks," James said. He found the stairs in a hallway behind the elevators and climbed to the second floor. Office number 245 was lit up, but the name plaque outside only had two names listed: Paul White and Xavier Young. James went in and smiled at the secretary.

"Does Bobby Tate still practice law here?" he asked her. "I didn't see his name on the sign."

She pursed her lips. "Bobby Tate is not in the office today."

"Well, that's all right," James said, pointing to his jacket pocket. "I'll just drop off this envelope real quick, and he can contact me when he gets in."

"Sir . . ." the woman called after him, but James was already striding down the hallway.

He expected Tate's office door to be shut, possibly locked. But it was wide open, and the office was bare. The desk was empty—not even a pen holder or a picture frame. The shelves held a few books, but the only personal thing James could see was a framed law degree from the University of New Mexico School of Law. One Bobby Tate graduated in 1965.

He glanced over his shoulder, but the blond secretary was right behind him. She crossed her arms.

"I'm going to have to ask you to leave," she said.

James knew her next move would be to call whatever security company the building paid, and he didn't need to make a scene. Not right then. He slipped her a business card. "You tell Mr. Tate to give me a call."

She didn't say a thing, only dipped her head a little and glared at him.

On his way out of the building, James stopped again at the desk in the lobby. The man was reading a newspaper—the comics section, from the look of it.

"I've got a question for you," James said.

"What can I help you with?" The man had a smirk on his

face but didn't seem bothered by his job. Maybe even enjoyed it.

"Bobby Tate, a partner at the law firm upstairs. You know him?"

"Nope," the lobby attendant said. "But I know what he looks like. Haven't seen him in months, actually."

"Is that so? People around here sayin' anything about it?"

The man looked over James's shoulder. Turned around to check the elevators.

"Sure. The cleaning staff and the rest of us. Rumors."

"Tell me about them," James said.

The lobby attendant fidgeted in his chair. "Are you a cop?"

"Just a curious client."

The attendant nodded. "Some people say he left to become a judge." He lowered his voice a little. "But other people say he left because someone found out he was actually an Indian. And now he can't get a job as a lawyer nowhere in Albuquerque."

"Huh," James said. "They say anything else?"

The man shrugged. "That's all I've heard."

James stuck out a hand, and the lobby attendant shook it. "Appreciate it," James said. "Take it easy."

As James exited, he retrieved the custody court case from his back pocket, unfolded it, and read over it again. He waited a good ten minutes until he was sure he was alone outside and that security had not been called before inserting coins into the nearby payphone and calling Lieutenant Lark's office.

"Lieutenant Lark. It's James Pinter. I've got a question for you."

"Pinter! Where are you?" Lark's voice was urgent.

"Albuquerque, actually. North Valley. Why?"

"You can ask me your question later. I need you at the corner of 1st Street and Kinley Ave. There's been a stabbing. Isaiah Winters is dead."

James went straight to the crime scene, but Lark had beaten him to it. Sanchez was there, too, looking like he hadn't slept in a while.

James showed his P.I. credentials, but the cop standing guard wouldn't let him cross the caution tape. So, he waited for Lark or Sanchez to notice him. It was Sanchez who finally did.

"Time of death?" James asked as Sanchez lifted the tape.

"Not exact yet, but between 1 and 3 a.m. City of Albuquerque PD got the call at 6:52 a.m."

As they headed toward the body, Lark noticed them.

"Glad I caught you in the city," Lark said to James. He took off his gloves. "One stab wound in the side. No weapons recovered."

"Do we know what Isaiah was doin' out here?" James asked.

"He's a few blocks from his place of work," Sanchez said.

"Who called it in?"

"Passerby. On the way to work," Lark said.

"Interview him already?"

"A woman. The city did briefly," Lark said.

James squatted down and studied Isaiah's body. Bruising around the neck and mouth. Blood under the fingernails. The body didn't seem to have been moved. No blood trail; it was pooled underneath him. Rigor mortis had set in, as expected. It had happened right here.

"Wanted you to take a look before we bagged him," Lark said.

"Appreciate that," James said. "You recover a wallet? Money, cards, anything?"

"City did," Lark said. "Bagged already with evidence."

James wondered if Isaiah had, in fact, been at work that night. Maybe Peter lived around here.

He stood. "Find anything else on him?"

"Just a set of keys."

"Have we talked to the bar owner? Coworkers? Anyone have eyes on him last night?"

Lark checked his watch. "Pinter, it's 9 a.m."

"Damn. I've been up since before the roosters. Probably two hours till they open at least. I'll handle it. I've got a friend of Isaiah's I'd like to talk to. No one's been informed yet, have they?"

"No. But Sanchez can call next of kin. Have them meet him at the morgue to identify the body."

James looked at Sanchez, who nodded. "An aunt, I think," he said.

"All right, well, maybe one of you fellas could help me with an address for this friend," James said.

"You can follow me back to the station," Lark said. "Say. What was that thing you wanted to ask me?"

"Oh. Right." James jerked his head to the side, signaling they should get some distance from the crime scene and crew. Finally, he said, "Duncan."

"What about him?" Lark asked.

"He married?" James asked.

Lark crossed his arms. "Not anymore. Why?"

"But he was?"

"He was. He and his old woman got divorced years back."

"You remember her name, by any chance?"

"Oh, yeah. He was always complaining about her. Couldn't forget it. Her name's Janice."

PETER

PETER HAD nothing to wake up for that morning. He'd finally been fired the day before—something he'd been expecting for months. He ought to have been more concerned about what came next. But mainly he felt relief. He could finally cut his losses. Find another job. Maybe even put this all behind him. Repair things with Isaiah—if Isaiah even wanted that. Now that he'd gotten what he needed, maybe he would disappear from Peter's life altogether.

Peter rolled over and looked at his alarm clock: 9:42 a.m. He was hungry. And a little ashamed of being so lazy. Rent wasn't going to pay itself, and he only had about a month's worth saved up. It wasn't like him to be so relaxed at a time like this.

He supposed it was simply because he was drained. He'd been so on edge for far too long. Looking over his shoulder. Afraid of being found out. Afraid of some retribution worse than losing his job.

It could still be coming. He knew that. Another reason to

hurry out of bed, to continue to worry. And yet, he just couldn't find the will to do it. His grumbling stomach finally gave him reason enough to get up, and he made his way to the kitchen to make himself some waffles with his new waffle iron.

He made three perfect waffles, stacked them on a plate, and loaded berries and syrup and whipped cream on top. As soon as he sat down to eat, the doorbell rang. And in that moment, he knew something was terribly wrong. He *should* have been worrying. He should've been doing something. Anything. Panic washed over him. His stomach rose into his throat, and his legs shook as he approached the door. He could see a man through the peephole. No one he knew or had ever seen before. Peter grasped the doorknob, but before opening it, he asked in the steadiest voice he could muster, "Who is it?"

"James Pinter, private investigator. I'm here on behalf of the New Mexico State Police."

Peter didn't believe him. Maybe he should try to go out the back. Force this man to break down his door.

"I was uh . . . Isaiah's private investigator," the man added.

Peter swung the door open. "Was?"

The man. This James Pinter. He looked so sad. So regretful. Peter closed his eyes. He wanted to go back to bed. He should've never gotten up. He should've laid in a world where his relationship with Isaiah was still repairable. Not in this one, where some strange man was about to tell him something that would turn his life upside down. Peter shook his head.

"Why don't you have a seat somewhere?" this stranger said.

Peter forced himself to open his eyes again. To walk to the couch. To sit down.

"Who did it?" he heard himself whisper.

"We don't know that yet," James Pinter said.

"How?"

"He was stabbed. Maybe ten blocks from here."

Peter's eyes filled with tears. A sob escaped his throat, and he covered his mouth with his hand.

"Was he here last night?" James's voice was gentle, but Peter broke down anyway. James let him cry. Didn't say anything. Didn't try to comfort him. Just sat.

Finally, Peter wiped his eyes with his sleeve. He stood and found a few tissues left in the bathroom. He blew his nose. It felt like his chest was being crushed. He wished this man would go away, but he also wanted justice for Isaiah. There was no one left except for Peter who could do that for him. He had to help. He went back into the living room and sat across from James.

"He wasn't here last night," Peter said. "The last time I saw him was on Saturday."

"How much did you know about what Isaiah did for work?" James asked. It was a strange question.

"He was a bartender at the Purple Dog."

"And was he there last night? Do you know if he was at work?"

"Yes. Probably. He usually worked Friday nights."

"But you weren't there last night? At the bar?"

"No," Peter said.

"Where were you?"

"Here," Peter said. "Drinking. Alone. I had just gotten fired."

James's eyebrows went up, and Peter realized he knew the whole story. Of course he did. Isaiah would have been smart enough to tell him. Still, it made Peter feel exposed. And like a fool.

"I assume someone found out I'd been taking documents, but I don't know how," Peter said. "I guess if they did, maybe I'm next."

"I'd like for that not to happen," James said.

That struck Peter as funny, and he laughed a strange, crazed-sounding giggle.

"Me too," he said.

"Have you got anywhere to go?" James asked. "Family to stay with? So you can lay low for a while?"

Peter looked around his house. Was it that serious? He didn't really want to leave. But, of course, it *was* that serious. Isaiah was dead. Isaiah was dead. He repeated the thought a few more times but couldn't believe it. It wasn't real.

"Okay," he finally said. "Should I tell you where I'm going?"

"Sure," James said. "But only me."

"Gallup," Peter said. "My parents."

"That's good. Closer to me, too."

"Where are you?"

"On the Navajo reservation."

"Do you know that's the last thing I gave Isaiah? Proof that money was getting sent there?"

"I know. The AG told me."

Peter nodded. He felt like he was dreaming. "Should I leave now?"

"Today, yes. I just have a few more questions."

Peter looked down at his hands. They were shaking, so he grabbed onto his knees to steady them.

"How long had you been gathering information for Isaiah?"

"Months. Almost a full year, probably." He still remembered the night they met.

"And you told no one else?"

Peter shook his head.

"When you got fired yesterday, did you tell Isaiah? Did you call him or stop by?"

"I wasn't sure what to say," Peter said. "I knew he would feel responsible. I didn't know how much he would care, though. He kept asking me why I would want to work for them, anyway, knowing what I knew. So, I hadn't told him yet, because I was afraid his reaction wouldn't be what I needed it to be. Even though I didn't really know what I needed it to be."

Maybe he *should've* called. Put his stupid feelings aside. Maybe Isaiah would still be alive if he had. Maybe Isaiah would've come over, called out of work—something. Maybe that would've saved him. Tears stung the backs of his eyes again. He wanted James to leave now so he could be alone with his grief. It felt so raw and big and intimate.

James wrote something. He ripped the piece of paper from his pad and handed it to Peter. There were a few phone numbers on it. James's and two more for the state police.

"You call me if you need anything at all. If you can't

reach me, try Sanchez. If you can't reach him, try Lark. You leave today, understand?"

Peter nodded. James stood and reached out a hand. Peter shook it.

"I'm real sorry for your loss."

Peter nodded again. He knew he wouldn't be able to speak. James turned and left, and Peter tried to decide what in his life was worth saving.

61

CECIL

Cecil supposed he should be thanking God he had two sons instead of just one. Ronnie's brain was like a wet log, unable to spark a flame.

He waited for him with the lights out. Not because he wanted to surprise him, but because he didn't need to see the indignation on Ronnie's face. It would make him too angry, and he wasn't looking to kill the boy.

It had been two days since Ronnie killed Isaiah Winters, but Cecil had only just learned of it and certainly not from Ronnie.

The sun had almost set completely when Ronnie came in. Earlier than Cecil expected. He heard Ronnie take his boots off. Sniffle. Clear his throat.

"Pops?" Ronnie shouted. Cecil didn't stand up. He waited for Ronnie to check each room.

"There you are," Ronnie said when he found him. Cecil stood then. Made his way to Ronnie in three strides.

"You are a Cody, yes? Part of this family now for twenty-two years?" There was just enough light left for Cecil to see the confusion pass over Ronnie's face.

He grabbed Ronnie by the back of the neck and hissed in his ear, "Don't you ever kill a man without my permission. Do you know what you've done? Do you know what I have to fix now?"

"What are you talking about?" Ronnie tried to pull away, but Cecil tightened his grip.

"The fag?" Ronnie guessed. "He was an informant. A fucking rat. Why do you care?"

"I don't ask you to think, do I? I don't ask you to make decisions. I ask you to follow my instructions. To be an obedient son."

Ronnie still strained to get away.

"Sit," Cecil said. Ronnie sat.

"This is not about treating you like a child as much as you think it is. It's about knowing your role. I ask Byron to make connections, because people like him and he doesn't have the stomach for violence. Like the vulture knows not to hunt, only to scavenge, you must also embrace your part in this."

Now Cecil sat down across from his son.

"The man you killed two days ago happened to be a client of James Pinter's. His own parents were killed not long ago, and Pinter is investigating the case."

"Oh shit. I didn't know, Pops. What are the chances?"

"I know you didn't know. I need *you* to know what you don't know," Cecil said. He took a deep breath. "This will not happen again. You did me no favor."

Ronnie was quiet for a moment. "He said something before he died. He said that Bobby Tate sent me. I asked him who that was, but he was too far gone to answer me. Probably some dealer with the Mexican gang. I can find out if you want."

Cecil shook his head. "Are your ears full of sap? You will do nothing until I tell you to. This is with me now."

Ronnie pursed his lips but said nothing else. Finally, he nodded.

62

BARBARA

WHEN LORRAINE FOUND out her nephew was not only back on the reservation but also a big, important judge, she wanted to meet him right away. That very day. And Barbara, who had a million other things to do, told her she would drive her to Window Rock to do just that. She wanted to meet Robert John, too.

Lorraine couldn't stop talking on the way. A few times, Barbara reached over and squeezed her hand, and Lorraine would laugh. "I'm a ball of nerves!" she said once.

The Navajo Nation's capital was an hour and a half from Shiprock, but it was a trip Barbara made frequently as a councilwoman. She navigated the streets easily once they arrived in Window Rock, and after they parked, she guided Lorraine by her arm to the large office building that contained just about all of the politicians and judges on the reservation. Barbara had her own office there. One she hadn't been to in nearly a month. The judges' offices were two floors above hers.

When they found Judge John's office, Barbara knocked

once loudly, waited only a second, and then turned the knob and cracked open the door.

"Judge John?" she called. She heard some shuffling and could see a sliver of his desk through the crack.

"Please wait one moment," a voice said. Barbara glanced at Lorraine, who looked like she might cry.

When Judge John did open the door, he looked puzzled.

"I don't have any meetings scheduled this afternoon. Are you ladies in the right place?"

And then, Lorraine did burst into tears. "Little Robbie," she said. "I never thought I'd see you again."

The judge's face paled. He looked desperately at Barbara. "Excuse me?"

"Judge John, this is Lorraine Claw. She's your aunt."

"My aunt?" The judge looked down the hallway as if for an exit route.

"You were born on the reservation to Allison Claw. This is your mother's sister, Lorraine."

"This is . . . unexpected," the judge said.

"Can we come in for a minute?" Barbara asked. *Since you just told us you don't have any meetings.*

"I . . . uh . . . all right," the judge stammered. "Briefly. I'm quite busy today."

He walked stiffly to his desk. His hair was cut short, not worn traditionally. He was of average height and stocky. He wore a button-down with a dark-green vest, which he tugged down as he sat.

"How did you . . . how did you find out where I was?"

"You're in a pretty public position here, yes?" Barbara asked, making a show of looking around. Lorraine was still standing. Perhaps waiting for a hug. Or at least, some sort of acknowledgment.

"I am . . ." But before he could finish, Lorraine jumped in.

"You were just a little thing the last time I saw you," she said. "So happy, too. So full of life. You used to make us all laugh, and you liked that. You liked being funny."

Judge John seemed speechless. Finally, he gave her a strained smile.

"I don't remember," he said.

A short burst of laughter came from Lorraine's mouth, and the judge looked startled by it.

"Of course you don't," Lorraine said. "Can I . . . can I hug you?"

John looked at Barbara again, and she looked right back and hoped that he understood she wasn't going to help him get out of anything.

"Okay." He walked awkwardly around his desk. She hugged him tight and sobbed into his vest.

"All right, then," he said twice, before Lorraine finally pulled away.

"You've done well for yourself, haven't you?" she said, looking around the office, wiping her eyes.

"I have," he said, sounding a bit steadier. He sat again, straighter this time, more in command of the situation. The shock was passing.

"So, your family was good to you," Lorraine said.

"They treated me like their own. Gave me everything they could."

Lorraine nodded. "Well, that says something, then. I've missed you. But maybe it wasn't all bad."

"My parents died, didn't they?" John asked. "I probably

would have, too, if I'd stayed." There was no compassion behind those words, Barbara noted. He was stating facts. His tone cold.

"I would like to think we would have protected you," Lorraine said. "But I guess we couldn't protect Allison. So, maybe you're right."

"Are you living well now?" the judge asked. "Do you need me to help you out in any way?"

Lorraine looked horrified. She still hadn't sat down. "You think I came here for money?"

The judge tilted his head to the side. "You didn't?"

Lorraine furrowed her eyebrows. "I know you don't know me from Adam, but I'm not that kind of person."

The judge looked at Barbara. "And you are a friend of my aunt's, I presume?"

"She is my constituent." It wasn't exactly true. Lorraine lived off the reservation, but Barbara considered all Diné her constituents. "I am a council member."

"Your name is?"

"Barbara Tully."

"Well, Councilwoman Tully. Lorraine. Aunt Lorraine. It's been a lovely surprise, but I really must get back to work. Perhaps we can set up another time to meet."

Lorraine looked a little less dazed now and maybe a little hurt.

"Soon?" she asked. "I'll leave you my phone number. I'm always around. Just an old lady now." She laughed, but it sounded forced.

Judge John gave her a polite smile. "Please do." He handed her a pen and paper.

When Barbara stood to leave, so did the judge. Lorraine

said her goodbyes and gave the judge one more hug. They were just about out the door when Judge John grabbed Barbara's arm.

"I'm not sure why you brought her here today, Councilwoman Tully. But I'm going to find out," he whispered.

"Brother," Barbara said, quietly but steadily. "I brought her here because family is a special thing. You are new to the reservation. We are all your sisters and your aunties. That is the Diné way. We are all happy you're home."

[63]

WAYNE

MONTICELLO, Utah, had snow on the caps of its mountains and a little on its sidewalks, too. The Bensons lived in a brick home not far off Main Street. Well, they had, at least. In 1952. Wayne wasn't so sure they'd still be there. He had tried calling before leaving Kayenta, but no one answered and there was no answering machine.

They had left early that morning, and after a two-hour drive, what Wayne really wanted was a coffee and a stack of pancakes and two over-easy eggs. Kay insisted on going straight to the Bensons first, though, since "old people were up early."

The woman who answered the door with the chipped red paint was indeed old. Possibly too old to be who they were looking for. She wore a curly white wig, and Wayne guessed she might be bald underneath. Her dress was too large and hung from her shoulders.

"Hello, ma'am," Wayne said. "I'm looking for a Betty Benson. Does she live here?"

"Well, that's me," the old lady said.

"My name is Wayne Tully." He glanced at Kay out of the corner of his eye. He had, again, asked her to let him do the talking, but he never knew with Kay. "I'm a police officer down on the Navajo reservation. I was wondering if I could ask you a few questions?"

The old woman squinted at him. "About that boy?" she asked.

"What boy?"

"The one we took in," she said.

"It is related. In a way."

Behind her, a tall old man shuffled into view. Betty's husband, Thomas.

"Thomas Benson?" Wayne asked.

"What's this about?" the man asked in a raspy voice. It sounded like he'd just woken up, but he was dressed for the day in pressed slacks and a dress shirt.

"They want to know about the Indian boy we had here all those years ago," Betty said.

The old man shook his head. "We're not talking about him anymore. Whatever he's done now, we aren't responsible. We weren't his parents, you know. His parents ought to have parented him. We only did what we could."

"Wasn't he with *you* for nine months out of the year?" Kay asked. Wayne was surprised she'd lasted this long. But he was glad she'd said it.

"That'll be all," the man said. He reached over his wife to close the door.

"Wait," Wayne said. "We aren't here about him, we're here about his father. Lester Tallsalt. Did you have any kind of relationship with him? Have you kept in touch?"

"No, but Cynthia did . . ." Betty started to say.

"Enough," Thomas grumbled. "Good day."

And then the door closed in their faces. Wayne turned and Kay followed. When they got in the car, he looked at her.

"What was I supposed to do, just stand there?" Kay asked.

"You're right," he said. "The guy's an asshole." He shifted the car into gear. "We're going to a diner now. Before one more word is spoken between us."

The only diner in town was starting to fill up. Still, they got a table, and every time Kay started to speak, Wayne shushed her. He would enjoy his breakfast in peace.

Finally, with a clean plate and a fresh, hot cup of coffee, he said, "So, do you think Cynthia is the girl from the photo?"

Kay nodded. "Their daughter, maybe?"

"This town's small enough," Wayne said. He waved down their waitress.

"Hey there . . ." He moved his head until he could see the waitress's nametag. When she realized what she was doing, she uncrossed her arms and grinned. "Ella! I've got a question for you."

He went into his back pocket and pulled out his badge.

"We're from the reservation, and we came up here to talk to some folks who used to participate in the LDS Indian Student Program. Do you happen to know the Bensons?"

"Oh, sure," Ella said. "Betty Benson. She was my mom's schoolteacher."

"Well, perfect for the LDS program, then," Wayne said.

Ella put a hand on her hip. "You would think. But that program did the darndest thing to their family."

We certainly lucked out with this waitress, Wayne thought. But that was how small towns were. You just had to ask. Ella—and everyone else in this town—was just bursting with secrets.

"Oh?" he asked.

She looked over each shoulder before answering. "Their daughter, Cynthia? She became downright ornery after befriending that Indian boy. And she's deaf, too. Can you imagine trying to yell at a deaf child? Anyhow, she's moved on now. To the big city. They don't speak anymore. Well, I guess she never really did *speak*. You know what I mean, though. They had a falling out."

"Do you know what it was about?" Kay asked.

Ella shook her head. "Only that the Indian boy had something to do with it. That was the rumor, anyway."

"And now she's in Salt Lake City?" Wayne asked.

"Salt Lake City?" Ella looked confused. "Heavens no."

"You said the big city," Wayne said.

Ella chuckled. "Not *that* big. She did move clear across the state, though. St. George."

"Huh," Wayne said. "Well, thanks. That's good to know. We'll make sure not to bring her up, then." He winked at Ella, and she blushed.

"That'd be smart," Ella said. "Big scandal around here." She picked up their empty plates. "Anything else I can get you folks?"

"Just the check."

JAMES

JAMES WAS at the *Albuquerque Journal*'s archives office. He had just hung up with the registrar's office at the University of New Mexico School of Law and was now making a copy of one of those newspaper articles that mentioned Bobby Tate. The one with his photograph.

When he was done with that, he drove to the police station. Lark was out, which suited James just fine. He wanted to peek into Duncan's desk and wouldn't mind doing so without someone breathing down his neck. The cubicle where Detective Duncan sat was part of a larger "pit" with other homicide detectives. It was empty today. As James sat in Duncan's seat in the corner, he thought again how stupid it would be for a homicide detective with as many years as Duncan to "forget" to put something into evidence. It was a cocked-up story. Lark must have known it. Duncan must have known Lark would know it. Maybe Duncan *wanted* to get kicked off the case. Or at least didn't mind if he did.

There was a photo of a teenage girl on his desk, half grinning, half rolling her eyes at the camera. His daughter. James

292 / LISA BOYLE

grabbed a napkin and opened Duncan's drawer. Typical stuff. Loose papers. Photocopies of reports. Notepads. Chewing gum and mints. Packets of sugar. A plastic knife and fork and napkin packet. A card with a kitten on it. He picked up the card and flipped it open. *Best wishes*, it said. And then someone had written, *On your last case with the New Mexico State Police.*

Just then, James heard footsteps in the distance. Maybe some other detective. Maybe Lark. He glanced at his watch. It was about time for Lark to show up. He stood, still holding the card.

"Pinter," Lark said as he approached. "You ready to grab lunch?"

"Sure am," James said. "Quick question." He held up the card. "I thought I would check in with your guy, Duncan. Saw this card on his desk. You know he was retirin'?"

Lark paused, and James took note of his expression. Then Lark shook his head. "If he's planning on it, he hasn't said anything to me."

James nodded. He slipped the card into his back pocket. "How 'bout that deli on the corner of Carlisle and Constitution?"

"I spoke with the owner of the Purple Dog and three of the bartenders who worked the evening of Isaiah's death," James told Lark. They were sitting outside by a fountain, eating their sandwiches.

"Was he working?" Lark asked.

"Sure was," James said.

"They notice anything unusual? Any special customers? Strange occurrences?"

"Not really. One of the bartenders said a few guys who Isaiah seemed to know stopped by to chat and order a few drinks. But they all agreed it was a pretty average night."

"Would he be able to identify any of those men?"

James shook his head. "I asked if he could describe them. He said, 'Not really. They didn't stay that long, and it's always kinda dark in there.'"

"Sounds like they knew exactly what Isaiah was up to. Protecting those customers' identities like that."

"You're probably right," James conceded.

"What else you got? Progress on Bart and Cathy Winters?"

James finished chewing a bite of his sandwich. "Gonna talk to the Navajo bank when I get back this afternoon. The warrant came through regarding the transfer of funds from Donald Andrews's account to the reservation."

Lark nodded. "Let me know what you find out."

"Will do."

Lark took a bite of his sandwich. James watched an orange-and-black bird land at the edge of the fountain. A Bullock's oriole. Rare. Especially this time of year.

"That all?" Lark asked after he swallowed.

"Yep."

[65]
CECIL

BOBBY TATE WAS NOT CONNECTED to any drug dealer or supplier from Mexico up through Albuquerque into the reservation. It was a forgettable name, but Cecil's colleagues were not forgetful people.

He must be related, then, to the murder of Isaiah's parents and, therefore, James Pinter's case. Which was good for Cecil and for Ronnie, because that's where James's attention was already. But Cecil Cody did not like to leave things to chance.

He was confident that Ronnie at least hadn't been sloppy. It could have been anyone, and if Isaiah had suspected this Bobby Tate, then Cecil would make it so.

He needed to speak to someone with connections to the same world as Isaiah's parents. He remembered the swearing in of one of the new judges of Jackson's court. Cecil assumed all of Jackson's picks had secrets to hide. Secrets Jackson could use to control them. Or they were, at the very least, vulnerable. Susceptible to manipulation. He knew this, because he knew what the new court was. They all did.

Cecil made his way to the judge's office early one morning. John. That was his name. Cecil knew a few John families, but they all lived on the reservation and had for his whole life. This John was a fresh face, and Cecil was a little surprised by Jackson's willingness to trust a newcomer. Though, he supposed newcomers might be easily molded.

The office was locked. Judge John wasn't there yet, and so Cecil waited in the hall. Just about no one worked Cecil's hours except for his sons. Up at 5 a.m. with Byron and not down again until midnight. Though, Ronnie was often up later than that, and Byron was making coffee before Cecil was even dressed.

Byron had been out looking for locations that morning. Jackson was introducing a new program and needed Byron to find a location for it. Preferably a building that could be repurposed. Jackson wanted to avoid building for this particular project, but if Byron couldn't find anything, they'd talk land plots.

Byron was in charge of these sorts of logistics for the Shiprock Chapter of ONEO—the social services arm of the Navajo Nation. The funding for this project was different, though, Byron had said. It was coming from a private, anonymous source. Not a government grant. Cecil didn't particularly like private, anonymous funders. He'd have to see what he could get out of Jackson later. Byron didn't even know what the project was about yet, which was also unusual.

Cecil was trying to guess what it might be when light, quick footsteps interrupted his thoughts. A stout man came around the corner. Judge John. Cecil watched him approach. He was not a man at ease. That much was clear.

"Good morning," he said to Cecil.

Cecil nodded once. "Judge John." He never had to introduce himself on the reservation, but he did anyway. "I'm not sure if you remember me from the council. Cecil Cody."

"Of course, Mr. Cody. Please come in." The judge unlocked his office door and switched on the lights. "To what do I owe the pleasure?" he asked as they sat.

"I've got a question about some goings-on in Albuquerque," Cecil said. "I understand that's where you were before you came to the reservation."

"That's right."

"And you practiced law there."

"Correct."

"Did you know of a Judge Winters? I understand he died recently."

"That's a shame," Judge John said.

"You didn't know?" Cecil asked.

"I wasn't aware."

First lie, Cecil thought.

"Did he have any dealings with the reservation that you're aware of?"

"It's possible," Judge John said.

Cecil leaned back in his chair. Intertwined his fingers and placed his hands in his lap. "What can you tell me about the man?"

"He was a children's court judge. And from what I could tell, a real piece of shit."

Cecil's eyebrows went up. "How so?"

"He had a reputation for keeping Indian kids on the reservation. Which sounds nice, until you realize what those families did to those kids. They offered absolutely nothing of value. Poverty, addiction, alcoholism. He never sent kids back into violent homes, but he didn't allow them a better life, either."

"You feel like he abandoned those kids?" Cecil asked.

"Let me give you an example," Judge John said, scooching closer to his desk. "Would you imagine that a grandparent who'd already raised a drug addict would be fit to raise her grandkids? Or an entire family living below the poverty line. Would you want an aunt or uncle to get custody of a child when they're already struggling to feed two of their own? It always seemed cruel to me. There are plenty of people out there who *want* children and have the ability to care for them."

Cecil said nothing. Long enough that the judge grew visibly uncomfortable.

"I see. Are you a parent, Judge John?"

John's face reddened. "No. But my parents—my biological parents—were not fit to raise a child. They died young. Abuse, alcoholism, from what I understand."

"And they were Indians?" Cecil asked.

"Navajo, yes."

"And your adopted family?" Cecil asked.

"Good people. I've had every opportunity in the world."

Cecil nodded. He could see the man's struggle. His inner battle. Cecil could feel it.

"Good for you," Cecil said. "We're glad to have you in such an important role here."

Judge John cracked a small, smug smile. The man was cocky, Cecil decided. Had it all figured out. And yet, he lacked any real confidence. Like a petulant child.

"How about Bobby Tate?" Cecil asked. He watched the judge's smile falter.

"Bobby Tate?" Judge John asked. He was trying to look perplexed.

"He a part of the legal scene in Albuquerque?"

"I . . . I'm not sure. Is this still related to Judge Winters?"

"You tell me," Cecil said.

"I . . . I don't believe I know of him."

Lie number two, Cecil thought.

"All right, then," he said. "This has been helpful." Cecil took a moment to look around the office. He would take his time leaving now that he knew silence unsettled the man.

"Can I ask you something?" Judge John asked. "Before you leave."

"What's on your mind?"

"You're on the council, so you must know her. A woman came and visited me here. A councilwoman, she said. She brought an aunt of mine with her. I'd never met the aunt. Didn't even know she existed. It was like this councilwoman was springing this on me. Trying to catch me by surprise or something. Do you know Barbara Tully?"

So, Barbara Tully had come to visit Judge John. How interesting. Now Cecil knew he was on to something.

66

MOLLY

IT WAS AN UNUSUALLY warm afternoon for late fall, and Molly and Barbara had gotten ice cream sandwiches at the convenience store after school. They ate them now on the steps outside Molly's trailer, waiting for James to get back from Albuquerque. The dog lay at Molly's feet, licking the ice cream drippings when they fell to the ground. Molly licked some, too, from her pinky finger.

"I can't believe Isaiah is dead," she said. "I only met him twice. But still. It's just so . . . shocking."

"I know," Barbara said. "He was so young still." She shook her head.

"I wonder what my dad found out from Bobby Tate," Molly said, popping the rest of the ice cream into her mouth. She wiped her hands with a napkin.

"Who?" Barbara asked.

"Bobby Tate. He was that lawyer that kept showing up in Judge Winters's cases, remember? And he was following Isaiah's . . . friend, too. Dad went down there to meet with him this time."

"That's right," Barbara said. "Now I remember the name." She paused. Wiped her mouth. "I went to visit some-one, too, the other day. Your dad asked me to find out about a judge on the reservation."

"Which judge?"

"One who approves adoptions to families outside the reservation."

"Like that Tallsalt guy used to do." Molly remembered her dad talking about that.

"Correct."

Molly started to bite her nails, then stopped herself. She was trying to grow them out for the spring dance. She already had a date but hadn't told James yet. Or Barbara. No one but Paula knew. Molly stuck her thumbs through her belt loops instead, to give them a place to be.

"So, what did you find out? What's this judge like?" she asked.

"Scared," Barbara said, chuckling. "Of two old women."

"You?" Molly asked. "You're not old! Do you think he's approving adoptions he shouldn't be?"

"Maybe," Barbara said. "I don't trust anyone on Jackson's new court. What's the deal with this lawyer Bobby Tate? He's following someone?"

Molly shrugged. "I guess. That's what Isaiah thought. He *might* have represented Janice Stone at one point, too. In a custody case."

Barbara's eyebrows went up. "Really?"

"Dad was going to try to find out. The woman's last name was redacted." Molly started to bite her nails again but twirled a piece of her hair instead. "Janice is pretty high on the suspect list, I think."

"I imagine so," Barbara said.

"Have you heard from Wayne?" Molly asked.

"They're in Utah. On a little road trip. They really need a break. I could hear how tired they both are."

Just then, Molly heard a car. She spun around and squinted down the road. Sure enough, it was James.

Barbara stood and wiped her hands and mouth. Private sat up and wagged his tail. *Dad's welcoming party*, Molly thought with a grin. Sometimes she was amazed that this was her life now. Like nothing she had ever imagined.

When James got out of the car, he hugged Molly, and she allowed it since only Barbara was around. "Well, if it isn't trouble one and trouble two," he said.

"You're one to talk," Molly replied, pulling away.

"I've got news about Judge Robert John," Barbara said. "Found out he was adopted, and I found a long-lost aunt of his." She put her hands on her hips. "We went to pay him a visit. I can't say he was too excited to see her."

"Oh yeah?" James asked. He put up a finger. "Hold that thought." He went into the back seat and came out with a newspaper article. He held it out to her. "Let me take a guess. Is this your guy?"

Barbara's eyebrows knit in confusion. "Yes, that's him."

"Turns out we were meetin' with the same person. Only, he doesn't frequent his Albuquerque office so much these days."

"Bobby Tate *is* Robert John?" Molly asked.

"That's right," James said. "Two names. Same guy."

67

LESTER

NOTHING THAT GEORGE had told Lester surprised him. Yes, ICWA had been passed, and that was a big win. The Indian Adoption Project was disbanded. But the people who headed it—the people who believed in their hearts and in their wallets that the only future for Indians were with non-Indians—those people were still out there, still doing the same things they had always done, just finding new ways to get away with it.

The LDS program had changed Lester's life. It had taken Roland from him for many years, and eventually he lost Roland altogether. But before that, Roland had changed Cynthia's life, and through her, Lester gained a daughter.

Lester was part of a larger organization. A national one whose purpose was to connect lawyers from across the country who were interested in seeing ICWA upheld and followed. They fought at their state level to make sure Indian children stayed with their tribes.

The Navajo Nation was blessed to have the legal system in place that it did. Their Tribal Welfare Committee had resisted officials from the Indian Adoption Project year after year. Lester was proud to have served it for so many years as a judge who was responsible for handling adoptions off the reservation. It was a penance, of sorts, for enrolling his own son in the LDS program.

But these people were wolves salivating at the gate, and ICWA was not made of iron, only words on paper.

With the information obtained from George, Lester's organization was able to find out just how Andrews was getting away with taking so many Indian children. Andrews's organization—the New Mexico Children's Agency—had drafted guidelines for their employees on "ways to spot neglect." It cited multiple children sleeping in the same room, for example. Or living in a single-parent home or with a non-parent relative. Eating food from a communal bowl or plate was another supposed sign. Things that weren't neglectful at all to Diné. Things that were often purposeful. These were the things being using against them.

Some of these new guidelines were vague, and Lester imagined that was intentional. Signs of poverty, for example. Who exactly determined what "proper footwear for children" meant? Depending on the season, and in areas where snakes couldn't hide, plenty of Indian children went barefoot.

In Utah, Cynthia was teaching Adriel sign language. Adriel seemed to like her, too, despite his anger at George and Lester. Lester didn't take it personally, but he knew it hurt George deeply.

George had made many mistakes. But Lester understood the cycle. He knew these people's methods. Lester had fallen for them once, too, after all, and lived the rest of his life regretting it. George would have to battle his own demons, but he wouldn't lose his son. Not like Lester had.

Now, they waited for Lester's colleague in New Mexico to prepare for George and Adriel to return home. They would need someone who understood what they were up against and who could legally practice law in New Mexico to protect Adriel. Lester often wondered if they all didn't continue to underestimate people like Donald Andrews. He couldn't help feeling a step behind. But how could one ever truly understand a man who saw children as pawns?

68

JAMES

THE BANK ACCOUNT information James was gathering that morning was certainly damning. And yet, it still didn't implicate the killer.

It was possible that Robert John—or Bobby Tate—had killed the judge and his wife. It made more sense than George Morris killing a woman he didn't even know existed and leaving his son's plush lizard at the crime scene.

James and Molly had spent an afternoon at the Albuquerque library going through the archives for anything related to Bobby Tate and his law firm. They learned that Tate had been a poster boy, of sorts, for Andrews's organization. A success story—and even worked for Andrews's group home and adoption agency early in his career.

It was likely Tate had been following Peter—or paying someone else to follow Peter—and learned what Cathy was doing before he'd even accepted the job on the reservation. Now, he was once again doing Andrews's bidding by approving Navajo adoptions that should never have been approved. Whether Andrews explicitly asked him to do so remained unclear. Perhaps Tate simply believed in the mission.

James had also been able to track down a marriage certificate between a Janice Stone and a Lawrence Duncan. When they divorced years later, Bobby Tate represented Janice in her custody case against her husband, proving that Bobby and Janice did indeed know one another. Perhaps they had a relationship of some sort—a close one. It was possible that Bobby had asked Janice to take that lizard to her ex-husband, to threaten him, to do whatever needed to be done to get that lizard into evidence and in so doing, tie an innocent man to both homicides.

Maybe—despite his instincts—James ought to let the man who now called himself Robert John take the fall. The man had done enough wrong. James was certain of that now, walking out of the bank with John's account information in hand. They were all guilty—Bobby Tate, Donald Andrews, Janice Stone. If not of murder, then of a scheme to steal children. But that was not the crime he'd been tasked with solving. No, James *did* need to pin the deaths of the Winters on someone. On the right person. He was close. He was almost there, but there were still pieces missing.

James was lost in his thoughts when he looked up and saw an older Navajo man leaning against his car. He stopped walking and straightened up, annoyed that Cecil Cody had gotten the drop on him.

"Mr. Cody. What a surprise."

"James Pinter," Cecil said. "I'd like to have a chat."

"Well then. How about you hop in the passenger's seat and we'll go to the buffet for breakfast?"

Cecil shook his head. "This is a private matter. Follow me back to my ranch."

"After you," James said. Cecil's ranch wasn't far, and though James knew the way, he stuck pretty close to the rear of Cecil's truck.

Cecil's dirt driveway was empty of cars. His sons must have been out. They had plenty of work to do, James knew, and even though Cecil was behind it all, officially the old man spent his days tending sheep and working for the council.

James watched his step as he got out of the car. He didn't want shit on the bottom of his boots again.

Cecil made them eggs and bacon and coffee, and James felt downright friendly with one of the biggest criminals on the reservation.

"So, what's all this about, Cecil?" he finally asked, placing his napkin on top of his plate.

"You've got an investigation going on, and I learned something concerning that I cannot keep to myself."

"Well, let's hear it."

"My son, Byron. I believe you've met?"

James snorted. "He had a strange way of introducing himself, but yeah. We've met." During James's previous investigation, Byron had followed him at a highway rest stop in the dark to threaten him.

"He's at ONEO," Cecil went on. "And Jackson has him working on a new project. Wasn't specific at first about what it would be, and the funds were coming from an anonymous source."

James nodded. Cecil sighed and turned his head. Gazed out the window.

"I knew something about that judge wasn't right."

"You talkin' about Judge Robert John?"

"That's right. He's funding the project. He's convinced Chairman Jackson to build a housing complex for pregnant, unwed women to access the services they need."

Cecil looked back at James. "Unwed mothers are not something us Diné have ever been concerned with. A baby is a baby. Doesn't matter whose. We all take care of it. We step up, because we know that child is our future. Only an outsider like John would suggest such nonsense."

James did not ask Cecil why he sold drugs to the future of the Navajo Nation. But he thought it.

"So why did the chairman agree?" James asked.

"He has his reasons," Cecil said. Fair enough. James knew that as one of the chairman's cronies, Cecil couldn't admit the corruption of the court.

"Do you know what else the judge does aside from serving on the Supreme Judicial Council?" James asked.

"The chairman told me he handles off-reservation adoptions. I know who this judge is. A coyote. A deceiver. He cites his sad origins for his interest in child adoptions. But he's selling our children. And now, he'll get them as babies."

James felt a shiver run up his spine. Cecil didn't have his reputation for nothing.

"You're angry," James said.

"Furious."

"I know you don't owe me any favors, but I'd be mighty appreciative if you would wait to do or say anything about this. I'm investigating a double homicide, as I'm sure you know, and now I've got a third body. But more importantly for the Navajo Nation, I intend to bring a case to the US attorney's office with all I've found on Donald Andrews and his violations of ICWA. Donald Andrews happens to be the original funding source of that project of yours. He's wiring money to John. I'd like you to keep this under wraps for now."

"US attorney's office, huh?" Cecil said. "I'm not sure I trust the US government to lift a finger for us."

"It's a foul business. I'd like to see them all get taken down, just as you do."

Cecil just stared for a moment, so James went on.

"I'm workin' with the New Mexico attorney general, too."

Cecil smirked. "El Gato."

"What'd you say?" James asked.

"That's what they call the AG. El Gato. The way he investigates. He pounces from in hiding. Some down in Albuquerque say he's a blessing. Others, a curse. Me, I'm not so sure."

"Shit," James said, scrambling to his feet. "Shit, shit."

"Did you forget something, Mr. Pinter? Or did you remember something?"

"Cecil, please keep this between us for now, all right? I have to go. But if you tell the wrong person, Judge John could get away with what he's done."

"Maybe you don't know me as well as you think you do, Mr. Pinter."

"Oh, I think I do." Then, James tilted his hat in parting and rushed home.

"You didn't tell me they call the AG El Gato," James said when Sanchez answered the phone.

"Yeah," Sanchez said. "They do call him that. What's that got to do with anything?"

"I'm packing some things up now, and then I'm coming to Albuquerque. I've got a stop to make, and then I'll be at your house. I need you to get started on a warrant."

"For who? For what?"

"CJ. The attorney general's son."

"What's this about, Pinter? What does CJ have to do with any of this?"

"I'll explain when I get there. We'll need a wiretap for his phone and a couple of concealed listening devices for his house."

"How am I gonna do that?" Sanchez asked.

"He's got an arrest record, doesn't he?"

"Small things, sure."

"Anything involving drugs?"

"A couple of marijuana possessions."

"Bingo," James said. "Get it done. I'll see you tonight."

James packed up just about everything he had on the case: the financial files from Cathy; the cassette tapes with Isaiah's recording and Janice Stone's, too; the intake list from the children's home; and Robert John's bank account wire transfers.

He put them in the trunk, got in the driver's seat, and went to pick up Molly.

SANCHEZ

SANCHEZ WAS SHOCKED by how easily he had obtained the warrant. He shouldn't have been, though. The city practically begged the state's narcotics division for help daily. Drugs had become such a problem that if narcotics wanted a warrant, they got one.

Sanchez tried to figure out what Pinter was thinking. Vasco's nickname—El Gato—was used among certain groups, mainly law enforcement and members of the community who had great respect for the man. Though criminals also sometimes used it mockingly. But what that—or CJ—had to do with this case, he couldn't figure.

When the doorbell rang, Sanchez opened it to find Molly holding two extra-large pizza boxes.

"Did you get the warrants?" James asked, behind her.

"Yes," Sanchez said. "But you've got to explain this to me." He shut the door behind them.

"Over pizza," James said, sitting at Sanchez's dinner table. Molly set the pizzas down carefully, and James flipped open the lids.

"Why CJ?" Sanchez called over his shoulder as he got some plates.

"You gotta trust me on this, all right?" James called back.

Sanchez returned with the plates and set them down on the table in a stack. James put a slice of pizza on a plate and handed it to Molly.

"I know how you feel about the AG. But I strongly believe he killed Judge Winters and his wife."

Molly stopped with the pizza raised to her lips and stared at Sanchez. He was breathless. And then he laughed. "Have you lost your mind?"

"Hear me out," James said. "Since the beginning, I've been thinkin' about who would have the balls to kill someone in their office right around dinnertime, leave the scene of the crime, go right to the judge's next of kin, and kill her, too. It's possible, but bold. And it's gotta be done within ten minutes. Someone with a personal vendetta is a solid explanation. Someone like George. Crime of passion, on a mission, isn't thinking straight, right?"

Sanchez stared at him in a stupor.

"But instead of that scenario, let's say there are two killers. One of whom is seen around the judge's office frequently enough that no one would bat an eye when they watched him walk in and out. And no one would think to even mention it to law enforcement—or anyone else, either. Hell, by the time the police arrive at the crime scene, they've already forgotten about it."

Sanchez didn't take his eyes off of James as he lowered himself onto a chair. Molly tentatively bit into her pizza.

"And the other killer?" James went on. "Just a young man tryin' to gain his dad's approval. The AG was the first to know about what Cathy was doin'. The financial statements revealed that NMCA gave a whole hell of a lot of money to Vasco's campaign for AG. Now, maybe Cathy thought Vasco had a moral compass that points north—that Vasco cared more about Indian children than that money—and she was wrong. Or maybe she hadn't uncovered Vasco's campaign name, Justice for All, so she didn't know it was him. Either way, big mistake on Cathy's part."

Sanchez scoffed a little but still couldn't form any words. James kept going.

"What I found in Duncan's desk wasn't a retirement card at all. It was a threat. To keep his mouth shut or else this would be his last case ever. With a little kitten on the front. El Gato. Well, el gatito, I guess." James chuckled a little. "Doesn't have the same ring to it. Either way, Duncan knew exactly who it was from."

"Wait," Sanchez finally spoke. "I thought Janice gave Duncan the lizard for evidence. How are Janice and Vasco connected?"

"I'd like to find that out," James said. "I've got an idea. A crazy little thought. Something I saw in Janice's office. I might be wrong, but we're gonna do our damndest to find out."

"But Vasco said his people were looking into Donald Andrews."

"He was lying."

Sanchez made a face. James had no way of knowing that. "He gave you that tip about the bank account."

"Because he wants us going after the Navajo judge for the murders. And I almost did. Listen," James said. "Vasco told us he didn't know about the ICWA violations, but Cathy would surely have told him. She thought he was on her team.

I think what *was* a surprise to Vasco at the café was how close Bartholomew was to involving the US attorney. I think that made Vasco's butt pucker."

Molly made a face.

"Sorry, but it did," James said. "The US attorney might just be someone Vasco can't bully. I hope he can't, at least, because Molly and I stopped at the US attorney's office on our way here and gave them all the evidence we've been gathering on Donald Andrews." James finally took a bite of his pizza.

"So, Vasco is doing all this for . . . campaign money?" Sanchez asked.

"Sometimes it's just that simple, my friend," James said after he swallowed. "Andrews has influence, too. He tells people to vote one way, and they do. He tells people the AG really is a friend to New Mexico's children, and they believe him."

Sanchez was speechless. He wanted to say no, this couldn't be true. Finally, he asked, "When Cathy came to him with this, why not just ignore it? Why kill the Winters?"

"Because he knew them. He knew they weren't quitters."

"No offense, Pinter. Excuse my language, Molly. But this is some bullshit." Sanchez couldn't help being pissed off. It was easier to be angry than to entertain this idea.

"I know it is," James said.

For a moment, the room was silent except for the ticking of the wall clock.

Sanchez shook his head. "I can't imagine CJ doing this. Just . . . killing Cathy like that. A woman he doesn't even know. But I guess I don't know him at all anymore. I haven't spoken to him in probably eight years?"

"That's gonna have to change," James said. "You're gonna have to speak with him." Molly grabbed another slice of pizza and looked back and forth between the two men.

"Why?" Sanchez asked.

"To scare him a little. Or maybe I should say to alarm him."

"How am I going to do that?"

"Make somethin' up. Tell him we have a witness that puts him at the scene of the crime."

They watched CJ leave the house, get into his truck, and drive away. Seeing him in person put a deep sadness in Sanchez's chest. CJ didn't look so great.

Molly kept watch while they set the wiretap and bugs. They tested the bugs by speaking to one another in the living room and having Molly listen in, the phone wires by calling from a pay phone. Everything was ready.

"Now remember," James said, "the goal is to scare him enough to call his father."

"And what if the attorney general calls me instead of going to speak with his son? Or what if he invites CJ to his house?"

"I don't think he's going to do either of those things. He doesn't want to talk about it around his wife or anyone else."

"What if he shows up at my house?"

"You won't be there."

If James was wrong about all of this, Sanchez would look like a real asshole, going to CJ's house, accusing him.

"You'll do good," James said. "I know it."

The next morning was cold and gray, and Sanchez wondered if the reservation would get its first snow of the year. Sometimes it happened this early. He remembered from his time in Gallup. He missed the snow.

He didn't wear his uniform. He went appearing to be a friend, even though he wasn't. The only thing left to do was knock. Talk.

CJ came to the door in worn bell-bottom jeans and a faded, striped tank top.

"Can I help you?" He looked exhausted.

"Hey, CJ. It's me. Gabriel Sanchez. Remember?"

CJ's forehead wrinkled in confusion for a moment before he broke into a slow smile. "Hey, brother. How you been? Come in."

"Thanks, man."

There was one small couch in CJ's wood-paneled living room and a pile of shoes in the corner. The television sat directly on the floor, and a single lamp stood on a side table next to the couch. There hadn't been many options for hiding the listening devices, and now, Sanchez resisted the urge to look right at them.

"How's everything been, Gabe?" CJ asked.

"Great, great. I'm, uh, with the New Mexico State Police now. How about you?"

"I heard. You know. Been working here and there. Looking for a gig right now. What brings you over? Just . . . catching up?"

"Actually, I came here as an old friend. To warn you." Sanchez rubbed the back of his neck, looking away.

"Warn me about what?"

"We're investigating a double homicide," Sanchez said.

"We have a witness." He paused. Cleared his throat. "A witness who puts you at one of the crime scenes."

CJ didn't say anything. Didn't move. But when he finally did look at Sanchez, Sanchez knew James was right. He almost cried. Right there.

"I don't . . ." CJ started. "I don't know what you mean."

Sanchez stared at him. He wished he could take him with him right now. Put him on a bus. Send him far away. To the East Coast. Anywhere. Just let him start over. James Pinter saw a murderer, but Sanchez saw a lost kid who only ever wanted to please his father and always felt he had fallen short.

"I think you do," Sanchez finally said. He wanted to say, *Don't do this. You didn't have to do this. Turn him in now. It's his fault.* But he couldn't encourage that. Not yet. They needed CJ to speak to his father. To call him as soon as Sanchez left.

Sanchez stepped closer. He clasped CJ's trembling shoulder. "As of right now, no one knows but me. But I wouldn't try to run. You won't get far."

CJ started to speak, but Sanchez interrupted him. "Don't say anything else. Trust me. Get a lawyer."

[70]

JAMES

THE PHONE CALL came shortly after Sanchez left. And just as James thought he would, the AG told his son he was coming over.

James knew it would unfold quickly, that they'd be stuck sitting, waiting in the car, listening and unable to leave. He had brought Pepsi and sandwiches and Slim Jims and apples and Ruffles potato chips. Molly munched on some now while they waited for the older Vasco to show up.

Sanchez said nothing. He ate nothing. James knew the feeling. Finding out that you really didn't know a person at all was jarring.

James took a bite of his ham and cheese sandwich.

"What about the others?" Molly asked, wiping her hands. "Bobby Tate and Donald Andrews?"

"It's with the US attorney now," James said. "We've got to hope Vasco's influence doesn't reach that far. We'll follow up, of course. But they can do much more with it than we can."

The car was quiet again. Finally, a crackle from the radio

transmitter. Faint voices. James signaled to Molly, and she started recording.

"When was he here?" the AG asked.

"I don't know. A couple of hours ago?"

"He doesn't have anything on you." The older Vasco's voice was calm.

"He says there's a witness!"

The AG sighed. "Witnesses are unreliable. It's nothing. Did you see anyone?"

There was silence.

"I didn't think so," the AG said. "Relax. We'll find this witness. They can be persuaded."

"That stupid lizard," CJ said. "I can't believe you did that. That's why they know something's off. It's that lizard."

"We had to connect Cathy with that Indian. It was the only way. The fact that the man had the misfortune to be the last one in the judge's office was a stroke of luck. One might say fate put him there. Put the lizard in Janice's possession. Or perhaps God did. She saved us with that lizard. Otherwise, we would've had to do a lot more work covering this thing up."

"Yeah, because she's such a close *friend*," CJ scoffed. "I ought to tell Mom. That's what I ought to do."

"You're forgetting yourself, CJ," the AG said. His voice was sharp now, threatening. "I am not the enemy. Do you want my help with this witness, or do you want me to throw you to the wolves? *You're* the one in question here, not me."

"Because you didn't have to worry about witnesses! It was probably easy for you to pull that trigger, too. Therapeutic even. You hated the man. I didn't even know that poor woman. The way she stared at me. The fear in her eyes." CJ paused. "I couldn't do it at first. I had to wait until she turned. She was trying to make it to the phone. And then I had to do it. I *had* to. I couldn't let her get to that phone." There was a muffled sob. It seemed like the AG was letting his son gather himself. Or maybe he had nothing to say.

"Gabe *knows* I'm a murderer," CJ finally said through clenched teeth. "Do you know what it's like to have a friend look at you the way he looked at me?"

"You always were too emotional," the older Vasco sighed.

CJ chuckled exasperatedly. "And you were never emotional enough. I hope this was all worth it for you. I'll be spending the rest of my life in jail."

"No, you won't. I explained. There was no other way. Once I knew what Cathy had . . ." There was a pause, and James wished he could see the attorney general's face. He went on. "Donald Andrews brings in federal money. He has friends in Washington. Friends in the church. He's a pillar of the community, and without his endorsements, without his funds, none of what I do would be possible. The whole state would suffer. You understood this before you agreed to help."

"I understood you needed me," CJ said. "And that you couldn't do it all yourself. And that I'm not good for much else." He chuckled again. "Not to you. And so, I thought, well, I can do this. I *will* do this. But I also thought you'd protect me when it came down to it. That's your end of the deal. You have to protect me now."

"I will. I will, son. We're a team. Put this witness out of your mind."

"And what about their suspicions? You told me yourself that a P.I. is working the case now."

"I'm hoping that little financial tip I gave him leads to the arrest of the Indian judge, Bobby Tate. It would be best for him to take the fall for all this. The least damaging for Andrews. A rogue, troubled, adopted Indian, who just happened to have ties to Andrews. Judge Winters was a thorn in Tate's side for years. The P.I. will see the money as payment for the murder, but Andrews will be able to honestly say that it's for the unwed mother's home. Easy enough to explain. The whole situation might even garner some sympathy for Andrews."

"And what about the lizard? How do they explain it?"

"Tate is on the reservation now. Same as this other man. This Morris. Tate could have taken the lizard. Or found it. Tate could have set this whole thing up just as easily."

James and Sanchez looked at each other. They had enough now. Sanchez looked a little pale. Queasy, maybe.

"So, you don't think I'll need a lawyer?" CJ asked his father.

"You'll have a lawyer. All the lawyers you want, son. But you won't need them. I'll talk to Gabriel tomorrow. Or maybe his P.I. I'll focus their attention elsewhere."

"All right," CJ said, but he didn't sound convinced.

"Get some rest," the older Vasco said. Then, he left, and Molly hit the button again to stop the recording. The van was quiet. Finally, James spoke.

"I'm sorry."

Sanchez shook his head. "Let's take this to Lark. Tonight."

71

SANCHEZ

IT FELT LIKE A DREAM. Like he sleepwalked into the station. Like it was someone else who called the head of homicide at home and told him to come in because they had arrests to make.

James believed that Lark already knew. He had seen the fear flicker across Lark's face at the sight of Duncan's "retirement" card. According to James, Lark was waiting to see what he and Sanchez would dig up. He would put it on them. Their successes, perhaps. Their failures, most certainly.

So, when Lark appeared to be surprised by the news, Sanchez spotted the small clues that told him it was an act, and he was glad James had spared him the disappointment.

But the tape, Lark *was* surprised by that. They had the AG discussing the crime with his son on record. Apparently, Lark hadn't expected this degree of success.

"This is . . . wow," Lark said. They waited for him to say more, but he didn't.

"I know, sir," Sanchez said. "I'll make the arrests tomorrow."

"How about you handle one and I'll handle the other?" Lark suggested. "We don't want either one getting spooked."

"All right," Sanchez said. "I'll visit the attorney general, then."

"You sure about that?" Lark asked.

"Pinter can back me up."

James nodded.

Sanchez knew he would not be sleeping that night, so when James and Molly went back to the hotel, he stayed at the station, finishing the paperwork, putting everything in order to take the judge first thing in the morning. He was no longer frightened by Vasco. He was just angry.

Sanchez waited by his radio for confirmation that CJ had been picked up before he and James walked into the attorney general's office with the arrest warrant.

When Vasco saw them, he smiled. "Just the men I've been looking for," he said.

"Sadly, we're not here for a social visit," James said. Sanchez felt like he suddenly had something stuck in his throat. He took a second to compose himself.

"Curtis Vasco, you're under arrest for first-degree murder and conspiracy to commit murder." The man was still smiling, and Sanchez could hear the quaver in his own voice as he went on. "You have the right to remain silent. Anything you say can and will be used against you in a court of law. You have the right to an attorney."

James approached the AG as Sanchez spoke.

"If you cannot afford an attorney, one will be provided

324 / LISA BOYLE

for you. Do you understand the rights I have just read to
you?"

Vasco said, "Oh yes, I understand." He still looked calm.
Clearly, he still thought they had nothing on him.

"Please put your hands behind your back," Sanchez said.
The AG complied, and James clicked the handcuffs around
his wrists.

"What's all this about, Gabriel? Surely this is a mistake."

"It's about you being a murderous, cowardly piece of
shit," Sanchez said. James raised an eyebrow in warning and
so Sanchez added, "Sir." James chuckled at that.

"Your P.I. friend has misled you," Vasco said.

Strangely enough, Sanchez realized he'd wanted to
believe that not twenty-four hours ago. He almost had. He
knew now, though, that the AG was goading him for information. He was already building his own defense in his head.

"You would think," Sanchez said, yanking Vasco by the
arm James wasn't holding, "that an attorney general would
know to keep his mouth shut while being arrested. I don't
want to hear another word."

Sanchez needed sleep. He was crazy with exhaustion. But his
adrenaline hadn't come down yet, and so he sat on the
balcony of the hotel room with James while Molly slept
inside. They were both drinking beers, and it was helping.

"I hate to say it," James said, "but this case is gonna be a
nightmare."

"I know," Sanchez said. "I'm willing to fight it out."

"You'll only be able to do so much," James said. "The rest

is up to those judges and lawyers, and they're all Vasco's buddies."

"I know." Sanchez stared at the night sky. The room faced away from the city, and it was dark out there. Peaceful. "You think he'll get away with it, then?"

"Well, I doubt he'll get a life sentence. I'll be shocked if it even makes it to trial."

"You mean the AG. But CJ . . ."

"We'll see just how bad of a father he is, I suppose."

Sanchez took a long sip of beer. "You think Lark will ask me to join homicide?"

James sucked his teeth. "I don't know. But I will say this, narcotics is a great place to get your feet wet. You see it all. There are so many criminals connected to the drug trade in one way or another. And as you saw, warrants are so damn easy to come by."

Sanchez smiled. "You just want a man inside narcotics."

"It's been nice," James admitted. "I know how much you want homicide. I'd be happy for you. But homicide is brutal. Day in, day out, seeing the absolute worst of people. I have no doubt you can handle it. Still, my advice is to get a little more experience under your belt. You'll get that in narcotics." James chuckled. "Now, me. I didn't have a choice. I had to do it all. I liked that though. Never knew what the day would bring."

Sanchez knew James was probably right. Working next to him made Sanchez feel like a real amateur.

"Did you get paid for this case? Before . . . you know . . . we lost Isaiah?"

"A little," James said. "Isaiah's friend, Peter, offered to pay the rest."

Sanchez sipped. "That's good of him."

"I'd rather not take it from him, but I guess I have to. I can't keep working for free."

"Lark ought to pay you, too."

James smirked. "I won't hold my breath."

"I'll see what I can do." Sanchez raised his beer in a toast, and James clinked it with his own.

72

KAY

KAY STARTED to sob before Adriel even noticed her. The woman who opened the door for her and Wayne stood to the side, revealing Adriel on the couch, reading something. But then he must have heard them, because he looked up, grinned from ear to ear, and ran into Kay's arms.

She fell to her knees that way, clutching Adriel, and he did, too. He let her cry into his hair.

"Oh, sweetie," she finally said. "I've missed you."

She didn't look for George when she finally disentangled herself from Adriel's little arms. And when George entered the room, she didn't acknowledge him. No explanation he gave would ever make up for taking her nephew. Or for the endless hurt he had caused families and struggling parents on the reservation. Struggling just like Linda—her sister, his wife —once had. Even though she now knew he wasn't a murderer, she could never forgive him, though she also knew she'd have to find a way forward for Adriel's sake.

She let Wayne speak to George and hoped that even though he hadn't technically broken any laws, there would still be some sort of punishment involved. Kay had been keeping a mental list of George's wrongdoings in case Wayne needed any help.

As soon as she stopped crying, Adriel tried to sign to her. She wanted desperately to understand, but of course she didn't. She turned back to the woman, Cynthia, to ask for a pen and paper. That was when she noticed the older man walking toward her. Lester Tallsalt. He wasn't looking at her, though. He didn't offer any kind of greeting. Rather, he looked at Adriel. He sat down across from the boy, on the edge of the coffee table.

"He's saying he missed you," Lester said.

Adriel gave the man a strange look. It wasn't quite anger, but something like it. But then he calmed. His brow smoothed.

"I've missed you so much," Kay said. "Are you hurt? Were you afraid? I'm sorry I didn't find you sooner."

"He says he's not hurt. He was afraid for a little while. And then angry. At me and his dad. He says it isn't your fault."

"Did you teach him this?" Kay asked.

"Yes," Lester said, finally looking at her.

"You learned so much so quickly," Kay said to Adriel. He smiled wide again.

"He's a very quick learner," Lester said.

"Why did you bring him here?" she asked.

"Cynthia doesn't know George. Doesn't have any connection to him. I thought we needed to get a little farther away. Buy ourselves some time. And I knew she could teach Adriel while we waited."

"Waited for what?"

"I'm part of a larger organization of lawyers dedicated to seeing ICWA upheld and followed. I'm working with a colleague in New Mexico to protect Adriel from what happens next."

Kay wondered what would happen next. She knew about the adoption papers. It was part of the reason she couldn't bring herself to look at George. She wanted to ask this Lester Tallsalt what he meant by that. But she also wanted to enjoy this moment with Adriel. She wanted that more.

"I read about your life," Kay said. "About what you did to your son."

"I can never take it back," Lester said. "But I can help other kids. I dedicated my career to it."

Kay looked up at Cynthia, who stood a polite distance from both conversations happening in her home.

"She taught you sign language?" Kay asked.

"She did. Cynthia is like my daughter. She was very close with my son. I had hoped they would get married. But Roland was such a lost and troubled boy. We all tried to help. But we couldn't."

"Do you know where he is now?"

"No. I received a postcard a year ago. He was in Nevada. I tried to go to the address, but he'd already left."

"I'm sorry," Kay said. She knew that as an elder, Lester had been through so much more than she understood. As they spoke, Adriel had slowly made his way into her lap and now rested his head against her chest.

"How will I learn sign language?" Kay asked.

"Adriel will teach you. I know he'll be great at it," Lester said.

Kay could feel Adriel's head shift and thought he had smiled at that.

Lester walked away, then, and Ariel sat straight up on Kay's lap, looking at her. He pointed his finger into her chest and made a sign.

"Kay?" she guessed. He smiled and nodded. Then he pointed to himself and made a series of signs.

"Are you spelling out your name?" she guessed. He nodded again.

"How about home?" she asked. "How do you do that one?"

He cupped his hand and touched it to his mouth and then his temple. Kay tried it next.

"Let's go there," she said. "I think it's time to go home."

73

MOLLY

MOLLY HAD GONE BACK to the juniper trees weeks ago. The berries she and Adriel had left on the ground were no longer blue but now brown like the dirt. The meat of the berries had indeed been picked away, and what was left were somewhat round, somewhat oval shells. She gathered as many as she could and kept them for when Adriel returned.

Now, she and Adriel sat on the floor of Kay's living room, threading strings through the beads Kay had made from the shells. They worked quietly and contentedly, making necklace after necklace. There wasn't a plan, exactly, but just the act of being together, finally, after so long apart, gave them joy.

The Navajo called these ghost beads, Molly had learned. They were thought to bring protection to whoever wore them, keeping them safe from evil. Molly imagined handing these necklaces out to every kid on the reservation.

She supposed she was glad the attorney general and his son had been arrested. That they would be tried and hopefully jailed. But she also realized how much work still needed to be done. She'd been helping Barbara with the families from the intake list the last couple of days. Not speaking to them. The matter was too delicate for Molly, an outsider, to be doing that. But she did help with the research. Tracking down the paperwork, the adoption records, the child services reports—which were actually NMCA reports that had just been stamped by New Mexico Child Services.

The work Molly was doing would help Adriel's lawyer, too. The children's journey through the New Mexico foster care system—and the Children of God Home—revealed Donald Andrews's methods. The guidelines for these social workers needed to be rewritten. They needed to be adjusted for the Navajo way of life. The way they raised their children. In a community. Most of all, this work needed to be re-delegated back to the government, who had a better chance of being impartial or at least held accountable. Who would, hopefully, seek out Navajo families first when searching for homes for these children.

She had also found herself thinking about Isaiah Winters a lot. He seemed to be forgotten in all of this. The Vascos had admitted to killing Cathy and the judge but hadn't said a word about Isaiah. James promised they would consider Isaiah's murder, too, while building the case, and they might be able to get a confession in a plea deal.

Molly had written a letter to Peter the night before. She told him how sorry she was for his loss. That even though she hadn't known Isaiah well, he had trusted her with information and treated her with respect, and she would never forget that. She told Peter that what he had done for Isaiah would impact the lives of so many children. She thanked him for his courage.

She finished another necklace, tied the ends together, and looked up at Adriel. He was still concentrating on his, his tongue sticking out just a little. Molly had never had a sibling. But she imagined this was how it felt. The love she had for Adriel. She waited until he looked up from his work and then she signed, "Beautiful."

74

JAMES

It was dark out, and Adriel was asleep inside George's trailer. George and James stood outside, James sipping a beer, George with his hands stuffed in his pockets.

"I can't ever repay you," George said.

"I don't need you to."

"You never told Kay that we spoke?"

James sighed. "Once I had a look at the case, I knew you didn't kill them. Can't stand to see a man framed."

George nodded. "I don't know where to go from here."

"You just focus on that boy. On bein' a good dad. We all make mistakes. Hell, I made a giant one for near fourteen damn years. I can't get that time back. You can't undo what you did, either. But I'll tell you what. Bein' a dad is the best job there is. It's a gift. You treasure that. You've got lots of years ahead with Adriel. Lots of time to show him what it means to be a dad, a man, a Navajo. A Christian, too."

George nodded again. "Kay will never forgive me."

"Maybe not. But she loves Adriel with every ounce of her being. You might not have a friend in Kay, but Adriel does.

He has a fierce protector with Kay in his corner. Use that when you need to. She'll do anything for that boy."

George breathed deeply. "Thank you."

James held out a hand, and George shook it. "Glad you're both home."

———

It was cold out now, the weekend after Thanksgiving. But still, a bead of sweat dripped down James's back as he sipped water from a plastic cup. He and Wayne were shooting hoops outside the station. Wayne took one more shot before wiping his brow and joining James on the bench.

"George said he'll testify to the US Attorney's Office," James said.

"He'll be working with Barb to get some of those kids home, too," Wayne said. "And helping to find others on the reservation doing what he was doing. And whatever else I come up with. He's real eager to atone, it seems."

James pulled his T-shirt away from his body. He was getting chilly now that he was cooling down.

"How about the AG?" Wayne asked.

"Both Vascos are out on bail. They expect the trial to be a real circus. If it even goes to trial."

"I bet."

"Haven't heard anything more from Cecil," James said. "But I assume he's got something to do with Judge John's disappearance."

"I'm sure. Word on the council is that John was graciously given the 'option' to quietly resign. But first he had to officially deny Forever Families' adoption request of Adriel Morris. Nobody has seen or heard from him since."

James whistled. "Sure do hope he isn't tied to a brick at the bottom of the San Juan River."

"Not sure I care to look into it," Wayne said, leaning his head back.

"Well, if John's out there somewhere, the federal government will find him. He's wanted in their case."

"They make any arrests yet?" Wayne asked.

James shook his head. "They're close, though. They've got what they need."

He squinted. In the distance, he could see the big rigs on the highway looking like toy trucks. A green one, white one, black one. That life was only six months past, but it felt like a lifetime ago. It was already impossible to imagine his life without Molly in it. He was in awe of the little investigator she was becoming. He shook his head in disbelief at how lucky he was.

Wayne got up and stuck out a hand for James to shake. "Good work, cowboy."

James smiled and shook Wayne's hand. "You too, LT."

AUTHOR'S NOTE

In response to more than one hundred years of Native American children being forcibly removed from their homes and sent away to either government boarding schools, religious boarding schools, or into the foster care system, the Indian Child Welfare Act (ICWA) was enacted in 1978 by the United States Congress, one year before this story takes place. The law states that if a Native American child is removed from his or her home by Child Protective Services, the state must find extended family members to care for the child, if possible, and if not, another member of the child's tribe. But a 2005 government report found that thirty-two states failed in some way to abide by this law.

Though not New Mexico specifically, some states have avoided their part in upholding the law by passing off responsibility to private organizations, who often profit from these children—sometimes by designating the Native American children as "special needs," much like in this book. Since its passing, ICWA has been challenged numerous times in courts across the country. One of those cases—*Haaland v.*

Brackeen—made it to the United States Supreme Court in 2023. The Indian Child Welfare Act was upheld at that time.

Beginning in the early 1800s, an unknown number of Native American children were forced to attend government and religious-run boarding schools across the country. The federal government has recognized 408 government-run boarding schools that operated between 1879 and 1969, while a separate nonprofit identified an additional 115 religious-run boarding schools, some of which operated as early as 1801. Evidence of physical and sexual abuse was found at many of the schools, and though school grounds are still being scoured in search of remains, the number of child deaths occurring at these schools is estimated to be in the thousands or tens of thousands.

When the boarding schools began to close in the 1940s and '50s, the Bureau of Indian Affairs (BIA)—part of the US Department of the Interior—understood they now had a new problem: families who had had come to rely on the services the schools did provide, such as food and clothing for the children, who could not provide those things themselves. Yet, neither the state nor the federal government was willing to step up and take on the additional expense of helping these children at home. In 1958, the BIA created the Indian Adoption Project as a solution, with the goal of adopting out as many Native American children as possible to non-native families who could afford to care for them. The project lasted for nine years and actively created a demand for Native American children among non-native families by focusing on the stereotype of the poor, uneducated Native parent who struggled with addiction. The project appealed especially to white, liberal Christian communities who touted inclusivity and were more likely to welcome a non-white child into their home. This demand for Native children among non-native families lasted for decades beyond the project's conclusion.

The Church of Jesus Christ Latter Day Saints (LDS), or Mormon Church, created a type of foster program itself during these years. The LDS Indian Student Placement Program operated from 1947 to 2000 and placed an estimated thirty- to fifty thousand mostly Navajo children with LDS families for at least nine months out of the year, oftentimes more. The objective was to send the children to attend the local schools in Mormon communities—much better schools than those that existed on the reservation. The explicit goal of the program was Native American assimilation. The creator of the LDS program said in 1962, "I firmly believe that tomorrow there will be no reservations."

Though I researched reservation life and Diné history thoroughly, this story is not meant to be a comprehensive account of life as a Native American or life on a reservation. As a white American of European descent, I couldn't possibly provide the authenticity that a native writer can. I encourage readers to seek out these stories, as well. Some of my favorite Indigenous authors are: Louise Erdrich, Tommy Orange, Diane Wilson, Arlene L. Walker, and Morgan Talty, though there are countless others.

While researching for this story, I read the following books: *Diné: A History of the Navajos* by Peter Iverson; *Dinéjí Na'nitin: Navajo Traditional Teachings and History* by Robert S. McPherson; *A Generation Removed: The Fostering and Adoption of Indigenous Children in the Postwar World* by Margaret D. Jacobs; and *White Mother to a Dark*

TORSNOTE

Race: Settler Colonialism, Maternalism, and the Removal of Indigenous Children in the American West and Australia, 1880–1940 by Margaret D. Jacobs. I also listened to season two of the podcast *This Land* hosted by Rebecca Nagle and produced by Crooked Media, and I listened to NPR's special series *Native Foster Care: Lost Children, Shattered Families*.

Thank you to my wonderful beta readers: my husband, Tim Boyle, who had a doozy of a time with this one; my brother-in-law, Joe Boyle, who is one hell of an Army investigator; and my wonderful sister who is so generous with both everyday legal advice and literary legal advice. Thanks for always answering my questions pro bono.

And of course, last but not least, the Bookstagram community! You all continue to amaze me with your dedication and support. Thank you so much for your lovely reviews and shares. It means the world to me.

ABOUT THE AUTHOR

Lisa Boyle has been writing stories for as long as she can remember. Born and raised in Finksburg, Maryland, Lisa received bachelor's degrees in journalism and international affairs from Northeastern University in Boston, Massachusetts. Lisa has held many different jobs over the years from cheesemonger, to educator at the U.S.S. Constitution Museum. Lisa lives in South Carolina with her husband and daughter. The first book in this series, *In the Silence of Decay* won the 2024 IPPY Gold Medal Award for Best Regional Fiction: West Mountain.

Sign up for Lisa Boyle's newsletter, and get your link for *To My Dark Rosaleen*, a short story prequel to Lisa's historical fiction series.

Did you love this book? Don't forget to leave a review!

9 781736 607794